THE NINTH GHOST BOOK

The Ninth Ghost Book

Edited and Introduced by
ROSEMARY TIMPERLEY

BARRIE & JENKINS
London

ISBN 0 214 66887 8

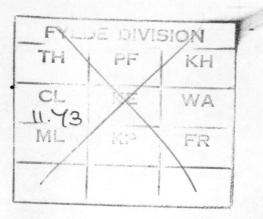
Printed in Great Britain by
Northumberland Press Limited
Gateshead

Contents

Introduction by Rosemary Timperley   7

GILBERT PHELPS   Who Were You With
                           Last Night?   13

CHRISTOPHER HOOD   The White Citroën   31

KIT PEDLER   White Caucasian Male   40

MAGGIE ROSS   When the Music's Over,
                          Turn Out the Lights   57

RICHARD SELMER   The Violet Lady   78

L. P. HARTLEY   The Stain on the Chair   103

KAY BATCHELOR   The Spirit Was Willing   114

ROSEMARY TIMPERLEY   Sister Varden   130

JOHN HYNAM   One For My Baby   149

JAMES TURNER   Love Me, Love My Car   163

JEAN STUBBS   Jarvey's Kingdoms   181

WILLIAM TREVOR   George and Alice and
                          Isabel   198

JOHN BURKE   False Harmonic   218

GILES GORDON   Crampton Manor   235

JOHN MOAT   Chope's Retreat   249

GEORGE MACKAY BROWN   Brig-o-Dread   266

Introduction

'Besides this earth, and besides the race of men, there is an invisible world and a kingdom of spirits; that world is round us, for it is everywhere.'

These lines come from Charlotte Brontë's *Jane Eyre* and are spoken by Helen, the character said to be based on Charlotte's elder sister who died young.

So—the world of spirits is everywhere, yet when we contact them, they seem to be only half there. A ghost is that creature which you glimpse out of the corner of your eye but vanishes when you turn to give it a straight look. It is that voice which is only half heard and stays silent when you stop to listen. It is that scent which tantalises your nostrils but has gone when you take a deep breath. It is that appearance of substance which you reach out to touch and find yourself grasping nothingness.

You would think that such a vague creature, there yet not there, would have very little influence over you. But its effect, however brief, is so strong that you always remember it. Even a person who has had only one ghostly experience in a lifetime will not forget it, though he may never speak of it.

One of the greatest problems which ghosts pose for

most of us is the way they can pass through solid things: they approach us through closed doors and brick walls, descend on us through plaster ceilings, and come wafting up through concrete floors. But this capacity to ignore matter and simply pass through it is not such a surprising factor to physicists who study the elementary particle called the neutrino.

The neutrino has no mass, no electric charge, and no magnetic field. It is not affected by the electric or magnetic fields of other particles as it flies past them. Travelling with the speed of light from the Milky Way or some other galaxy, it will pass through our earth as if it were empty space. There's a gallant little ghost if ever there was one! It may be passing through your skull at this moment and neither of you a whit the wiser.

An eminent astronomer said about it: 'A neutrino brain might suspect our existence from certain secondary effects, but would find it very difficult to prove.' And isn't that just the way a human brain suspects the existence of ghosts but finds it difficult to prove? He adds: 'Our universe is no truer than that of the neutrinos—they exist, but they exist in a different kind of space, governed by different laws.'

The ghosts in this book, however, are a lawless lot. Instead of staying quietly in their own kingdom, they have started to explore ours—catching a glimpse of us out of the corner of their neutrino eyes—aware fleetingly of the sound and the scent of us—and perhaps having a ghostly chuckle at the clumsy way we walk round each other or bump into each other instead of simply passing through each other. If they can feel pity, they surely pity us for having to drag our fleshly bodies around wherever we go. Perhaps one whispers: 'This place must be Purgatory,' and another: 'No. It's Hell.'

So here they are to speak for themselves, our new

family of ghosts, who found their way to the printed page by creeping into the minds of the writers, pressing this lever and that in the buzzing brain factory, and thus appearing, clothed in words, for you to read. Picture them first in your mind's eye before you meet them in the pages to come:

✓THE MISCHIEVOUS MINX who got her man.

✓THE HITCHHIKER who found himself.

THE DROWNED MAN who bewitched a nurse.

THE SINISTER SWEAT on the furnishing fabric.

THE POPSY who popped in for a pop song.

THE BEARDED INCUBUS who attempted rape.

THE SNOW-SHADOW seeking a grave.

THE GROCER who tried to buy heaven.

THE TRAVELLER whose passport was a poem.

✓THE MUSICIAN who came back for murder.

THE LUMINOUS HAND which gleamed in the night.

✓THE MISTY SHAPE which filled a wife with wonder.

THE CROUCHING FIGURES in the creepy cottage.

THE ARTIFICIAL GHOSTS who found believers.

✓THE BRAIN with the boot button eyes.

THE BELL which rang without stopping.

My thanks to everyone who has helped this haunted volume on its journey from me to you—writers, publishers, printers, paper-makers, chaps who do up parcels and knot string, van drivers, postmen, dogs who don't bite postmen, and the ghosts who came as tourists to have a look round, and then stayed to lend an invisible hand.

By the way, don't forget that each time you sit down in a chair, a ghost is probably sitting there already.

Rosemary Timperley.

THE NINTH GHOST BOOK

GILBERT PHELPS

Who Were You With Last Night?

'Who were you with last night?' Miss Nisbett sang the question, in a rough approximation to the tune of the old music-hall song. It was meant to be mocking. She had once entertained hopes of Mr Pidgeon, but he had snubbed her by completely ignoring her small advances —the extra lump of sugar in his tea, the biscuit in his saucer. He had made no comment, either, when these favours stopped. He kept a tin of biscuits in a drawer of his desk, and as he was inclined to put on weight, he preferred saccharine to sugar anyway. That was a long time ago, before Mr Pidgeon had become chief clerk, but Miss Nisbett had not forgotten. She made a habit of these little digs.

Her eyes widened now, for she had actually caused Mr Pidgeon to pause on his way to his office.

'What do you mean, Miss Nisbett?' he said.

'Last night, about ten, near the *Mariner's Arms*.'

'Yes ... Yes, I had a drink at the *Mariner's Arms* on the way home.'

'Well, I saw you with someone.'

'You couldn't have done, Miss Nisbett.'

'Why not?'

'Because I was alone, Miss Nisbett.'

'You usually are,' she agreed tartly, 'but there was some-body with you last night.'

Mr Pidgeon shook his head. 'Oh no, it must have been someone else you saw. I was alone, quite alone,' he said, walking towards his own office.

'A man—a tall thin man!' Miss Nisbett called after him, an edge of exasperation in her voice. But Mr Pidgeon went into his office and closed the door behind him.

'Who were you with last night?' Miss Nisbett sang in a savage voice, pounding the keys of her typewriter as if she were operating a machine-gun.

Mr Pidgeon shook out his raincoat and hung it, with his bowler hat, on the hook behind the door. He opened his umbrella and laid it carefully on the floor. It took up so much space that he had difficulty in getting to his desk. Once there he took out the brief he was copying and set to work. For some reason the song Miss Nisbett had been singing was still running through his mind. 'Who were you with last night?' he hummed. What was the second line? Ah, yes, 'All in the pale moonlight'— something like that. He couldn't remember any more. 'There was no moonlight anyway,' he muttered to him-self. 'Only this confounded drizzle.' He glanced at the open umbrella. In the heat of the close little office it was beginning to dry, and wisps of steam rose from it. Steam was rising, too, from his raincoat. The smell of the material blended with that of the dusty briefs and law books ranged on a rack against the far wall.

Mr Pidgeon began to cough. His bronchitis had both-ered him a good deal this winter. He controlled the cough, but his breath sounded very odd. It wheezed and whispered round his chest, interminably it seemed, like smoke trapped underground. It sounded almost as if *two* people were breathing ...

Yes, of course, that was why he had listened to Miss Nisbett. It was last night, on his way home from the *Mariner's Arms,* that he had first noticed this curious double-breathing effect ... It was strange that it was last night, too, that Miss Nisbett had imagined she had seen him with someone ...

He opened the drawer of the desk where he kept his tin of biscuits. A bottle of bronchial mixture was there too. He took a good swig from it, and was about to return it to the desk when his eye again alighted on his umbrella. The steam had spread out now in wisps and filaments. These drifted to and fro aimlessly, and yet with an unexpected appearance of activity—like wasps which have been disturbed and don't know where to settle. Then they seemed to steady themselves into a tall, wavering outline, or rather, half an outline. Towards the top, a wisp of steam protruded to the left, and began to wave up and down, almost like the branch of a tree, or (a ridiculous fancy!) a gesticulating arm. He glanced at his raincoat hanging on the door. The steam rising from it was behaving in exactly the same way. It, too, rose almost to the ceiling. It, too, extruded a branch like filament, but to the right. Then as Mr Pidgeon coughed again, agitating the atmosphere, it detached itself and began to drift towards the other wavering column of steam.

Before the two halves could join, Mr Pidgeon had hurried over to the window. It had not been opened for years and he had to struggle to raise it. One of the sash-cords crumbled like soot, but reaching back to the desk he found a rubber and wedged it beneath the upper section of the window. It held steady and he returned to his desk. The view of a semi-basement area, occupied by a row of dustbins, and ending in a blackened brick wall, was hardly inspiring. The air was chilly on his shoulders —but at least it circulated strongly enough to disperse the steam from the umbrella and the raincoat.

Mr Pidgeon worked late. He didn't have anything particularly urgent to do, but in a solicitor's office it was always easy to find jobs that might just as well be done now as later. As he worked he kept glancing at the open window. For some reason he could not place, he didn't want to leave until the drizzle had stopped. At one point he thought the 'pale moonlight' of the song really had arrived, for the area suddenly filled with silvery light, but it was only the street lamp outside the office that had just switched on. The rain, so fine as to be almost indistinguishable from mist, was still falling.

Reluctantly he locked his desk, closed his umbrella and hooked it over his arm, put on his raincoat and bowler, and went into the outer office. He was quite pleased to see that Miss Nisbett had also been working late. She was just putting the cover over her typewriter. She glanced up at him with the usual ironic expression on her pinched little face—and received her second surprise of the day. Mr Pidgeon had stopped, and there was a contortion on his plump and usually expressionless face that bore some resemblance to a smile.

'Er, nasty drizzle outside,' he said.

'Yes,' Miss Nisbett replied. She was too surprised to say anything more. She put on her ridiculously girlish jockey-cap and her shiny red plastic macintosh.

'Nice colour, that,' Mr Pidgeon mumbled. 'Nice and bright!' Miss Nisbett stared at him, her mouth open. Was he paying her a compliment? He was staring greedily at the red macintosh, and his smile this time was one of unforced approval. What was more, he was waiting for her.

'I believe we live in the same direction,' he said, and courteously held open the office door. She was so stunned it never crossed her mind to remind him that in fact they had been near neighbours since childhood.

Mr Pidgeon was not a stimulating companion. He hardly addressed a word to her. His behaviour, too, was distinctly odd. To begin with he walked on the outside as, naturally, a gentleman should, holding the umbrella over her head. But when they reached Burough Avenue, which was long and little frequented, he suddenly changed places—and changed them several times more before they reached the end of the road. She could see no reason for these antics, apart from the fact that, the road being unprotected by trees or houses, the drizzle was more persistent there, coiling round them in a fine and, it seemed, remarkably mobile spray, first on one side, then on the other. Perhaps, she told herself, his behaviour was a form of shyness. She knew that he lived alone and that, no doubt, made him somewhat eccentric. In addition the poor fellow was obviously unwell. He was wheezing and gasping like a broken-down old cart horse.

'You'll have to get that chest of yours seen to,' she told him, when they reached his garden gate. 'You're making enough noise for two!'

Mr Pidgeon jumped as if she had stuck a pin in him. 'What's that? What's that?' he said, peering nervously around him.

'Just what I said—you need something for your chest.'

'Yes, yes,' he muttered, and darted through the gate, up the garden path and into his house without another word. Miss Nisbett stared for a moment at the closed door, then shrugged her shoulders and walked on. Her own home was only a couple of turnings farther on.

*   *   *

Mr Pidgeon ran from room to room switching on the lights. When he reached the lodger's room, which was at the end of the upstairs landing, he was out of breath and sat down on the edge of the bed—uncomfortably, because the bed was unmade, the hard mattress neatly rolled and secured with a leather belt, the blankets stacked with barrack-like precision. Everything in the room, indeed, had a barrack-room neatness, and bleakness. Old Perkins could never forget that he had been a regular soldier. He had insisted on 'putting his room decent' on that last morning, padding round in his old grey army socks (he would never wear slippers), his tall, emaciated figure cringing slightly at the waist, where the growth in his liver hurt him, his gaunt face obstinate, while the ambulance waited below and the men with the stretcher argued with him. He was glad enough to be laid on the stretcher when he had finished, though. His face was as grey as the socks. But the eyes he fixed on Mr Pidgeon were as piercing and commanding as ever. Obediently Mr Pidgeon had leaned over the stretcher.

'Now mind!' old Perkins had said. 'I want to be buried at Parkton Combe!'

'Yes, Arthur, of course, Arthur,' Mr Pidgeon had mumbled. The old man's eyes regarded him sternly as he was carried away. He died in the hospital forty-eight hours later...

A remarkable old man in his way. Straight as a dart (except when the pain gripped him) with a springy, almost bouncing stride, and a habit of waving his arms about when he was excited. He was over eighty when they took him to the hospital. A good twenty-five years older than he was, Mr Pidgeon reflected. Twenty-eight years older than Doris, that would be. A big difference in ages. Not too big for Doris, though ... Old Perkins had been their lodger when they lived at Parkton Combe,

which was Doris's birth-place. He had come with them
when they moved into the town. One of the family by
then ... too damned much one of the family! Mr Pidgeon
remembered the first time he had caught him and Doris
together. In the very bed he was sitting on now—though
how it had accommodated the two of them he didn't
know: Doris was a large woman. Old Perkins was working nights at the time, and Mr Pidgeon had brought
him a cup of tea in order to wake him for the night
shift. And there was Doris lying on her side in old Perkins's bed, her hips humped up, facing the wall and
snoring peacefully, while the old man sat upright, his
long, muscular arms clasped behind his head. Even so,
his feet stuck out of the end of the bed.

Mr Pidgeon's hand had been shaking so much that
the cup had rattled in its saucer, slopping some of the
tea. Old Perkins had not moved, but his eyes had held
Mr Pidgeon in a fierce stare.

'Put it down!' he barked, jerking his head in the
direction of the bedside table. Mr Pidgeon hesitated for
a moment, but the old man's eyes did not leave his face.
Meekly Mr Pidgeon did as he was told.

'Now go!' the old man said. He poured the slopped
tea back into his cup and began to sip it, but without
for a moment taking his eyes off Mr Pidgeon as he
backed to the door.

Mr Pidgeon had not seen much of Doris in their big
double bed after that—though even now he sometimes
puzzled over the problem of how she had managed in
old Perkins's single one ... Old enough to be her father
—disgusting! She had gone first, though, killed in a road
accident ten years ago, and buried, of course, at Parkton
Combe. It had not occurred to Mr Pidgeon to turn old
Perkins out of the house afterwards. He had become a
habit, a fixture. He kept the house tidy, too, and did

most of the cooking. In any case, old Perkins wouldn't
have gone if he *had* asked him...

He'd got his own back on the old bugger in the end
though! He had allowed the hospital authorities to bury
him in the municipal cemetery. He had been hard put
to it to keep a straight face at the graveside.

He went back downstairs, prepared and ate his supper,
then watched the television. Before the next programme
started he decided he had better refill the coal-scuttle.

The coal-shed was at the end of the little paved back-
yard. The drizzle was still falling, but he felt cosy in the
light that spilled through the kitchen window and the
open door. On his way back, he noticed how the light
fell on the fine drizzle round his shoulders so that they
looked as if they had been picked out in phosphorescent
paint. A moment later he saw two other streaks of light
in front of him, and some two feet higher. The wind
sighed through the still bare branches of the apple tree
in his plot of garden, and agitated the drizzle. It seemed
to swirl above the two bars of light into the semblance
of a circle, then drifted downwards into a series of wavering lines. One of the lines, just below the left-hand bar
of light, began to lift up and down, like a gesticulating
arm. Mr Pidgeon breathed fast. His chest creaked like
old leather. Echoes filled it, as through a series of caves.
He could have sworn he could hear them whispering,
over and over again, 'Parkton Combe! Parkton Combe!'
He dropped the coal-scuttle and ran indoors. He locked
and bolted the door and went straight to bed.

The next morning he was relieved to find that the
drizzle had stopped. Indeed there was even a pale lemon
sun struggling to break through, though with its rays
lopped off by cloud it looked more like a moon. As he
left the house he caught a glimpse of Miss Nisbett's
shiny red macintosh ahead of him, and set off in pursuit.

He liked that macintosh. It cheered him up; besides, it produced a bright glow, and nowadays he was like a moth, drawn to anything bright ...

By the time Miss Nisbett had reached the corner there were only a few yards separating them. He called out to her. She stopped and looked back. Her eyes alighted on him, with a gleam of recognition. Then they switched to his left, somewhere above his shoulder. She nodded briefly, as one might to a stranger one has seen before, but to whom one has not been introduced. The expression on her face, as she turned the corner, seemed to say: 'You don't want *my* company, because ... because...'

His heart thumping, he put on a spurt, determined to catch her up. He felt hot. The sun had more strength in it than he had thought. It was drying the damp pavements and the puddles in the gutters; the steam was swirling round his feet. There was a shop just before the corner. Something was reflected in its plate glass window, something at his side, an outline, wavering but distinct as if composed of astonishingly accurate smoke-rings, the outline of a tall, rangy figure, striding beside him with springy steps, an arm upraised in an angry, threatening gesture...

Mr Pidgeon's heart nearly stopped. His breath came in painful gasps, and each gasp tailed off into a whisper which sounded like 'Parkton Combe! Parkton Combe!' He turned and ran back home.

He did not appear at the office the next day, or the day after that. He sent no message, but Miss Nisbett made his excuses. 'I expect it's his bronchitis again,' she told Mr Parsloe, the solicitor who employed them. 'It's been bothering him a lot lately.'

But on the third day Mr Pidgeon arrived at his usual time. 'You're looking much better,' Miss Nisbett told him. 'Your cough's gone, and you're breathing quite easily,' but he only nodded and walked past her. 'I expect this nice spring weather has bucked you up!' she called after him, but he paid no attention. He was back to normal. Miss Nisbett felt a spasm of irritation. That was back to normal too, but she wasn't sure whether she was glad or sorry. On the whole she was glad she hadn't teased him again about his tall, skinny-looking friend.

With the English climate, of course, it didn't do to be over confident, but it really did seem as if there was going to be an early spring. The days were clear and bright, with only a touch of frost in the mornings, and hardly any mist at night. Mr Pidgeon felt a different man. He was careful not to be out too late, but his bronchitis had practically disappeared. It must have been quite bad, he told himself; a bit of a temperature with it too, making him light-headed; that would explain those ridiculous fancies. But these too he soon forgot. He looked ten years younger, Miss Nisbett told him. He raised his eyebrows, to show that he disapproved of such familiar remarks. He was a solitary by nature and habit, and he wasn't going to let her intrude on his privacy.

In the last week of March he received the usual invitation from Doris's Aunt Emily to spend the week-end at Parkton Combe, so that he could mark the anniversary of his wife's death by putting flowers on her grave. He had never accepted the invitation, and in fact hadn't seen Aunt Emily since the funeral, though he always sent her the money to buy flowers on his behalf. But she was the only one of Doris's relations he had liked, and to his surprise he found himself hesitating. After all, it *was* a lovely spring; he had been out of sorts, and a week-end in the country would do him good. On the other hand, at his age it was unwise to alter one's routine. He would be expected to talk, and he had got out of the habit of talking. He decided in the end to write his usual polite refusal.

He took the writing-pad from behind the television set. As soon as he raised his pen, however, he was seized by an unaccountable, and quite unaccustomed spasm of anger. The anger communicated itself to his hand. He found himself driving it across the paper in wide, sweeping gestures, as if it didn't belong to him, as if, rather, it was a ball he wanted to hit as hard as possible, in order to relieve his pent up feelings, or a squad of soldiers he wanted to drill at the double. When he read through the letter he was surprised to see how unusually large and bold his writing was. He was surprised, too, to see that he had, after all, written a letter of acceptance.

Saturday was calm and bright. The crocuses in the front garden were already beginning to wilt, and the daffodils had turned towards the sun. As he boarded the train he was quite glad he had decided to go.

The station at Parkton Combe was a picture. Raised slightly above the surrounding countryside, bathed in sunshine, and with quite a lot of the daffodils in full bloom (he remembered that it was always winning 'Best Kept Station' awards) it looked like a floodlit stage. The light, though, had a brittle quality, and it was decidedly colder.

'Don't like the look of the sky,' the station-master said, as he handed in his ticket. 'Up and down, that's the weather this time of the year. "Ne'er cast a clout till May is out," my grannie used to say!'

Mr Pidgeon nodded. He had not yet discarded his winter underwear, and he had brought his overcoat.

Parkton Combe station was far too small to merit taxis,

and there was no bus, but he quite relished the three mile walk to Aunt Emily's cottage, on the far side of the village, on a rise overlooking the churchyard. The sun was still shining, though the air was growing more chilly, and the sky-line to his right had turned a sullen, liverish colour.

He turned up the collar of his overcoat and set out briskly. It grew colder. The road under his feet, although still golden, had a hard, metallic look, as if the winter frost, after the brief uncurling of its fingers, was again tightening its grip. Gradually the sky became more overcast. He had covered about a mile when the last brightness faded from road and sky alike, and snow began to fall.

'It won't be much,' he told himself. '*Surely* it's too late in the year for a heavy fall.' But the flakes, large and flat, mockingly like petals in shape, went on falling. Moreover, they were settling. Ten minutes later his footsteps no longer rang on hard asphalt; the snow came over the soles of his boots. It fell with a soft murmur. His breathing was making a murmuring sound again, too; this wretched bronchitis, it always played him up in bad weather. He noticed that epaulettes of snow had already formed on the shoulders of his black overcoat.

With an effort he turned his head. Surely the outlines of another pair of shoulders were etched in snow beside him? But there were so many snow-flakes now, and they were swirling round him so fast, that he couldn't be certain, and he was able to keep the thought at bay. He quickened his step. A tall spiral of snow on his right seemed to detach itself from the falling white curtain and to roll along beside him. The murmur of snow sounded like breathing. He fancied he could hear muffled footsteps.

A moment later, as he rounded a bend in the road, he

laughed with relief. He had forgotten how quickly one came upon the village. A minute later he was walking along its single street. Most of the inhabitants were indoors, but the few muffled figures that passed him nodded or murmured a greeting, country fashion. Several dogs were barking, and the engine of the van outside the grocer's was coughing and spluttering. Everything seemed cheerful and normal, and by the time Mr Pidgeon had reached the end of the village street he, too, was in a cheerful frame of mind again and able to scoff at his fears—especially as he could see Aunt Emily's cottage on the brow of the hill facing him, the windows glowing with the promise of a log fire within.

He had forgotten that it was farther away than it looked. The village dropped away abruptly, as if it had fallen into a pit. He was once again in open country with fields, in which the snow was already drifting, on either side. The road seemed to climb away from him, interminably. It was rapidly growing darker. The red glow at Aunt Emily's window had faded, as if the fire had burned itself out. He tried to hurry, but the snow was well above his ankles now, even in the middle of the road. He thought he could detect a slight shuffling noise beside him. He stopped. The noise stopped too ... Perhaps he was mistaken. He hurried on, but the shuffling sound had increased in volume. It had taken on an urgent, impatient tempo. He forced his eyes to focus on a spot a few feet in front of him, but after a while he could not resist the impulse to raise them, to glance to his right ...

He gave a trembling cry. There was no doubt about it this time. A wavering column of snow flakes, in the semblance of a man, was keeping pace with him. There was so much snow along the lines of the shoulders that the wild idea passed through his mind that he would lift his

hand and brush it off—and then shuddered at the
thought. A dab of snow had also formed above the shoulders, at a point where one might suppose the top of the
head to be. There was something grotesque, almost
comic, about that dab of snow bobbing up and down.
He broke into a peal of hysterical laughter—and
wished he hadn't, for the flakes immediately beneath the
dab of snow began to whirl round and round frantically,
like particles subjected to an electrical charge; then they
disposed themselves into the appearance of head, ears,
nose, eye-sockets—and last of all, lips that twisted as if
uttering unheard of threats and obscenities.

He screamed and tried to run. The figure kept pace
with him. It was, moreover, gaining substance every
moment. It was, not only the head and shoulders that
were marked out in snow. Snow was thickening, too,
along arms, legs and trunk. It was like a skeleton gradually reassuming its flesh, only the flesh was made of
snow. Suddenly, to his horror, footmarks appeared beside his own, only footmarks rapidly growing wider and
deeper under an ever-increasing bulk. His heart thudding,
his lungs rasping he forced himself into a stumbling
run. The monstrous club-feet clumped along beside
him.

He reached the churchyard. There was a change. The
huge footmarks were no longer parallel with his own,
but ahead. The thing was outpacing him. He counted
the footmarks up to six, then lost track of them. He
peered through the snow and could see nothing. For one
wild, hopeful moment he thought he was alone again.
Then he collided with something hard and, as the snow
curtain parted for a moment, saw a tall white column
directly in front of him.

At first he wondered whether he had strayed off the
road towards the churchyard, banging into one of the

pillars that stood on either side of the gate, or even, perhaps, one of the effigies inside the churchyard. But in the same instant he knew what it was. The thing was completely filled in now, and as solid-seeming as marble. It grew as he watched, faster and faster until it towered above him. Apart from this rapid accretion, it was at first quite motionless. He almost wished it would move: there was a terrible menace in the way it stood there, barring his path and regarding him (for he felt it had eyes to see) in a still concentration of fury and malevolence. A moment later his wish was granted. The figure began to sway, slowly at first and then more and more rapidly. Suddenly an arm was raised in a fiercely commanding gesture. He followed the direction in which it was pointing, and saw that the gates of the churchyard were indeed almost directly opposite.

But now the other arm was raised as well, and both arms were gesticulating, wildly, angrily, threateningly. A gust of wind came whistling through the trees of the churchyard, causing the snowflakes round the gigantic figure to rotate furiously. They seemed to be dipping and screeching, like so many hungry sea-gulls. Then a hollow, roaring noise proceeded from the pillar of snow. Something cold and heavy thudded on to him, rolling him over and over. The whiteness turned black.

When he awoke he was in a small cottage bedroom. The window, almost level with the high bed in which he was lying, looked out over a dazzling landscape of snow. The sky was blue and cloudless. He put up his hand to shade his eyes, and someone drew the chintz curtains. He realised it was Aunt Emily: she looked exactly the same. 'Hello, dear,' she said. 'This is a funny way to arrive after all these years, and no mistake!'

'What happened?' Mr Pidgeon asked.

'Oh, Tom found you—or rather he found your bowler hat! *You* were completely buried—but he had you out in a jiffy.'

'Tom?'

'Tom Jordan—don't you remember? He lives in that cottage next to the churchyard. He says he heard a kind of roaring noise—snow falling from the top of the wall, I suppose—and went out with a torch. Lucky he spotted your bowler!'

'What day is it?'

'Sunday afternoon—three o'clock. The doctor gave you something to make you sleep. He'll be looking in again later.'

'Did he ... did he find anything?'

'Who, the doctor? Just a few bruises...'

'No, no! Tom Jordan, I mean.'

'Nothing but a lot of snow!'

'There wasn't ... there wasn't anyone else?'

'No, of course not! What a funny thing to say!'

'You're sure?'

'Of course I'm sure! You came alone, didn't you?'

'Yes ... Yes, I suppose so...'

A door opened and shut below, and brisk footsteps sounded on the narrow stairs.

'That'll be the doctor now,' Aunt Emily said, and left the room. Mr Pidgeon heard the two of them whispering on the landing.

The doctor came in alone. 'What's this I hear?' he said as he was examining Mr Pidgeon, 'about someone else being with you?'

'Oh nothing. I must have been dreaming.'

'H'm, yes ... Well, you're all right physically, but obviously you're strung up after your experience. You'd better stay here for a few days.'

'Oh no, I must get back tomorrow ... What's the weather forecast?'

'Eh, what's that?' the doctor said, regarding him curiously. 'Well, it's fine enough today, but the radio says there's more snow on the way, some time this month.'

'Then I *must* get back!'

'That would be most unwise.'

'I know what I have to do.'

'You do, do you?'

'Oh yes, I know exactly!'

It was fortunate that Mr Pidgeon worked in a solicitor's office. It needed some manipulating, and it used up a sizeable slice of his savings, but before the month was out he was standing beside an open grave in the churchyard at Parkton Combe, next to that of Doris, as old Perkins, in a brand new coffin, was being lowered into it. Apart from the clergyman and the undertaker's men he was the only one there—and he would hardly call himself a mourner. On the contrary, his heart leaped with joy as the first handful of earth pattered on to the coffin. It was another cold day, with a still, leaden sky. Winter was reluctant to let go. Most of the daffodils had been destroyed by frost, and people were worrying about the fruit crop. And something else was pattering on the coffin —large flakes of snow.

Mr Pidgeon had expected it. All the same, his body stiffened. The snow fell fast and steady. Before the service was over it had begun to settle. As the clergyman closed his prayer book and turned away, a gust of wind came whistling through the trees. It caught the powdery snow at the rim of the grave and whirled it upwards, into the shape—to Mr Pidgeon's eyes at any rate—of a tall, thin man, swaying slightly at the hips. Then the wind, subsiding, laid the scurry of snow back on the grave, as gently as if it had been a wreath.

Mr Pidgeon returned to the churchyard that evening, before he caught his train. Now the snow completely obliterated the clods of raw clay. It obliterated, too, the dividing-line between old Perkins's plot of earth and that of Doris. It lay thick and white—and as silent as the graves it covered.

CHRISTOPHER HOOD

The White Citroën

I was sitting beside the N.7., on the other side of Aix-en-Provence, during the last half hour of a May evening. Everything about me seemed charged with that lucid sense of existing entirely in the storm-eye of the present, an impression which I fought against, since it implied that by growing up in the shifting grey damps of England I had been deprived of something essential.

I was eating some bread with soft cheese from a round box—I always forget the name. It's about the only French diet which isn't colossally expensive and it's really quite nice and almost wholesome.

My litre of Ordinary Wine, (so funny in English) almost finished, had dispelled any delusions of urgency which I might have held about anything. Since dawn of that day I had travelled perhaps a hundred miles—no, kilometres. Getting lifts in France is like panning for gold.

I swallowed the wine and slid the bottle and the ends of my bread and cheese into my bag. I brushed myself down and stood up at the edge of the road, the bag aligned carefully against my shoes, a slow cigarette crackling quietly in front of my mouth.

Faithful to the compulsive lore of hitch-hiking I determined to try the next thirteen cars before using the ends of the daylight to find a good place to sleep. In front of me was a field of early sugar cane, with about half a barn in the far corner, its tumbled grey walls pale bronze in the falling sun.

I would look it over, I decided, if no lift turned up. Sometimes, of course, one carries on travelling after nightfall, but I couldn't be bothered. And the barn appealed to me strongly. I remember thinking that it had the quiet dignity of anything whose decay is entirely unchecked. That's the kind of mood I was in. It was clearly a perfect place to sleep. Unless it turned out to be a field workers' shit house. That's one reason you want a bit of daylight to look these places over.

Thirteen ungenerous cars duly drove past. Sixteen actually—a burst of nine, a five minute space, and a string of seven. I crushed my dog-end on the road and slung my bag up to my shoulder.

I am still unable to determine the cause of my sudden decision to try just one more car before exploring the barn. It certainly occurred when I heard the desperate, flat-out whine which was gathering towards me through the still invisible distance. But this was the trigger, not the cause. I am now bound to entertain the possibility of supra-logical forces—fate, doom, predestination. But at the time I hesitated, tossed a mental coin, and reluctantly felt that the appalling compulsion to travel had turned uppermost.

So I set down my bag and composed my stance and my face to look inscrutably engaging. The car ripped into view around the distant corner. It proved to be a Citroën 2.C.V., ivory white beneath broad smirches of dark yellow dust. I pulled my thumb back and forth, sure that it would tear straight past, but at something after the last minute the anchors were thrown on. Streaks of hot rubber pencilled themselves down the road, the back wheels lurching heavily towards the front. Its skid miraculously checked, the car stopped ten yards the other side of me. I ran up and opened the door. I said, '*Est ce-que vous allez . . . ?*'

'*Oui,*' said the driver, starting off.

I jumped in, hauling my bag after me, and slammed the door. He was already moving into top gear. The engine note climbed sharply to a whine as we gathered speed. And this was the point where the usual confines of reality were left behind. Because the sound never levelled off. It kept getting higher and higher. So, as far as I could tell, did our speed. The clock was broken, but we certainly weren't slowing down. When I glanced sideways the middle distance was a vague flicker and the road-side a deepening blue smear.

The features of a nasty corner grew rapidly across the windscreen. I was still thinking we would obviously slow down for this when we pelted straight into it as fast as ever, and as we screamed out the other side I was still waiting for the crash.

Nothing was an obstacle. Corners, cars, lorries, hills—everything taken at a speed which never let down—which always increased, steadily, insidiously, continually—the whine of the engine pushing at the brink of audi-tory perception.

Those cars have a gait like an old camel with heredit-ary syphilis. With all the bucketing around I had my right arm thrust through the window, clinging to the roof for all I was worth.

He never put the headlights on, even when it was pitch black. My God, I thought, he can see in the dark. It didn't seem at all unlikely. Approaching cars droned their horns and swished by, stabbing brilliance and shadow over his yellow grey skin, coarse greying hair, rigid grey eyes.

A fairly sharp turn, lurching and screaming, and we had left the main road. Something like trees either side, and steep hills and hairpin bends. Occasionally a glimpse of lights far below. One or two angry, astounded drivers forced off the road possibly, but it was too chaotic and too fast to see. Still a steadily increasing speed. Oddly enough I wasn't scared. Numb, possibly. Also the usual laws of physics seemed to have been suspended. I wasn't really thinking at all. I was just *there*. We can't crash, I thought, because if we were going to we would have done already. It was almost soothing. I began to enjoy it, anyway.

'*Ici*,' said the driver out of the blue. It was his second word to me, addressed towards the windscreen.

Where? I thought. What? I flexed my legs and straightened them rigid, and took a firmer grip on the roof with my right hand. We didn't slow down but time appeared to. We were climbing a hill. Stone walls to our right and left, holding back earth. A gully. Olive trees at the top, possibly. Sharp right hander, lights beyond— screaming into it, left hand side of the road.

Brightness. Noise. Spinning in brightness. Ripping. Shrunk body. Exploding. A roar of breath.

And Nothing...

There was something poking me in the ribs. A jackboot. Belonging to a motorcycle dick.

French phrases were bounding off beside my ears.

It was daylight.

Eventually I managed to sit up.

This cop had his hand out, talking continuously, imprecating.

Ah. I fumbled around for my passport. He glanced inside it, nodded, gave it back and got on to his Harley-Davidson and roared away.

Then everything came into my head at once. The drive, the car. The crash.

It was ridiculous to be still alive. I felt all my bones carefully. I was shaking all over. Nothing was broken, or even scratched.

'It's ridiculous,' I said aloud. My voice worked, too.

I lit a cigarette, consumed about half of it, and stood up to take some bearings.

And there over the road in front of me was a field of sugar cane with a broken down barn in the far corner. And there in the ditch was my empty wine bottle, while lying on the grass was my bag.

'A dream,' I said immediately, but it somehow wasn't plausible. I went over myself meticulously for any sort of change: scratch, tear, anything. I even went through my bag. Nothing was altered.

Eventually I discovered that my ring was missing. I'd worn it on my right hand. It was a large, heavy silver ring, depicting an octopus. He had seven tentacles—one of them was broken off.

But rings fall off—get stolen. There was nothing, I told myself, swinging my bag on to my shoulder and walking off, to prevent me from thinking it was a dream.

But there on the road were the skid marks the car had made when it stopped.

I went down to the south coast. I don't know why, but that's where one always ends up. I would lie on the beach, transfixed by the scalding sun, and feel the vast fabulous plateau to the north of me, without being able to get up and go off into it. If I wanted to write diatribes against industrial society, I thought to myself bitterly (O, every day) this is what I would describe. The reward. The goal. The dream fulfilled. Never mind the penalties; slums, prisons, dropped wombs, petty money-grabbing, hatred. Describe the aspirations and that's enough.

And so I pissed the time away, wandering up and down the coast, getting sunburnt, getting fed up, getting drunk occasionally. Here and there the natural beauty of the place still strong enough to take your breath away. Rounding a corner, a dark green hill shattering down into the brilliant flat sea: a boat skimming its shadow over blue and ochre rocks: the black chill before dawn, the lights of a harbour, voices thrown gently across the bay.

As for the question of the White Citroën—it was an insoluble problem, so I shelved it. Memory behaves oddly when you're on the bum. Yesterday often seems like last year. It's partly because you're always moving.

It did trouble me, the thought of it, and the crash, but only vaguely. It gnawed at me.

I suppose about three or four weeks went past. I was getting misanthropic and I noticed that I was spending too much money. It was time to go back. I decided this one evening when I was in Nice.

So I walked out to the appropriate side of town and took up a position by the road. It had been dark for several hours when I got a lift.

It was one of those huge French lorries, lit up like Christmas trees, which seemed to be equipped for travelling weeks on end through the trackless wilderness.

I ran up and opened the door.

'*Est-ce que vous allez vers Paris?*' I shouted. The noise of the engine was colossal.

'*Oui!*' he shouted.

Quite incredible luck. I jumped in and we crawled off.

It was nice, perched up in the dark cab behind sharp headlamps, eating through the night. Noisy and soporific. I liked the driver. He was friendly without being imposing. We exchanged cigarettes and pulls of Coca-Cola (his) and watery French beer (mine) and occasional shouted pleasantries.

He managed to convey to me that he'd have to stop once or twice, '*aux montagnes—pour* something *les* somethings.' To pick up some kind of fruit, was the impression I got. After that he was going to Paris '*tout droit*'. I smiled and nodded. After a while I fell asleep.

Once or twice I started gently awake with the grinding of low gears up mountain roads, and with the hushed slam of the door whenever he stopped to something the somethings, when I made half-hearted offers to help him load up which he graciously declined, and I would fall asleep again as we ploughed off into the darkness.

Then abruptly I became completely awake. I felt that I had just been thrown from an unremembered nightmare.

But the undertone of horror, instead of dying away with the expansion of wakefulness, increased with it. I searched about for ordinary tangible things to reassure myself, and each ordinary tangible thing filled me with panic.

We were driving through a kind of Alpes Maritimes one horse village, dark, its silence ground and pounded up by the noise of our passing. I shifted, trying to restrain the sea-monster which seemed to have got itself shut inside my rib cage. But there was no visible reason for my fear. It was now definite, overwhelming fear, but with no sign, flavour, intimation. Nothing. The driver glanced at me, and I gave him a kind of shaky smile.

He beamed back. '*Pas encore de stop,*' he said, '*on regagne la route; et après—Paris, tout droit.*'

'*Bon,*' I said, '*formidable.*'

I was going mad. The word 'terror' came into my head once or twice. There was no escape from it, like very bad toothache. But it had no name, no shape, no kind of baggage at all. I wanted to shout at him to stop the lorry. That was it. But why? What the hell could I say?

I stared out of the side window. It was somehow difficult to breathe. There was some sort of cultivation along beside the road.

The engine grinded its note downwards and we started down a hill. The road dropped between the land on either side of it, between stone walls which held the earth back. Suddenly much steeper, approaching a sharp left hand bend. I was rigid, voiceless; inside my brain a vast, electric-blue scream. It was just as we came into the corner. Right on the wrong side of the road something hurling itself into us. The lorry driver threw on the anchors instinctively, which made us slew head on into the wall.

There was a huge three seconds of black silence. The pressure had gone from my head but my heart was beating wildly, as if trying to pump it up again.

I climbed out. He got the lorry started again and backed away; flicked on a spotlight fixed to the top of the cab.

The thing we had hit was a Citroën 2.C.V. It was crushed against the wall like a dirty white horned insect, lurid with blood and oil, burst open. The lorry was dented in, and the headlamps were smashed. That was all. We'd been going slowly, and hit the car kind of side-on in the corner.

The driver leaned out of the cab.

'*Ils sont morts*,' he shouted, '*certainement. Viens! L'essence! L'essence!*'

He was right, of course. They must certainly be dead, and it was a miracle that the petrol hadn't blown up already. But the thing I had noticed was a human fore-arm. Probably it was still connected to the remains of the passenger in the black inside of the wreck. The spotlight had caught it—the right arm, thrust through the win-dow, its crushed fingers still clutching at the flattened twists of the roof.

And on the ring finger, a large silver ring. Depicting an octopus with seven tentacles, one of them having been broken off.

It took me a long time to turn away, but when I did, I ran like the wind. He had given up shouting to me and had backed the lorry right up the top of the hill.

As I reached it the car blew up.

KIT PEDLER

White Caucasian Male

Simon Anderson had no great hopes. As senior lecturer in the microbiology department of a teaching hospital, he spent most of his day with medical students who had already begun to frighten him with their sense of youth and attack. In between monotone and pedestrian lectures, he would perform obsessional experiments which he pursued for months at a time. About once a year, he was able to collect enough material to publish in a minor scientific journal where the quality of the editorial board was sufficiently low to ensure that his work would be accepted with a minimum of criticism.

His life conformed to a surprise-free ritual which kept him for ever having to look out at the clamouring world beyond the laboratory window. To see his name in print when the journal was published gave him one of his few remaining pleasures. He was quite unaware that one of his more aggressive colleagues had once remarked that: there are two sorts of research—the effect of A on B and good research. Poor old Simon, he had said, will always do the A on B sort.

Poor old Simon.

His day followed a rigidly established pattern. After leaving a bleakly resentful wife with a perfunctory kiss, he would cram on a very old hat and set off into the harsh morning light, bending his tall angular frame against the onslaught of noise and motion from the city.

In the laboratory, his entrance would evoke little reaction. Technicians would merely look up, smile and nod briefly, partly out of friendship and partly so that they could register his presence as a natural completion of the daily scene.

His subject was cell culture.

It is one of the odd quirks of nature that although humans are strictly mortal—beginning to die from the moment that they emerge from the womb—their cells, if grown separately from the body in special culture flasks—are for all practical purposes immortal. Once seeded out, they continue to grow until the time comes when they have to be put in a second container holding fresh medium.

For example, the cells from one human donor, started some twenty years ago, live on in nearly all the biological research laboratories of the world and it has been estimated that the gross weight of all the tissue from this one donor alone probably exceeds thirty tons. The original host of course is long since departed, his own flesh returned to the damp compost of the grave.

Simon worked with a particular family of cells of some ten years vintage. Originally taken from an accident victim in San Francisco, they had, in similar fashion, been grown and reseeded so that anyone who wished to do work on isolated brain cells would choose them as a standard. Since scientists need to achieve a certain minimum of ego-satisfaction, the cell strain had been dubbed with the name of the man who had first taken the tissue from a corpse on a post-mortem table in San Francisco. The cells were called: 'Wegner 414', but the body of the unidentified accident victim was blankly labelled: 'White Caucasian Male, name unknown'.

Simon's particular interest was the development of organs from individual cells. How is it that in the embryo, a small knot of primitive cells forms into a heart, a lung, or a muscle? The question has never been answered but it is certainly to do with complex chemicals called organisers. Minute amounts of these strange compounds can cause flat sheets of dividing and unspecialised cells to turn into parts of organs.

Anderson had made small but definite progress in this area and most of the workers abroad who used the Wegner 414 strain had received samples of his compounds for use on their own cell cultures.

Late one afternoon, Anderson slumped exhausted on his laboratory chair after a particularly gruelling seminar where a student had tried to turn a perfectly ordinary discussion on virology into a political debate. Almost without being aware of his movements, he inoculated a particular culture of Wegner 414 cells with his latest organiser, clipped it on to the slowly rotating wheel inside the incubator and left to face the fluorescent hell of the underground and supper with his wife and children.

It was the crossword in the evening paper which started the whole train of thought. There was no doubt, he was getting slower. There was once a time when he could get it nearly threequarters finished by the time he reached home. Now, he looked down at the crumpled paper on his knees and realised that he had only completed about seven clues. He looked up at his wife working through school exercise books piled on the floor beside her.

Ugly bitch! The violence of the thought shocked him slightly: she didn't really do any harm.

The crossword—he *was* getting slower, no doubt about it. To hell with it, there was still one thing left.

Anderson was a minor expert on port. Catching the habit on occasional visits to the senior common room at Oxford, he wrote occasional articles about the different vintages in a popular medical journal.

He sat gazing at the ruby glow of a Fuortin '59, the aroma of the last sip still exploding delectably in his nose.

Forty-seven! At forty-seven you could go up or down. Down to retirement—a small lab. party—cheap sour wine in plastic beakers—a contrived gift—don't do anything I wouldn't do Simon eh?—Oh God!

Up—what to?—'and now Professor Anderson is to address us on...' Applause, head bowed in humility, walking up to the rostrum, admiring eyes—brilliant chap Anderson.

Up or down? Down! Where else for God's sake? A formal obituary in the *British Medical Journal*: '...prolonged career of teaching and research ... will be greatly missed by his colleagues.' Missed! Who the hell by?

Nobody really understands the genesis of originality. Some innovators were probably certifiably insane, others were romantics and yet others had an equal parts mixture of imagination and logic. Their motivations are totally unknown.

In Simon's case it was partly the stark realisation of the choice between the two future paths open to him, partly the gulf between him and his wife and partly the seductive headiness of the Fuortin '59.

He was lying in bed visualising the molecular structures of his organisers and trying to see round a particularly severe problem, when the solution quite simply occurred. It just popped up in his mind like the sign in a cash register. But then it stayed, as obvious and as simple, as if he had always known it. But he hadn't and neither had anybody else. He turned it over and over in his mind—it couldn't be that simple. He lay awake staring at the dim outline of the ceiling light. The new molecular shape was right—it was almost certainly the answer. Not even a very difficult piece of chemistry. Someone must have thought of it—but no, there was no record. He was sure there was no record in the literature.

Slowly, reluctantly he gave in to the belief that he had had a genuine original idea. My God what would they all think? Old Anderson—thought he'd had it years ago —old Anderson, I'll be damned!

By two in the morning he had solved the remaining technical problems and by three he was visualising his nameplate on the office door: 'Professor Simon Anderson F.R.S.' Shortly before he fell into a restless sleep, he had glimpsed brief images of the wigged and powdered Nobel prize ceremony: the King shaking his hand. He no longer minded the lumpen form of his wife hunched beside him.

The next two weeks passed in an intolerable fever of excitement and anxiety, as he set up the apparatus to make his new organiser.

He began to reach the lab. early and to start work furiously at his own bench. Students at his seminars noted the change; there was a hooded confidence in his movements. One, the political joker of a previous occasion, tried the same ruse and retired pale and silent after a verbal onslaught from Anderson which left him bereft of reply.

Finally, it was done. In a sealed glass ampoule, there was a faint white smear of crystals. Ten one thousandths of a gram, just enough to cover the head of a pin. Delicately, with the most intense concentration, he broke the neck of the ampoule, poured in an exact amount of a pale yellow fluid and shook the ampoule until the crystals dissolved. Then he took out the culture flask of Wegner 414 and examined it under a microscope. A flat sheet of cells. No sign of any organisation. No order. He made careful notes, then, with a syringe, he gently placed two drops of fluid on the edge of the sheet of cells. Finally he sealed the flask, put it on the rotating wheel and gently closed the incubator door. There was nothing to do but to wait.

He went home as quickly as possible, snapped once, massively at his wife, poured out half a tumbler of non-vintage port—there was no point in wasting the good stuff—and sat down in front of the television set to try and relieve a near intolerable mental tension.

A research laboratory has a definite and regular daily rhythm. During the early hours of the morning, night cleaners whisk around the floors and mop down bench tops, carefully avoiding complex tangles of apparatus, labelled with urgent felt pen notices—'DON'T TOUCH', 'KEEP OFF' and 'DANGER'. After the cleaners have gone, there are a few hours of austere disinfectant-smelling quiet, then the first technicians arrive, changing from the bright colours of their city dress into the white-coated anonymity of the scientific acolyte. Then follow the junior scientific staff and finally the director who marches in, eyes flicking round to make sure the daily cycle is progressing well.

Gradually, the early morning silence is replaced by the clatter of glassware, the whirr of motors and the harsh sibilance of air jets. The smells of after-shave and hastily applied scent give way to the sharp tang of organic chemicals and the sour-meat smell of incubating fluids.

At intervals, there is a smell of illegally brewed coffee

and by the time the lunch break has arrived, the cool tidiness of the early morning is replaced by piles of dirty glassware, stained bench tops and crumpled paper.

During the afternoon, the pace is less hectic and just before the staff make ready to go home once again there is an almost ritual winding down. One by one, gas jets are snapped off, switches are clicked off, motors sigh down to silence and panels of coloured indicator lights flicker and die.

As the last technician leaves, he usually pauses by the door and looks carefully round to see whether there are any signs of activity. Finally, he locks up, leaving the great complexes of apparatus to pulse quietly under automatic control and to tend the microscopic aggregations of living tissue which they enclose.

There is almost complete silence, save for the occasional momentary click and rustle of a refrigerator automatically switching itself on and sometimes a faint creaking as hot metal cools. The orange eye of a neon indicator light will sometimes snap open in the dimness, startling the late visitor. But otherwise, it is as if the tense sinews of knowledge and skill embedded in the hard outlines of the equipment relax and rest in the darkness.

Anderson's experiment was enclosed in a small glass tube clipped on the slowly rotating wheel inside the damp, foetid womb of the incubator. Inside the tube, the cells were just beginning to sense the presence of Anderson's new compound.

Slowly, as the hours of the night slid away, the shapeless cells which had previously formed a continuous sheet of quite primitive tissue began to undergo a change. As the wheel rotated, the tube turned so that the fluid slowly washed over the surface of the quietly sensing membranes of the cells. Each unit in the flat sheet began to change its shape and move away from its neighbour.

Surfaces separated and the tiny envelopes of near perfect efficiency began to slide and undulate over the wet inner surface of the tube.

Minute protoplasmic fingers felt their way stealthily as each cell began to search for the surface of its neighbour. Gradually the fingers found a particular area of their neighbour's surface and remained attached so that by early morning the original flat sheet of cells had transformed itself into a network of interconnected units each one of which resembled a minute octopus. As the connections became more firmly established, soft signals began to travel around the net. Cell communicated to cell, speaking in an ancient staccato language of electrical spikes. Small currents began to flow around the growing colony until an almost imperceptibly tiny pulsation began.

No one understands how the brain works. Millions of cells are lumped together in a soft and vulnerable mass of tissue which can sometimes create great works of art and sometimes only just control the body in which it is resident. No one has been able to depict the difference, nor do they even know how many brain cells it is necessary to assemble to generate control or for that matter— intelligence. By the same token, no one can understand the genesis of delusion.

Anderson slept badly and by the time he was ready to leave for work he had already been physically sick with anxiety. On the way to the underground station still trying to fight down a recurring nausea, he gave only a cursory glance at a middle-aged man sitting in a blue Jaguar almost opposite to his front gate. As he crossed the road the man's eye flicked up from a newspaper and then almost as quickly cast down again.

Hard, boot button eyes.

His hands shook uncontrollably as he withdrew the tube from its clips on the wheel. Under the microscope, he focused down on the cells ...

Over the succeeding minutes, all his tensions and anxieties were swept away by an all infusing warmth. The back of his neck prickled, tears welled into his eyes and all the resentments and repetitive dullness of the years slid away in a great crescendo of feeling which he was totally unable to control. It had worked!

He sat immobile, tears streaming down his cheeks. A technician touched him gently on the shoulder asking if she could help, but he stayed still, alone with the experience, until suddenly unable to contain himself any further, he grabbed both the hands of the startled girl, held them briefly to his cheeks, then stumbled awkwardly to his feet and rushed from the room.

The following weeks were an agony of repeat experiments. All his obsessional traits rushed back into action. Each detail was properly logged and analysed. Each milligram, microlitre and wavelength recorded.

To his colleagues, the change was amazing. He walked with a spring, his voice took on a new authority and his movements at the bench were deft and economic. Opinion about the nature of his change varied, but most were agreed that he had acquired a mistress. 'Fancy old Simon —never have thought it—devious old bastard! Old Simon.'

One evening after a particularly heavy day, he was

relaxing alone in his living-room, when, on impulse, he walked to the window, parted the curtain and peered out.

A dim figure hunched in the driving seat, alone. No lights.

He sat down trembling. For God's sake! It was only twice, get a hold of yourself. Who could it be? Perhaps Gordel in Munich had heard rumours—bloody old Nazis —he might well send someone ... Now! Just a minute, let's reason this out. You're overtired, you've seen one man in one car outside your home just twice. So it's someone waiting for his girl-friend in the flats opposite and it's not the C.I.A., the Russians, Gordel or anyone else. It's just a middle-aged sugar daddy waiting for his girl.

And a paranoid tendency is an occupational hazard among scientists.

And the notes! God you left them in the drawer, it isn't locked. What if Rayburn finds them. He'd see in a flash—he's a good chemist, he'd know. He'd steal it all right—miserable opportunist...

Frantic with anxiety, he drove himself to his feet and paced the dark empty house. At one stage, he almost reached the point of telephoning for a taxi to go back to the lab. and retrieve his notes.

He heard the car drive off.

The telephone rang.

Furious at his panic and his weakness, he wrenched it off the hook. Silence, then the sound of a dozen different conversations echoing far away down distant lines. He listened, the skin on the back of his neck crawling. Someone, immensely far away, was calling his name: Anderson, Anderson, Anderson ...

He slammed down the receiver. In the silence of the room, the shadows fluttered around the pool of light from the standard lamp. His forehead was cold with sweat, his chest ached.

In the morning, it took him an age to open the bathroom window and look out.

No car. The early sun warmed his face. He felt sheepish.

Rayburn probably wouldn't have understood the notes. Anyway, he wouldn't have bothered. Who'd want to steal his experiments?

Over the ensuing weeks, his experiments built towards a climax. He sent samples of his new compound to colleagues in other countries, so that the effects he had seen could be confirmed. Each new batch seemed to produce a better specialisation in the cells from the 'White Caucasian Male'. Each cell developed finer branches and threw out more profuse connections with its neighbours.

One afternoon, at the microscope, he felt a presence behind him. He turned. Rayburn!

'What're you up to Simon? You're going like a mad thing?'

Perhaps he *had* read the notes. A mad thing. 'Oh I'm still trying out some new organiser variants—nothing much to show yet, I'm afraid.'

'Can I see?'

Rayburn bent over his shoulder and peered into the microscope trained on one of the tubes. Anderson snatched the tube away.

Then, hesitantly: 'Sorry, it's been out of the incubator too long already, I—er don't want it to get cold.'

He jerked the incubator door open and clipped the tube in position. Rayburn studied him gravely.

'Not overdoing it are you, lad?'

Lad—lad! Condescending bastard.

'No—no I'm fine—it's just a bit tedious that's all.'

He must have seen! Rayburn was looking down at his

notes. As casually as he could, he reached over and closed the notebook.

'Look, I'm sorry Tom—I've got an awful lot to finish today.'

Rayburn gestured at the incubator: 'Want to watch it Simon.' Then from the door: 'Take it easy.'

Take it easy. Don't do anything I wouldn't do—lad! Bloody hypocrite. 'Good night, Tom.'

He almost dropped the tube as he took it out of the incubator again and put it under the microscope. In the dim green light, he peered at the tiny motes slowly drifting in their nutrient. The nuclei in the cells were like eyes staring up the tube into his head.

White caucasian male, name unknown.

Eyes in the cells—a network of eyes.

White caucasian male, name unknown.

Wegner 414—the brain culture.

White caucasian male.

Multiple eyes.

It was then that he experienced the first vestiges of the pain. It simply entered his head, way beyond any possibility of control.

As if it didn't belong to him, he watched his hands stretch slowly out over the bunsen flame, he saw the flame curl and lick round the outline of his thumb. The flame sputtered and changed colour. Pain slammed through his head. He snatched his hand away and screamed.

The ugly probe of the pain drove through his body as he waited to cross the road to the underground station.

Eyes in the cells, white caucasian eyes. He stepped off the kerb ...

A car slewed sideways, tyres screaming, someone

grabbed his arm, pulling. The car disappeared round a corner. A blue car, a blue Jaguar.

By the time he reached home, the pain had gone. His thumb ached, but the deep elemental pulsing in his head had gone. He began to think more rationally.

There are a lot of blue Jaguars, it's a mass production car. Metallic blue is a standard colour. The man outside the home was waiting for his girl-friend. Rayburn is stupid. The material works. The others I've sent samples to will confirm it. All those other cultures will soon be showing signs of organisation. Seventy-four different cultures will soon be developing. Where are they? Let's see, New York, Melbourne, Odessa, Paris, Munich—yes Gordel should have got it going by now. Soon get confirmation.

All those other cultures. A world net.

In his dream, giant writhing cell masses fingered their way up to engulf him. There was a wet, glaring eye in each cell. Twisting, entwining, pulsing, pulling him down. In the background a pallid figure on the white tiled post-mortem table, the top of its skull lying like a ragged pink helmet on a separate trolley.

The pain began on the way up the stone staircase to the laboratory. As he opened the door, it flooded into his head. He sat down at his bench trembling, then looked at the incubator. As he walked over, the pain grew more intense and changed from a deep tugging discomfort to a shrill, agonising beat. He opened the incubator door and it streamed out at him.

Anguish and death.

Fighting the intolerable sensation, he groped in the darkness for the tube, pulled it off its clips on the wheel and stumbled over to the bench. Fumbling awkwardly with his bandaged hand for a bottle of concentrated acid, he pulled the cap off the tube and poured the fuming oily liquid down over the surface of the culture.

The pain snapped off as if someone had pulled a needle out of his brain.

The culture dissolved under the searing attack of the acid and the pain stopped...

Communication between people is usually by means of language. Sometimes the especially sensitive will learn about the feelings of another by the lift of an eyebrow, the poise of a hand or a swift movement of the eyes. Language can be spoken, or it can travel directly between faces. There is little difference between the two, but all are agreed that it can happen. Where disagreement starts is whether brain can talk directly to brain, whether there may not be another more ancient and undefined language which travels secretly across the ether enabling one person to receive knowledge of another's behaviour without involving either the senses or the spoken word. Orthodox scientists largely reject this possibility because it is not easily amenable to experiment. Anderson was never unorthodox, so he was bound to experiment.

It took him just over a week to restart a new culture of Wegner 414 and inoculate it with his new organiser. An obsessional trait will always overcome fear. This time there was no doubt in his mind. The pain returned. It grew worse as he approached the culture in the incubator and diminished as he left.

Gradually, the influence of the cells seemed to reach out beyond the laboratory walls. At first, the pain only started as he got to the laboratory. Then he began to be aware of it in the road, then in the underground and finally, he could just sense the deep grating tension in his own living-room. There was no place to hide from the white caucasian male. From the post-mortem slab in

San Francisco to a London laboratory, from the dying cells of an unidentified accident victim to immortality in a flask—in *many* flasks. In flasks all over the world!

He conceived a vast global network. They were everywhere! New York, Melbourne, Odessa, Paris, and in Munich. Gordel had several cultures!

As the jet descended towards Munich, the stewardess gave only a cursory glance at the unshaven figure hunched awkwardly in a seat at the rear of the aircraft. He looked ill, she thought, but not like a bomber. She looked at the tremor of his fingers and forgot about him.

It started in the square outside the Krankenhaus where Gordel had his laboratories. Slightly at first and then more sharply as he approached the supercilious stone façade of the main research block. Then at the main entrance, a flood of burning agony poured into his brain ...

He ran.

Lebrun's laboratories lay tucked away at the edge of a wood near Marcousie south of Paris. He was already over conscious of the noise of his shoes on the gravel as he approached through the tall silent pines. There was no pain. A cool wind fanned gently over his face. No pain. His spirits began to lift.

Maybe Lebrun hadn't got a culture growing. He must have; he'd written. As he walked on, the sharp scent of the woods calmed his ragged senses. There was no pain. He stopped for a moment savouring the clean air, then sat down on a pile of logs at the side of the path and reflected on the long weeks of experiment, the strain, the uncertainty. He recalled his wife's disbelieving expression when he told her that he had been called away urgently to Europe. He worried briefly about the cost of the fares, then looked up at the bright shafts of sunlight streaming through the misty trees. Gradually, the calm of the wood soaked into his mind, brushing away the jagged edges of his tension. They were only cells—a sheet of developing cells. It was totally unlikely that they were behaving in any brain-like way. It was ridiculous to suppose that they could have any influence on his own mind. His feet curled in his shoes with embarrassment and shame as he recalled his previous fantasies. All the people in the lab. must have thought he was crazy. Bloody fool way to behave. Oh God they must have really thought he was mad.

There was no pain. Of course there wasn't any pain. He got up and walked on towards the laboratories tucked away at the foot of the hill.

As he passed between the two pitted stone griffons guarding the steps up to Lebrun's institute, he felt the first tug at the base of his skull. As he walked on, it grew until shining spears of agony stabbed through his head. He stopped. The whole area seemed deserted. The stark branches of the trees were woven into an enclosing net, preventing escape. Behind him, the path stretched back through the woods, the outline of the most distant trees lost in a blue haze. The pain showered down on him from all directions. It probed in intolerable bursts of intensity. He stumbled and began to run back down the path. The trees knotted their branches together like cells—like eyes—to bend down, to give pain.

The car rounded the griffons, its tyres crunching in the gravel. He turned.

Light metallic blue—the characteristic shape. He stood transfixed. The soft rumble of the exhaust grew to an urgent crackle, stones shot away from the rear tyres. The black cell net of tree branches swooped down. The car loomed. He lurched round searching for escape. The pain stunned him. He froze.

The figure at the wheel, naked, pallid white, the crude post-mortem stitches on the chest. The top of the head open like a cup.

Eyes in the woven branches. Eyes in a net of cells— pain and eyes.

Hard, boot button eyes. Pain and failure.

An overwhelming compulsion forced him back into the path of the car. The great chromium teeth leapt at his chest...

MAGGIE ROSS

When the Music's Over, Turn Out the Lights

That day she almost told him. What stopped her was not the desire to be secretive, but rather the conviction that between them was such complete understanding that words might distort or even shatter it. No, not shatter ... Already she could feel the thoughts coarsening as she tried to define them. Nothing between them would ever break. She was not afraid. But what she most desired was the continuance of a relationship in which the subtlety and strength of silence counted for as much— or even more—than a million intimate conversations.

It had always been that way between them. If there had been times when she might have liked to ask more about his feelings, she had learned restraint. When she had asked and he had politely answered, she had known the mistake was hers: she hadn't been sufficiently sensitive to understand without the questioning. In those distant days she'd thought she'd seen the hint, the glint of something like alarm in his eyes as he told her she should know his feelings instinctively. And she did. It was obvious. Nothing was in doubt. How could such a relationship as theirs have areas of shadow? If she hadn't told him yet it was only that she was waiting for some moment when his attention would be hers completely. Then she

would speak about it, and he would understand. At once
he would put her fears to rest and reaffirm their closeness.
Meanwhile she would wait patiently, hoping he might
save her by noticing himself that something out of the
ordinary was beginning to bother her.

Beginning. Only beginning. The merest cloud floating.
A shadow floating over her head. Or rather *his* head,
since he seemed to be involved from the very start. But
how to tell him? It floats? Over your head? No. Inaccurate. It seems to be there where you are ... wherever you are. Alongside you. Around you ... But was it?
Wasn't it only the faintest image of something shadowy
which seemed to follow him? Was it anything? That was
the worry. But when he came home from the shop didn't
it enter like a second shadow? Electric light on or off.
Sunlight or rain. No, not even like a shadow. It accom-
panied him at a distance as if in response to the turn
he always made as he closed the living-room door. As if
it manifested itself along with his smile. As if it faded as
his smile changed, so that when he came close it was
hardly visible, and had vanished as he kissed her.

'A good day, darling?'

'Not so bad.'

Lately it was always the same. The usual pleasantries
about the day and work and how he and she had been;
she trying to think of ways to show her involvement in
what he did. He liked to talk about optics, the difficult
cases he'd dealt with that day. She always agreed that
prompt diagnosis was important. She was pleased for him
he'd lately discovered a case of tunnel vision. With professional pleasure he prophesied that the patient's sight
would surely diminish to pinpricks of light. She told him
again how good he was at his job and asked, as was
customary, what else had been happening in the optician's
world.

'Only the usual set of hypochondriacs, wasting my time.' And, he added, the usual boys and girls from shops and offices in search of novel lunchtime amusement.

'I hope you're kind to them,' she said, and he looked at her sharply. 'Not many tests today?'

She was ready to be sympathetic, but he gave her that extra brilliant smile she knew hid some irritation, and told her business was brisk enough. She avoided furthering the subject for fear she might misjudge him. Her own over-sensitivity might be the fault. Once he had told her so, long ago when they had spoken more freely about such matters. How strange that there had been a difference in those early days. She had forgotten how imperceptibly things can change. He had once told her that her reactions were too sensitive. In those distant days before she'd learned to like the silences, there had been abrasive moments of question and evasive answer. And his confession that such super-sensitivity might only succeed in pushing them apart. Now she wondered whether she might dim the brilliance of his smile by telling him of her problem there and then: whether she could change the coldness in his eyes with an appeal for aid. It wasn't going to be easy. There was a chance, despite his naturally affectionate nature, he wouldn't see she might need help. For a moment she wished she was one of his patients—some unknown girl impulsively pouring out her feelings and fears because, in his white coat, the strange optician looks so attractively reassuring. She thought how unusually handsome he looked. And remote.

It was better to wait for a while. She must marshall her thoughts and try to find a more scientific way to tell him how it was beginning to colour her life. She must find facts. Dates. When had it begun? Had she noticed it first only a few short weeks ago? Not before? Hard to think back over six or seven years and be sure ... Perhaps it had come before and passed unremarked, coinciding with those grey, murderous moods of hers when she had felt ... what was the word? ... bereft...

It was becoming frustrating to discover her inability to be accurate. Memories, ideas, feelings, words all floated through her brain in hazy convolutions. If she tried to grasp at them she was left with tiny pricks of pain as if she had clenched on a cactus. The pain of what should be pleasant memory: the holiday in France which had been so immensely enjoyable. Yet now it came to her clouded. Only the faintest suspicion of a cloud, but hovering over that holiday as if the sun which had shone so bright had become masked by impending rain. And other times and other holidays which, in retrospect, she now saw through a thin, grey veil which hovered and held like a canopy over her husband's head. If she closed her eyes she could see him last summer, clearly standing on the battlements of the castle at Hvar, his arm encircled by a twining mist. She rushed at it and beat it away and watched it float down to the pavement below and vanish without trace. He said she had sunstroke and made her rest. So long ago. The photographs in the neat album revealing nothing but the sunny smiles.

And now it had started again. A few weeks ago. Exactly when? She remembered his coming home cheerful. At dinner he'd spoken a great deal about an old gentleman's macula which was giving him cause for concern. Yet after a while it had seemed to her he was speaking on a subject which interested him no more than marginally, while in reality his mind was wandering to other things. It was then that her eyes gradually became aware of something cloudy floating directly behind him, a few feet from the table where they sat. At first she thought she might be liverish, due to the richness of last night's meal and the ensuing restless night. But she came to the conclusion that what she was seeing moved in a way quite separate from the functioning of her eye muscles.

She mentioned the thing to him immediately. Not liking interruptions he replied abruptly that everyone suffered from floating vitreous matter from time to time, continuing with his tale of the faulty macula as if she'd seen nothing. She could have sworn the shape was too large to be contained within her own aqueous humour. It hovered at the door, staying for some time and distracting her from trying to ascertain the cause of his distraction. Later, when they sat together and she played to him, it went and didn't appear again that night.

A few evenings later she saw it again. He seemed to bring it with him, this second shadow, which grew with the brightness of his smile, then faded the nearer he approached. When he held her it vanished, yet at times she thought she could see it still, quivering in the corner of her vision as if struggling against departure.

And with the passing days it seemed to come more frequently and stay longer. Always the same. Always hovering and quivering and moving in with him like an obedient dog overjoyed at his return. Or a well-trained alsatian ready to defend its only master. She was beginning to give it form—a dog sometimes, sometimes an ape. A cat ... a tree ... a typhoon gathering. Even when it wasn't there she thought she saw the shadow of its shape growing stronger, more assured. But it had no shape. It wasn't a tree, an ape, a dog ... Or it was all these. At times its shape was extraordinary ...

Thoughts rose in such confusion that only on later consideration could she see how often her conclusions were contradictory. What had she pushed over the parapet that sunny Yugoslavian day? It was no dog. No dog waited in the house all day for his return. She never saw it then. Only the shadowy memory which made her tense as she

entered rooms, prepared for something to spring out
from behind closed doors. When she sat practising her
music, seeking distraction by playing the guitar, she tried
to pretend she wasn't listening for other sounds in other
rooms. If, beneath her fingers, she felt the tremor of an
alien vibration, she put it down to her own incompetence
and a nervous disposition which music always seemed
to heighten. It was as if she was afraid of her own fear.

She told her friend it was getting worse and asked her
what to do. Juliet said: 'Define the fear,' and didn't scoff
at her confused explanations. 'Perhaps it's in the house,'
she said. 'We'll search it out and pin it down. And kill
it.'

They searched the house together—just for a game,
Juliet said. They peered at floorboards looking for stains
of ancient blood, tapped walls which might be hollow,
hung garlic across the central heating vents and laughed
like children. Both were half-hoping for some small mani-
festation but there was nothing. They played the game
of search and disappointment to the end, arriving at the
same conclusion, that one of them might soon have a
mental problem.

Juliet came more frequently to see her friend, to share
her increasing unease; to listen to her troubled conjec-
tures; to try distracting her with music. She bought and
brought new sounds to supplement her friend's collection, sounds so amazing and so loud that nothing should
survive them.

Headphones clamped to their ears they sat together
side by side in the afternoons, letting the incredible
Hendrix guitar sweep over them, giving themselves up
to the embrace of Can and the Soft Machine. They
worked their way through the Stones and Beefheart and
Focus and Yes and Bowie and Rory Gallagher as if life
depended on it. And for a few hours each day the music

beat out an approximate happiness. And if, from time to time, the singers cried out at the pain of insecurity and loss, their words gave reassurance that others were aware of how blurred the margins of madness were.

'Why doesn't he notice anything?'

'Why should he? You're normal enough.'

'He smiles sometimes as if he knows.'

'But you haven't told him yet?'

'No.'

'Then he doesn't know.'

She gripped Juliet's arm. 'He's getting careless of me.'

'And you're getting obsessed by him. You should take a job and get your mind on other things.'

'"Opticians' wives don't work"!'

'Of course he cares. Look at the records he brings home...'

'That's what I mean. He never used to. It's making me nervous.'

'Then you must tell him straight what it's doing to you.'

'He hates speaking about intimate things...'

'You'll have to run the risk of upsetting him.' Although why he should be upset she couldn't see. Since he couldn't detect his wife's suffering for himself, she supposed he must be preoccupied. It was understandable that professional problems might take precedence over the nervous behaviour of a neurotic woman. She could see how irritating it might be to have a wife of such microscopic sensitivity since (in her private opinion), he was lacking in it himself. Her advice was to wait for an opportunity when she had all his attention.

He himself had told Juliet how busy he was at work. She refrained from mentioning his wife's worsening condition, with the excuse to herself that the matter was very personal. Instead she tried questioning him obliquely on visual anomalies in the highly strung. In answer he bewildered her with lectures on thyrotrophic exophthalmos and scotomas, becoming quite excited at the prospect of her as his patient. She was forced to admit her interest was only mildly academic and very dilettante and she was not to be taken seriously in any way. His books gave no clues to her friend's condition. She worried over rod cells and the effects of myopia, frightening herself with diagrams and accounts of ocular disorders. Either nothing was wrong. Or everything.

'You'll have to ask him for a sight test.'

'He's always testing my sight. He used to gaze into my eyes nearly once a week with that awful opthalmoscope. I was his practice ground! Dropping drops into me. Making me stare at Ishihara plates!'

'When did he last test your eyes? Properly, down at the shop?'

It was two years or maybe more.

'Too long. Ask him for a test this evening.' She was worried for her friend.

The shape came again that evening. It came in with him through the door, clearer by far than it had ever been. It moved as he moved—breezily and fast as if it was capable of taking his mood. Apologising for his lateness he came towards her holding out his arms. He had almost reached her when she saw the oncoming cloud beside him. She shouted 'Look out!' thinking they would be in collision. At her warning he swerved away from the swinging door, unaware of what she'd seen. The thing swerved with him. She closed her eyes and felt his arms close around her trembling body. He didn't seem to notice how she shook. He asked if she'd missed him. When she opened her eyes the shape had vanished.

He told her she mustn't look so gloomy, because today he had something extra nice for her. These days she always looked a little sad, so he wanted to surprise her with a special gift. He couldn't help the hours he worked, so it would while away the times of his absence a little better. He knew how music pleased her. He thought it an excellent hobby. And she deserved a better guitar than her present one. Here was an instrument worthy of the musician she could become. Now she must practise seriously. Not knowing about the finer points himself, he'd taken the advice of the girl in the music shop who had assured him that this guitar was the equal of any Ramirez—whatever that meant. Now she could occupy herself happily for hours.

For an instant she thought she saw the merest wisp of a cloud go sailing past his face as he put the beautiful instrument into her hands.

He said he liked to think her happy while he worked. He suspected she wasn't too pleased with the present state of his affairs, and he was sorry. Lately, he said, the tiny lines between her brows were becoming noticeable. There was a slight reddening of her conjunctiva. He wouldn't like it if she lost her looks. Now she really had no excuse for frowns.

'Might it be a good idea if I came and had my sight tested?'

He looked surprised, briefly shook his head and asked whether the gift had displeased her. He'd spent a lot of time and money searching for tone and quality.

'It's beautiful.'

'I knew you'd like it. She suggested I buy an electric guitar! But you know what these girls are—mad on noise. Heavy Rock and all that!'

'I like it too. You know I do.'

'Yes, but you must admit it's not really your scene. I

can't see you as a groover!' He laughed and walked away from her. 'Sitting with your ear glued to the amp at some tatty Rock concert!'

'But we've been to concerts...'

'I see the classics as more your style.'

'Don't you like Rock any more?'

'I didn't say that.' There was slight irritation in his voice. 'For somebody who's just received a present, you're remarkably argumentative.'

'I'm sorry darling, but I'm confused. Of course I like the classics. It's lovely to learn to play a piece of Renaissance music properly. But I like listening to music that's really modern. And really overwhelming.'

She wanted to explain how necessary it was to drown the beating of her blood. To still the tingling in her skin which seemed to spread through her entire body whenever she paused for thought. She wanted to be taken over by a beat as primitive as the urgent fear which daily rose in her the closer the time to his homecoming. She wanted a wall of sound to protect her from what she was beginning to think of as a malevolent force.

'The neighbours don't appreciate the blast!' he said.

'Are your tastes changing?' she was trying to keep her voice light.

'Not necessarily.' He opened the door and walked towards the kitchen. 'It would be nice if we ate soon, don't you think?'

She followed him. 'Please don't think you have to keep buying all those records for my sake ... If you don't like them.' She was inexplicably worried. 'I thought you really loved Rock music. I mean ... We used to enjoy it so much and ...' He began to set the table, rattling the knives and forks.

'It would be nice,' he said, 'if we dropped the subject

and ate. And it would be nice if you, my darling, enjoyed yourself a little more.' He smiled brilliantly at her. And she could see behind him that the outline of the cupboard was half obliterated by the shadowy shape of a person, smaller than he, but smiling just as brilliantly.

'We must keep you happy,' he said. The shape vanished. 'It's worth a lot to me.'

She fetched the plates and put them to warm. When she stood up, he was at the refrigerator. 'I can always tell her you don't like the guitar and take it back,' he said. Beside him she saw the vertical cloud formation begin to take shape again. She saw the outline of a body. Saw what looked like trousers the colour of smoke. And above them a smock of a lighter shade, criss-crossed by refrigerator shelves and the plastic jars inside. She saw a pair of hands materialise, moving so transparently that through them she could see the drawer marked BUTTER. And the smile coming and going more strongly than the other features, reminding her of Alice's sinister Cheshire cat. She stood very still, watching and wondering why the creature moved its body from side to side and its hands in circular motions. She wondered what sex it was.

'Please don't upset yourself, darling.' His fingers were pressing her shoulder. His face came between her and the cloud. He straightened and her vision was clear. Nothing but the refrigerator door and the bowl of salad in his hand.

'I think I don't feel very well,' she said. 'I shan't eat anything tonight.'

'Now what's the matter!' He was getting inordinately angry. 'You know I hate to eat on my own!' He banged the bowl on the table. 'I've never seen such a foolish mood. Are these my thanks?'

She said she was sorry and sat with him, making a pretence of eating while he reiterated in increasingly vehement tones that he could always return the wretched guitar.

To please him she began to practise seriously, sitting by herself in the trembling afternoons trying to make sense of crochets and semibreves; forcing her fingers to mute notes she would rather have ringing a thousand-fold stronger. Forcing a calm she no longer felt, until dark thoughts and fears overcame the good intentions. Then to the telephone in sudden panic to speak to her friend and be reassured by her sympathy. More and more frequently she rushed from the house and met Juliet in some noisy place of calming banality, to tell what the previous night had been like, to diminish the madness in torrents of talk. To repeat over and over what it was she thought she was seeing.

She said it was human. It had a face. The shade of a face surrounding a smile. It had hair like a brief brush-stroke across a wide brow. And hands which moved. She'd seen them held out to him as he walked towards the bedroom door. When she called goodnight they disappeared into darker woodwork.

'And you really don't believe in ghosts?' she asked Juliet.

'Of course not! But I will if it makes you feel better.'

'I think I'm getting worse. He keeps looking at me strangely.'

'If you believe he loves you, you'll tell him,' Juliet said.

'He mustn't think I'm ill. It would upset him terribly. He doesn't like sick people. Some of his patients disturb him dreadfully. He's sensitive like me. That's why he married me—we're so alike. We're very close.' Juliet nodded. 'I feel as though I'm part of him. When he speaks to me sometimes, I tingle.'

Lately she had realised that the tingling was the fore-runner to something worse. When she tingled the cloud came. Lately she found herself waiting with horror for the sensation to spread, moving upwards through her neck, lodging where spine and skull meet. As the cloudy shape solidified she could feel the tingling spread through her head, splintering her sanity. 'I want to rush at it and stop it. Hit it. Kill it. But it's always on the other side.' She'd tried looking away, but it came and caught her unawares. Often he'd be in mid-sentence when its shimmering form hovering like a heat-haze appeared behind his shoulder.

'You're afraid to tell him,' Juliet said. 'Are you waiting for him to notice what's wrong himself?'

'Yes.'

She didn't want to say that in her opinion her friend would wait a long, long time.

'But these days he seems too busy to notice anything...'

These days he spoke about work from the moment he arrived home. While still removing his coat he would begin speaking excitedly about what was happening at the shop. With feigned enthusiasm she asked about his patients, the health of the receptionist, the tempers of the dispenser and the delivery man, and the latest factory errors. She could see how such trivialities pleased him. His conversation, so concerned with life's realities, made her ashamed of her personal weakness. She would try to be more like him—strong and clever and practical, with no use for the morbid areas of introspection. Yet with every attempt she could feel the distance grow between them, and found the pretence of sanity more difficult.

At night she watched him in the bedroom stripping his

shirt while still carrying on what had become a virtual monologue. He didn't seem to notice any more that by the evening's end she had ceased all conversational pretence and was silent. He seemed a stranger. She looked at his brown back but refrained from touching him. Only a few nights ago she had sat beside him on the bed, caressing him, while he continued speaking about presbyopia as if he felt nothing. Was she really going mad?

She asked him one evening: 'Do you think I'm going mad?'

'Why on earth should you?'

'What? Go mad?'

'No—think you're going mad. You're very ordinary really!' Then he laughed and she joined in with relief. She thought she would tell him about the apparition soon.

She thought about nothing else. During her solitary evenings, when the passing of time had been measured by the length of several long-playing records, she tried to ascertain the ghost's exact movements: it either stood, or floated somewhere near him, often in the corner of the room, but close and often closing in. When he sat it stood behind his chair. It hovered near the mirror when he shaved.

He was shaving late one night when she saw its reflection beside him in the glass. The smile was coming and going ferociously. He heard her gasp.

'What's the matter, darling?'

'Nothing . . .'

He turned back to his shaving unperturbed.

'I thought I saw a ghost.'

'Looks like it too!' he said without turning his head.

'A female ghost.'

'Jolly good!' He was wiping his face on a towel. He was going towards the bedroom.

She followed slowly, trying to summon the courage to speak.

At the bedroom door she stopped, startled by the sight of another woman standing in their bedroom watching her husband get into bed. She saw her for less than a second, the female form fading as the man pulled the sheet over his shoulder and settled. Trembling she undressed and slid into bed beside him.

She heard his heavy breathing. 'I'll describe her, if you like.'

'What . . . ?'

'Your ghost . . .' After a pause she continued: 'She's fairly tall with cropped, shining hair. Young too. Twenty-ish . . . Can ghosts have ages, I wonder? She often wears different clothes. Today she's wearing a dress which clings. I didn't see it properly. But I know her face. A wide mouth and a big smile.' She paused again. 'Funny, isn't it? Although she smiles I feel her animosity. Do you know what I mean?'

He groaned and put out his arm to pat her. 'When did you say you wanted your eyes tested?'

The following day he brought home another record. 'James Brown for you!' he said. 'Supposed to be fantastic. Bit too noisy for me though!' He left her to listen and went to do something to the car, returning immediately to ask her to lower the volume. He said the neighbours might not appreciate the finer points of Mr Brown's voice. She kissed him and he hugged her, unaware that over his shoulder she was looking straight at a shadow of a smiling woman.

'I love you,' she said defiantly.

He looked surprised. 'I love you too!'

On the day she went to the shop they were very kind. The receptionist gave her sympathetic smiles as if in reassurance. The dispenser took her coat and asked most sweetly after her health. Her husband led her into the consulting room as if she were an invalid, and spoke in tones usually reserved for the old or partially deaf. His room with its dark panelling, soft carpet and quasi-clinical air suited him exactly, she thought. His attitude was different from at home: here he was dealing not with his wife but with any female patient with neurotic tendencies. He seemed so tough and disciplined that for the first time she recognised that there might be another side to his character. She wondered how a ghost would fare in such a chill atmosphere. So far there were no signs of her, although there was light enough from the chart to see into the corners of the room.

She read the test-type perfectly with both eyes, insisting she could see PRINTED IN ENGLAND at the bottom of the card. He asked if she could confine her levity to a more appropriate time.

'Now I must look into your pupils,' he said.

'How nice! What colour are my eyes?'

But all he said was that she was too tense. She was being difficult. Before he could examine the retina he'd have to put drops into her eyes. She wanted to explain it was his closeness in the confining dark which was tightening her nerves. She imagined herself a stranger feeling the touch of his knees on hers, his sweet breath in her face as he directed his blinding light which would penetrate right to the centre of her mind. How could any woman fail to respond?

She felt the drops. The room had gone dark. They waited in silence for her pupils to expand.

'I can see her feet!' she said suddenly. 'I felt her come! She's in here now! She's standing behind you!'

She heard him turn. 'I can't see her!' he said. 'And the door's still closed! Where is she now?'

But she'd already gone.

He told her she was too fanciful. They were alone. She must sit very still and be quiet and not get hysterical about absolutely nothing at all. He was a busy man, and had other people waiting.

He continued the test and she wondered where his patients were. Nobody had entered the shop. Outside no sound except the quiet conversation of the receptionist and the dispenser. And the steady rhythm of the air conditioning beating out what sounded like a tune by Spooky Tooth.

The telephone rang and she heard a voice saying the optician was busy testing his wife's eyes. The receiver replaced. Then silence outside. Not even conversation. And she could hear the distant roar of highroad traffic.

'Your eyes are perfect, my dear. Your macula is quite delightful! There is no sign of high blood pressure, diabetes, cataract, glaucoma or a squint! I could correct a very slight astigmatism, but the lens would be weak indeed.'

'I shan't wear spectacles,' she said. She was afraid she might see his ghost more clearly.

'Good! I'm getting rather tired of what you can see already.'

He showed her into the street and told her to be careful going home and not to talk to strange women without substance. At the corner she turned to wave and saw him through the window shaking his fist vehemently at the receptionist.

Instead of going home, she phoned Juliet. She said she was Cassandra doomed forever to be misunderstood. She said the frustration was killing something inside her brain. She felt a wild and murderous desire to hit out at what was always out of reach. It was worse than when she'd tried to push the shadow over the ramparts at Hvar. The thing was more attainable and yet more distant. And her husband didn't understand. 'She's become a barrier between us. If it weren't for her, he'd understand. She's trying to separate us!'

'Ghosts can't hurt you,' Juliet said. 'They're in the mind.' But she said no more on the subject, afraid for her friend's sanity. By the sound of her voice she needed practical help. Or at least, distraction. 'We'll go to a concert,' she said. 'A nice, noisy one. You'd like that, wouldn't you?'

'I think I would. I can't stay at home...'

'There's a Rock Festival on at the Round House.'

It was hot. Somebody said the temperature was at boiling blood heat. When they arrived a band was already on the stand with the amplifiers up to a roar. The two women fought their way through the crowded outside corridor, pushing through the pillars until they could glimpse the stage where a group was tearing up the air. On stage a boy in buckskins was performing spectacular embroidery with his arms while the band created amazing riffs and runs, and the audience shouted encouragement. On the floor below the stage the usual clusters of dedicated listeners lying quietly smoking and rocking to the beat, oblivious of the trampling feet. A few people managing to dance against the stream of others pushing past to gain seats on the ramps behind. People by the hundred—singing, shouting to friends, coughing in the rising smoke, scrambling good-humouredly for room. The balcony above was already crowded, the rows of faces peering down and glowing rainbow colours in the strobe lighting; watching the movement of the crowd below—

the swaying phalanxes of bright colour and shade which filled the great circle with a pattern of people as exciting as if this night was the culmination of a prehistoric rite which might build to an unforgettable climax.

The music was going to be good. It rose and shrieked to the rafters and came down to loosen the body and dement the mind. They felt themselves caught up in the atmosphere, and were content to move with the majority, gently progressing in the press until there was space to stand for a while and listen before moving on. Close together they shuffled, Juliet's hand through her friend's arm, her mind both on the music and on the trembling energy she could feel beside her. Occasionally a shudder passed through her friend caused, she hoped, by the passion of the band and nothing more sinister.

In a slow and halting perambulation they kept up their own rhythm as number followed number. Across the floor to stand by the stage and let the amplifiers reverberate through their bodies in a deafening beat; through the joyful dancing girls to the outer edges where the shadows were darker and the voices as vociferous as the singers, until they were performing a slow series of circumscribed movements to which the music kept accompaniment. And in them both a rare excitement.

Not until an hour or more had passed was there some slackening in the progression. By then most movement in the central area had slowed. The earlier bands had gone and everyone was waiting for Black Sabbath. Road managers were setting up complicated arrangements of drums and mikes and amps, while a disc jockey tried to make himself heard above the din. Then from the loudspeakers came the recorded voice of Jim Morrison reliving 'Weird Scenes Inside the Gold Mine' for an audience who, since his death, had never forgotten him.

Test lights were coming up and glowing, reflecting

like blood on the massed faces looking down from the gallery.

'What a crowd,' Juliet said. 'Shall we go upstairs?' She felt her friend go rigid beside her. 'What's the matter?'

'That's her!' She was looking up and she saw her. Clearly. Recognisable. She knew the shape of the face. The brush stroke of hair. The wide, wide smile. And the hands moving in time to the music. She was up there between the pillars of the gallery, looking over the balcony. She was moving in time to the beat. She was smiling. She was pleased. Her face was the colour of blood, and it was malevolent. 'See! Up there! She's up there . . . !'

With alarm Juliet felt the arm she held begin to tremble as if charged by a thousand electric volts. Then numbness as her hold was released and she found her own hand holding on to nothing. Her friend had escaped and was already throwing herself forward like a maniac. She watched the crowd hurled back and tumbling and heard the cries of anger and astonishment at such brutal behaviour. Helplessly she watched her friend fiercely moving through them towards the black shadows. Someone murmured about madness. She kept her eyes on the place where her friend had gone, trying to detect her in the crowded darkness swept suddenly by lights which contorted and disguised the sea of heads. A small scuffle near a pillar on the other side: angry shouts coming from the corridor leading to the stairs . . .

She stood very still waiting, looking up to the gallery for signs of disturbance. Jim Morrison had begun 'When the Music's Over' to the clash of drums and cymbals being tested on stage. She saw the same mass of faces and undulating arms patterned in garish colours by the strobe lighting; faces made expressionless by the changing flow of purple and green, and running red blood light. A microphone wailed, echoing a shrill cry.

Up in the gallery a section of the crowd had turned. They were facing some disturbance, jostling and jumping to see what was happening.

Amid the music, a woman's voice high pitched, coming from the depths of the gallery. The freezing fear in her blood because she recognised the voice. Around her people were beginning to look up.

Many saw what happened and spoke about it afterwards, but the stories varied. Some said the woman with cropped hair seemed to fall backwards over the balcony to her death unaided. Others, more numerous, said they saw her being pushed by the crazy-looking woman—the one who leaned over to stare at her victim lying broken on the floor below. Some asked why the man hadn't intervened to save her since his arm had been round her at the time.

Juliet saw and remembered only the look on her friend's face: the look of horror changing as she looked down, to a wide smile of relief. Now she would be free of her husband's apparition. And she saw him as the house lights went up, shocked and pale, standing beside his wife, his hand mechanically stroking the coat he held of the woman who had fallen.

RICHARD SELMER

The Violet Lady

If you were to see Alec Hudson now, his attentive face studying the build-up of complex charts at the Forecasting Centre, you might find it difficult to visualise those same features in the depth of a January night some years ago confronted with the macabre and unbelievable.

At that time he was an undergraduate studying for a science degree at the west country city of Somerbury, and had the scientist's scepticism about reports of ghosts and paranormal forces.

Morton Row consisted of an attractive terrace of twenty early Georgian houses with parapets and dormer windows, several of which were owned by the University whose imposing entrance shared the opposite side of the street with two or three shops, chiefly dealing in antiques, and a finely-preserved half-timbered inn, *The Drake's Head*. Despite the bustling and occasionally boisterous activities of the students, the road, a cul-de-sac, managed to preserve an essentially eighteenth-century style and dignity.

Most of the rooms let out by the colleges were shared by two or more students, but Hudson was allocated a small room to himself at the rear of the third and topmost floor of No. 18. Being of a rather retiring and studious disposition, he was pleased with the seclusion it afforded compared with the more populous lower floors.

He found that the uninterrupted quietude of the evening hours was essential if he was to make a success of the study of the kind of mathematics which now came his way and for which he had no natural talent. It was during one such brain-wearying session that he first heard the harpsichord.

Earlier in the evening there had been a commotion of calling out and knocking on doors among his colleagues downstairs, but this had been a prelude to the departure of most of them into the November night, leaving behind an unusually silent house.

Nibbling his pen and struggling with a statistical problem between the covers of what was ironically called 'Elementary Mathematics', he gradually became aware of a distant musical tinkling. Despite his application to the work his wayward senses were alert for any slight stimulus which might offer an excuse to relax the effort of concentration, and he found himself listening. At first he thought it might be a musical box, but it persisted too long; paused for an instant, then resumed, steadily fingering out a slight elaboration of the same theme. Recognising it now as a harpsichord, Hudson pondered idly over hearing such an unlikely instrument. That it might be a radio or record player never entered his mind—perhaps the desultory nature of the musical phrasing suggested something other than a planned performance.

His listening was soon interrupted by the swelling roar of a low-flying jet, and by the time its slow thunder had died reluctantly away the music had finished, leaving nothing between Hudson and his unsolved problem.

He thought no more of the incident and it was not until about the end of January that he once again heard the mysterious performer.

As on the previous occasion most of the occupants of the house were out and it was a very still, frosty evening. Again Hudson leaned over his books with his mind temporarily released from the present and drawn into the curious aura of the past which surrounded the sound. It seemed to be drifting from the direction of No. 19 next door.

Five minutes must have passed when, without any preamble and apparently from the same source, a bellowing shout arose. It was a man's voice, but raised almost to a scream. Muffled by the dividing walls the words were undistinguishable but sounded like 'Get away, get away!' repeated in a rising and maniacal yell. Three or four rapid and heavy footsteps followed, terminated by a heavy thud and a queer jangling sound as if the keyboard had been dealt a smashing blow with some heavy object.

Hudson felt a little shaken at the sound of this violence, apparently in a neighbouring house, but his sense of shock turned to puzzlement as against all expectation, he heard that the music continued without the slightest indication of any interruption. Running to the window he raised the sash and leaned out into the freezing night, looking towards No. 19, but the topmost windows were in darkness. Lights showed in the lower windows of both 19 and 20, but his ears could catch nothing apart from the faint 'boxy' sound of TV sets. When he withdrew his head he found that the instrument had ceased playing, but feeling uneasy and no longer in the frame of mind to study he decided to make himself coffee in the kitchen downstairs.

Though normally rather shy, he was this time happy to find company there, and particularly so as it happened to be in the person of Anne Meredith, a pharmacy student who shared the large front room in the adjacent women's wing of the big house with Marion Dawling from the School of Art. The latter was a small, thin pallid girl with short black hair cut to a straight fringe above a pair of square-framed spectacles. Very quietly spoken and not in the least 'Bohemian' in her ways, she nonetheless produced the most startling canvases encrusted with violent and liberal applications of the brightest oil colours.

Anne, on the other hand, was of medium height and inclined to be plumpish. Not particularly pretty, she was, however, attractive in a cheerfully open-faced manner, with rather unruly hair of a lightish brown colour, errant strands of which she frequently needed to brush aside with a small but practical-looking hand.

Unlikely room-mates though they might seem, the two girls came from the same small town in Devonshire where they had grown up together, and were inseparable friends.

Hudson was already more than a little captivated by Anne, but rarely succeeded in seeing her as he did now, without her companion.

'Got a stinking cold,' she explained, her pleasant west-country burr thickened with catarrh. 'Marion is up at the College painting scenery for the Dramatics crowd. I usually give her a hand but thought I'd better stay in as it's turned so perishing nippy tonight. I suspect that she wasn't altogether sorry either—my delicate little cloud-effects always seem to get over-painted with the most ferocious-looking trees.'

'I can see that I shall have to give you a little instruction on how to depict some equally ferocious-looking clouds,' laughed the future weather-man.

As they sat sipping their coffee, Hudson casually mentioned that some of their neighbours seemed to have had a terrible row and wondered whether she had heard anything.

'No,' she answered, 'and it can't have been the top floor of No. 19 as the flat is empty: I happen to know that,' she added, 'because Marion was keen on a room with a north light when we first came up last year. At that time girls were occupying the lower floors, but even so the Bursar was very cagey about it all and simply said that it was not available to students.

'The same thing happened again this year when one of Marion's male colleagues made a similar request ... so, no one lives at the top of No. 19.'

The remainder of the College term passed without any further mysterious sounds to disturb Hudson's studies, and the whole affair passed to the back of his mind, submerged by the weight of work and by his slowly progressing friendship with Anne Meredith. He had managed to secure her company on several of the idyllically fine evenings of that early summer, for this was 1959, when the sun rose and set in the same clear, hot sky day after glorious day, week after week, with hardly a break.

In idle moments he speculated about the reason for the emptiness of No. 19, and his interest developed a more personal element when he noticed that, unlike his own quarters, the top back room next door opened on to a balcony.

Now like most keen weather-men, Hudson liked to make and record his own observations, and considering that the space he had seen would make an ideal spot for the exposure of a few simple instruments, he resolved to make a request for permission to move into the room next door when the autumn term came round.

He had anticipated a little difficulty in arousing sympathy with the unusual reasons behind his request, but it soon became clear that any obstacle which might exist seemed to be connected with the place into which he hoped to move.

James Heddon, the Bursar, was a laconic Yorkshire-man, tall with a tight, frizzy mass of reddish hair greying at the temples. Normally ready with brief responses of rather earthy humour delivered in a deeply nasal accent, he now sat frowning behind his heavy-sided spectacles, his strong head inclined towards his blotter.

Picking up his ballpoint pen, he held its ends wedged between his two forefingers, and appeared at first to address this rather than Hudson when he eventually spoke.

'Maybe you'll think this a lot of tommy rot, and I'll forgive you if you do, but there is something about the top room of No. 19 that I reckon you ought to know.

'I can quite understand how you weather-minded folk have to play around measuring rainfall and the like, and there is no objection to your using your digs for the purpose, but that room hasn't been occupied for the last ten years, and there's a reason, for what it's worth.

'During the last war, No. 19 and several other houses in Morton Row were requisitioned by the Army and when I myself was demobbed at the end of 1945 and took this position, the College was negotiating with the lessors to take possession of that house as we already leased the adjoining property.

'I happened to meet the Ordnance Corps Captain whose men had just vacated the building. We had a jar together in the *Drake* and a chat about the recent war, but then he made a rather strange remark about hoping that my students settled down better in the house than his soldiers had. I asked him what he meant, and he told me that there was already some story about the place being haunted by a "Violet Lady", whatever that might signify.

'He soon began to hear rumours that peculiar sounds, weird music and so on, had been heard by men billeted on the top floor, and one day an official request was put in by two of the men to be transferred to the main barrack quarters—normally regarded as the coldest and most uncomfortable of places. They claimed that one of them had seen a woman in old-fashioned clothes disappearing through a wall.

'The request was granted and the top rooms at No. 19 remained empty until the College took over.'

The Bursar leaned back in his chair, thrusting his large hands into trouser-pockets.

'Now I've been in the Forces myself,' he resumed, 'and I reckon soldiers can be as superstitious as sailors, given the right circumstances. The crowd I was with used to have an expression, "Swing the lamps", when they were told what they thought to be a particularly tall story.

'Well, though I didn't say so, it sounded to me as if this officer had been the victim of a typical "Swing the lamps" kind of yarn—not that I wouldn't have acted as he did at the time—and decided to let out the rooms regardless, accommodation being too precious to waste.

'The first two occupants of the top flat were a couple of girls studying botany. Several months passed and I forgot all about the whole business, as nothing happened to bring it back to mind. Then one day in the New Year something did happen which brought the matter up again rather forcefully.

'The two girls had come across a cheap carpet in the market and were busy tearing up dusty remnants of its predecessors which were firmly tacked down in places, when one of them caught her heel in a small loose piece of floor boarding which came right out. Glancing down in the hole that was left they found this.'

The Bursar leaned sideways and, pulling out a small drawer beside his knee, picked up a tiny object and placed it on his blotter. Hudson took it up and studied it with interest. It appeared to be a type of pendant made of some brassy metal, but not heavy enough to be gold. About an inch long, it had four elongated triangular sides with the lower corners turned out into blunt points, giving it a somewhat bell-like appearance. One face seemed to have a stone missing as there was an oval-shaped indentation surrounded by a line of minute jewels. At the pinnacle was a split ring with an open join, suggesting how the owner may have come to lose it from her neck-chain.

Heddon took it back and resumed his story, meanwhile regarding the curious bauble with a quizzical expression as he twiddled it between his finger and thumb.

'This lay on the table beside one of the girls when she went to bed that night, and for some reason she couldn't get to sleep. After about an hour or so she chanced to open her eyes.

'She was startled to see a woman's hand stretched out from above touching the table where this was resting—just a hand and forearm seemingly glowing in the darkness.

'At first the girl thought it must belong to her roommate, but when she listened she could hear her friend breathing in her sleep on the other side of the room.

'She could find no breath to scream, but managed to reach up and switch on her overhead lamp. She was making a kind of shuddering noise in her throat and the other girl awoke and ran to her ... There was no one else in the room and the door had remained closed.

'They came rushing over to me in the morning saying they wouldn't spend another night there, come what may.

'The young lady who found this is now my wife, so I suppose I owe something to it; but she won't have it in the house!

'Afterwards I thought it best to leave those quarters untenanted. About that time some alterations had been

taking place in the Science Wing and we found the space
useful for some of the chemi. lab. equipment.'

The older man carefully replaced the little piece of
jewellery in the drawer and after closing it looked up at
Alec Hudson in a very direct manner.

'Well, Mr Hudson,' he recommenced in a more formal
tone, his accent very noticeable, 'do you still wish to
move into that room? I'll not stop you if you're keen on
it. The place has been kept in good repair, though there
may still be some junk about.'

Hudson had been enthralled by this anecdote, and was
surprised to find that the Bursar—normally a reserved
man with a somewhat aloof attitude—seemed pleased to
have a listener to an account of events which he had
probably rarely mentioned to anyone.

It was a bright autumn day and bars of hazy sunshine
from the tall windows warmed the sides of their faces
and necks, making any idea of the supernatural seem
very insubstantial and difficult to credit.

'Yes, I'll take it,' Hudson replied, straightening a little
with his decision made; then after a slight hesitation,
added: 'Perhaps it might be as well if I shared with
someone in case I get to imagining things.'

Heddon picked up a hard-covered notebook and ran
his finger down a page.

'Young Marsden—he's coming up on Sunday week to
study for his maths degree—very stolid, down-to-earth
sort of character; I'm sure you'll find him the right kind
of company, and we could fix that day for your change-
over.'

They walked to the door, and as an afterthought Hudson remarked that Miss Dawling had mentioned an interest in the room in question, and for the first time James
Heddon laughed outright.

'Why not hang up a couple of her paintings there?—

that should frighten away any self-respecting apparition!'

'Thank you,' was the reply, 'but I'd rather risk the apparition!'

Though laughing, he was conscious of a slight inner chill as he recalled the strange sounds which had certainly seemed to originate from the place into which he was now going to move. At the same time and despite all he had been told that morning, in his heart he could not imagine anything of a similar nature happening to himself, and considered that all such phenomena must have a natural explanation.

It was partly this challenge to the pride he took in his sense of realism and logical thought that had decided him to persist in his request. He was also still looking forward to setting up his modest weather observation post on the little verandah, and resolved to collect the necessary equipment from his home next weekend.

Two days later he stood for the first time before the heavy black-painted panels of the door which guarded the room in No. 19. Moving the key-flap he inserted the key into the mortice lock and with some difficulty turned it. The big door creaked open and Hudson breathed the stale air of the top room. Its odour possessed the usual close, dusty, slightly mildewy tang of a long-disused confined space, but there was also a hint of another element which he could not identify—a faint perfume, saccharine-sweet and slightly acrid. He recalled the girl students who had occupied the room, but as if his nose could perceive a dimension it seemed to tell him that this was a scent of long, long ago.

Perhaps it is no coincidence that when we wish to ascribe to a place an aura which makes upon us a particular mental impression we use the same word 'atmosphere' as we do for the air around us with its many evocative odours, some consciously noted, others not.

The room itself offered a similar appearance to his own next door, with a comparatively low ceiling of decorated plaster mouldings; but here the windows to his right descended to the floor, giving access to the balcony. There were two iron bedsteads, and in the shadows at the far end a sombre and massively-pedimented wardrobe from a bygone age.

Taken all round, he decided that it could turn out to be a very reasonable room for two students, providing he could disregard its eerie reputation. There was present, however, a tangible if mundane, reminder of what he had been told, in the form of an incongruous collection of objects. Arranged along the floor between the fireplace and the window, and on top of the dust-cloth-covered table which intervened, were a multitude of wooden burette stands, their uprights tilted this way and that where their rectangular bases had been dumped carelessly overlapping one another. With their open wooden clamps outstretched, Hudson thought they looked rather like the water-carrying broomsticks in Disney's 'Fantasia' version of 'The Sorcerer's Apprentice'.

Absorbed in these reflections, he started when a voice suddenly spoke close to his ear.

'Not thinking of taking our haunted room, surely?'

Turning sharply he came face to face with another youth, black hair sleekly parted, hands in dark blazer pockets, regarding him with upraised eyebrows.

'That was the general idea,' he replied, adding, 'I'm not too worried about the stories, though: Alec Hudson's the name.'

The other pulled from his right-hand pocket a fin-like hand and extended it with something of the gesture of a Chicago gangster producing a revolver in an old-time movie.

'Stan Jepson, first floor front ... No, a load of nonsense, I would say, just because a couple of girls had some sort of nightmare or hallucination. Anyway, welcome to these portals.'

After a few more words he turned back down the stairs, but then with an odd sort of laugh he halted for a moment and turning his head called out:

'I hope you don't find the good-humoured ladies too much of a disturbance.'

Before Hudson could demand an explanation for this baffling remark, Jepson had gone.

The next few days were spent in tidying the room and moving his property from next door. He made a couple of trips home and returned with a raingauge and a home-made thermometer screen which he carefully set out on the verandah. On the Sunday he was due to take possession of the room, he encountered a thick-set, dark-haired youth a little older than himself struggling up the stairs with a couple of heavy cases, who proved to be Phil Marsden, his co-tenant.

Hudson, who normally preferred his own company, was relieved to find that his companion had a friendly but unobtrusive manner, and the arranging of their various effects went ahead in a most amicable fashion.

Conversation touched upon the reputation attached to the room, but Marsden revealed that he was completely agnostic towards the entire concept of anything of a spiritual nature, and whilst sharing this view with regard to the existence of ghosts, Alec felt they were getting too close to the delicate ground of religious belief, where they were bound to differ. Wishing to avoid any such contentious subject so early in their acquaintance he confessed his true reason for wishing to have company in the room and soon found himself in complete harmony with his new companion concerning the possible effects of an over-active imagination.

As is not uncommon in a strange bed, Hudson did not sleep very well on the first night, but lay awake for long stretches of time staring into the darkness. Nothing, however, of an unusual nature came to trouble him, though occasionally he became aware of the faint, mysterious perfume. It was vaguely familiar, but try as he might, he could not put a name to it.

Many nights passed thus without a hint of any unnatural disturbance. Only once did he awake at dawn with what he thought was the resonance of the bass strings of an instrument which had been struck a moment earlier, but it faded too quickly for him to be sure. At the same time there was a noticeable chill in the air and on rising that morning he was very puzzled to find that the inside wall thermometer read only 52°, whereas outside on the balcony his Maximum and Minimum thermometer assured him that the lowest temperature all that unseasonably warm night had been 56°. Despite long discussions with his colleagues and checking on the accuracy of the instruments, no explanation was forthcoming.

Towards the end of the Christmas vacation Hudson was proud to announce his engagement to Anne Meredith, and to celebrate the occasion there was to be a party at his new address, but in the midst of his happiness there was a curious moment of quite another feeling just before the guests arrived.

Entering the room, Anne sniffed at the air with a half-humorous expression and turned to bring her nose into contact with the dark wave of his well-groomed hair.

'Well, that's a relief—I thought you were indulging in Violet Hair Oil: it must be Phil, then.'

The identification of the elusive odour and the co-incidental recollection of a remark of the Bursar's activated a queer fibre of unease in Hudson's mind. His reply provided a poser for his fiancée:

'How long do you think a perfume can linger in a room—one year, ten years . . . a hundred?'

The Spring Term commenced grey and dreary, Christmas gaiety forgotten as if it had never been, but for Hudson, with his cherished future wife living so close, the Season of Goodwill seemed to linger on.

He applied himself with renewed vigour to his studies, and found Phil Marsden an invaluable coach in matters mathematical. A few words from him and the most mind-gumming perplexities could be resolved into orderly propositions.

Their quarters felt to reflect in its mood only the personalities of its two occupants and the idea of any strange entity within its walls seemed untenable. Any traces of unaccountable perfume were effectively neutralised as Marsden formed an attachment for a pipe of the Sherlock Holmes variety, the exhalations from which Anne claimed to be detectable two doors away.

It was about this time that Hudson learned something of the history of Morton Row and in particular of his own address.

Jepson, his downstairs neighbour, was the raconteur and the scene was the capacious lounge bar of the *Drake Inn*. Seated by a round glass-topped table laden with an assortment of partly-consumed drinks were Alec and Anne, Phil and his fiancée, and Jepson with Marion Dawling; the latter couple having struck up a rather unexpected liaison.

The dissertation had been triggered off by Hudson's referring to Jepson's enigmatical remark some months ago about No. 19 and 'good-humoured ladies'.

'There is,' he commenced, 'quite a story attached to our present residence, and like many other valuable pieces of information, I obtained a lead on it from the aged char who "does" for us in the mornings.

' " 'Ope yur comfortable here, me dear," she says one day, "but you wouldn't ketch me up there after dark, not fur no money," and indicated the ceiling above with her mop handle.

'She went on to tell how more than a hundred years ago a woman was murdered in the little room where the cleaning-things are now kept: that it was once a music room and it was said that from time to time the deceased returned to play the harpsichord, "Though you can see fur yurself," she said, "thur bain't be no 'arpsichord, nur nothing thur now 'cepting my brooms and buckets—yet that's been hurrd and recent-like too." '

Jepson turned to Alec:

'From another source I learned that the music was said to be that of "The Good-humoured Ladies" from Scarlatti—hence my remark to you when we first met.

'Now, as you know, I am studying Law, and I decided that it might be a useful exercise to ferret out the past history of No. 19, Morton Place. I did so and very rewarding it turned out to be.

'I established contact with one of the local magistrates. Some of them are crusty old devils, but this one couldn't have been more helpful, and together we delved through masses of past Court Records; and he also introduced me into the local newspaper office where I could look up early back numbers.

'Early in the eighteenth century, Jonathan Morton, widower, a successful and ingenious engineer and a wealthy landowner purchased this section of the town from the Duke of Somerbury and built an estate bordering on the College and including Morton Row. No. 19 he took possession of as a town house for himself and his two daughters, Yvonne and Clara.

'They were a musical family and used to invite small gatherings of friends to perform on the top floor of their house. It seems likely that the front room where the cleaning materials are now kept was used as a kind of stage. It was, and still is, divided from the other room (yours, Alec) by a folding wooden screen in place of a solid wall.

'Yvonne, the elder daughter, married and left her father's home, but she proved to have made a desperately unhappy match. Her husband, Henry Pritchard, had inherited a considerable fortune, but was an inveterate gambler and an unlucky one at that, as he was soon heavily in debt. In addition, he seemed to have possessed a violent temper as there were several records of his appearing in court charged with riotous behaviour and damage to property, incurring warnings and sharp fines. Possibly his influential connections may have saved him from imprisonment for a time, but one night after a wild drinking session he was involved in a fight with a club owner who had ordered him to leave and the latter died from a head injury received as he fell.

'Pritchard narrowly escaped a murder charge, but a brilliant counsel saved him and he served five years for manslaughter—a light sentence for any era, and especially so in those harsher times.

'When he was released, Yvonne apparently tried to make a fresh start with him, but this was doomed to failure as Pritchard could not settle to any sort of work for long and constantly bore down on his wife for funds. There was a final quarrel and she left him to return to what was now her sister's house in Morton Row, following the death of their father.

'Not long afterwards, Clara and her maid returned one afternoon from attendance on a sick relative, to find Yvonne lying on the floor beside the harpsichord in the music room ... She had been strangled and her jewel box was found to be empty.

'When Clara had left in the early morning, she knew that Yvonne had been expecting a visit from her husband during the day following receipt of a letter from him. Clara had strongly advised her sister to refuse to see him again, as on a previous visit there had been a violent row, again over money, but Yvonne was loath to sever all ties with a man with whom, despite all, she still felt some affection.

'The police soon traced Pritchard for questioning, but he denied having visited 19 Morton Row on the day of the crime. However, after interviewing some local people, several witnesses were found to testify that he had been seen in the vicinity on that very morning.

'Both he and the sisters were well-known and Yvonne was spoken of as the "Violet Lady" because of her practice of wearing a bunch of violets at her throat as long as these were in season.'

At this Jepson signified that his own throat required a little attention, which was willingly provided.

He continued:

'The most damning piece of evidence was found when the police searched Pritchard's rooms. He had been working at a book-binder's for a few weeks, and attached to the sole of one of his boots was a patch of some sort of glue. Imbedded in this was a tiny polished reddish stone, which was readily identified by Clara as a jasper from a pendant frequently worn by Yvonne since her childhood. The stone had in it a curious feathery marking resembling a "Y", which was quite unmistakable.

'None of the other jewellery was ever found, but it was assumed that Pritchard had disposed of it already. He then admitted visiting No. 19 but denied the murder and theft, despite all the evidence, and the absence of any other person in or near the premises at that time. The only other occupant, one Samuel Rodgers, who rented rooms from the sisters on the ground floor, could prove that he was at his work at the crucial time. He was personal secretary to Sir Percival Vance-Quebec, a local bigwig, who gave evidence that the young man had never left the office all that morning.

'Henry Pritchard was found guilty and was hanged, protesting his innocence to the last.

'Clara later married Samuel Rodgers, but she was very soon widowed. According to the records of the inquest he had been troubled by visions of the murdered woman, and the supposed sound of her at the keyboard instrument. Because of this the couple were arranging to move elsewhere, but a few nights before they were to leave, Rodgers had a kind of seizure—he smashed a heavy poker on to the harpsichord and fell dying in the music-room of what was probably a stroke.

'No. 19 seems to have remained empty for some years after that, and since those days the upper floors have been seldom used, while the ground floor has been mostly utilised as offices for various firms until the whole place was requisitioned by the Army in 1940. You know the rest.'

For a few moments the table was an island of silence in the surrounding sea of chatter, then Marsden's fiancée remarked:

'You've certainly got a good lawyer's memory for names, but one of them is vaguely familiar to me. Wasn't Vance-Quebec involved in some kind of international vice racket of the time—white slaving or something—using a legit. business as a cover?'

'That transpired later,' replied Jepson; then speaking more reluctantly, his eyelids hiding his downcast eyes:

'While I was doing all this research I had a very odd experience—trifling, maybe—and you can make what you like of it.

'To verify some of the dates, I visited the Morton family vault which is in the Old Town Cemetery. There was a rusty iron gate and a flight of broken steps down to a small mausoleum. It was dank and musty-smelling and seemed colder than it was outside.

'I shone my torch and found the tombs of Yvonne Pritchard and her parents, then I swung round and made out the names of Clara and Samuel Rodgers, but as I looked I suddenly heard a kind of dry click behind me. It was only faint, but I can't begin to tell you how eerie it was in the utter silence—I was petrified—but at the same time I noticed something else. Across the name "SAMUEL RODGERS" were four spidery scratches from above to below—maybe they could have been made with a gardening fork ... but what gardening tool could start the two centre scratches an inch or two higher than the outer ones?'

No one seemed disposed to suggest an answer, and Marsden was the first to speak, excusing himself and his partner from the company as they had a five mile scooter ride to make to her village home, and he had noticed recent arrivals in the bar beating snow from their coats.

The others left shortly after, to be faced at the outer door with a chokingly-freezing snow-filled gale. They stumbled across a street already more than ankle-deep in places and bidding each other hasty goodnights parted to their respective rooms.

Not unexpectedly, Marsden had not returned by the time Hudson took to his bed. The wind roared and thundered round the roof tops, while the snow hissed against the window-panes like a muted sand-blast.

There came to his mind the recollection of the piece of jewellery shown him by the Bursar and he reflected upon the probability of the incriminating jasper stone belonging to the empty setting in it.

Eventually he drifted off to sleep, but to uneasy dreams engendered by Jepson's story of the vault. He seemed to hear the same dry click and then awoke quite suddenly.

He immediately sensed that there was something odd and tense in the atmosphere of the room. The gale had abated leaving not a whisper, and the silence was velvet deep, but as he lay on his side staring at the wall with its washbasin faintly illuminated by the dimly snowlit ceiling, he knew without doubt that there was some presence behind him. Not daring to move his head, but with his heart beginning to pound, he rotated his eyes downward until he could see Marsden's bed against the wall—empty!—He was alone except for . . . ?

Then he caught sight of something which caused his body to freeze as if the sheets were of one with the snow outside.

On the corner of the foot-board of his bed there rested a palely gleaming object—a delicate white hand. Even as he saw this through the throbbing reddish circles within his own eyes, the remainder of the spectre gradually glided into his field of vision.

From the hand ran a faintly-glowing forearm, then a dark, shortsleeved jacket and above it a thin white face, the lips and eyes black in the general phosphorescence. Against the throat was a shadowy cluster from which seemed to spring wave after wave of the cold, earthy scent of violets.

Even to Hudson's shattered senses, the attitude appeared to be not threatening, but somehow meaningful, as if intended to convey some thought or idea to him.

How long the figure remained standing as if regarding him he could not afterwards say, but probably no more than a minute or two, then it began to fade gradually and recede towards the wardrobe against the old folding wall.

Immediately he started to hear the faint, almost misty tones of a harpsichord as if from far away. Gradually the melody settled imperceptibly into one deep chord repeated several times—distinctive, sombre and with a peculiarly discordant element in its tone...

Then silence again.

Breaking from his trance, Hudson jerked on his bed-side lamp and turning on to his back lay panting and staring at the ceiling, while trying to organise his mind for a normal sequence of thought.

Thus he remained until morning brought a clatter of footsteps on the stairs and the entrance of Marsden:

'What a night—two miles pushing the scooter through drifts—here, what's the matter?' as he caught sight of his room-mate's still strained countenance.

Hudson's account followed in somewhat disjointed fashion but Marsden obviously thought that it was merely a nightmare, despite assurances to the contrary.

At breakfast Hudson sat nursing his cup, still ruminating over all aspects of the mystery of their room and its culmination in last night's events.

'I think we should examine that little front room from top to bottom to see what we can find,' he determined.

It was a Saturday and a little later, joined by Jepson, Marion and Anne, who was full of concern over what had befallen Hudson—even though she was inclined to share Marsden's views on the matter.

They made their way into the former music room with its row of brooms, mops and buckets lining much of the walls. Marion's eyes were, however, drawn to the wall farthest from the door. This consisted of heavily decorated plaster-work, shining with white gloss paint. On either side of the centre, about three feet from the floor was a deep niche, as if intended for statuettes or possibly busts of composers.

She stepped across and after pausing to gaze down at a curious curved line of faint marks on the floorboards by the wall, hooked her fingers into the panelling just below the righthand niche.

It occurred to Hudson that as a part of her art studies she might also be familiar with architectural detail.

Her sharp eyes now fell on the parallel rows of beading which ran along the wall immediately below the two niches. Turning to Jepson, she asked if he had a penknife and when he nodded she indicated that he should run it along above and below the two moulded ridges about seven inches apart.

'Vandalism!' he cried, but trusting her he complied and cleared the paint from two faint seams which were now visible.

Once more hooking her fingers into the panelling she gave a powerful tug and was rewarded with a creaking movement as a broad oblong band of the wall bordered by the two rows of beading and about four foot six inches long, started to swing out from a hinged point nearer the window.

With the young men helping, a further heave produced a vertical carved supporting leg, strongly constructed but cunningly concealed in the ornamentation of its surroundings. It was mounted on a large caster hidden behind a tiny hinged flap in the wainscoting. Another similar leg followed.

Now the whole structure swung out smoothly and was revealed as a keyboard instrument of the harpsichord family, sometimes known as the 'virginals'. The end nearer the wall was firmly supported by a horizontal, triangular iron plate, about a foot long and rooted in a massive hinge just inside the panelling.

In an awed silence Jepson raised the cover on the side facing the window to expose a short keyboard. The flat keys were black and the raised ones white, reversing the familiar piano arrangement. On the edge of the cabinet and across several of the keys ran a dent which tallied with part of Jepson's narrative.

Still not quite steadied from his nocturnal experience, Hudson pressed a rather nervous hand on to the keyboard. The sound produced was so hauntingly familiar that for a moment he felt a wave of faintness. It was of the exact tone he had heard previously.

The others were hardly less affected as they all realised that no human hand could have played the instrument where it must have remained hidden in the wall and forgotten for generations—and yet it had apparently been heard by a number of persons over the years.

Curiosity or some less obvious compulsion prompted him to explore the notes in search of the exact sound of the final chord he had heard in the night. At last with a somewhat unmusical grouping of the fingers of the left hand, he reproduced that same sombre, slightly jarring set of harmonics.

Simultaneously, Anne, who had been leaning on the wall close beside him, uttered a little exclamation, and indicated the end of the harpsichord which faced the gap from which it had been taken.

A thin pencil of smoothly polished wood had suddenly extruded for a couple of inches as if released by some mechanism operated by that particular combination of notes.

Still wondering, Anne pulled on it gently and to her surprise it came out attached to the side of a drawer which when fully opened extended nearly to the wall ...

but it was the contents which caused the greatest astonishment, for these consisted of a collection of jewellery which glittered dully through a light covering of brownish dust; and also a leather-bound notebook.

Hudson picked this up and opened it. After leafing through a few pages he looked up and spoke to Jepson:

'I think this may be an end to the story told us last evening,' he said, handing it over opened at about the middle.

What met Jepson's gaze was a journal or diary written in a flowing, old-fashioned hand, the paper yellowed and ink brown with age.

Reading aloud from the last entry he commenced:

'... All alone once more now Henry has departed. As I had expected, it was only to beg of me for money, and ended as it always does with high words and lost tempers. Poor Henry—he is really just a very naughty spoiled boy who has never grown up. Strange how I still love him, but at the same time cannot tolerate his presence for long—how is that possible?

'I hardly like to admit it even to myself, but after his last visit I missed a diamond brooch—and he knew where my jewel box was kept. This time I have concealed my valuables in the hidden drawer which poor dear Father made for me so long ago before Clara was born, and which remains my own secret, even from her, till this day.

'If I am weak, she is doubly so to be taken up with that scoundrel downstairs. I know he wishes to have her hand in marriage, but I have forbidden it, that she shall not make the mistakes I have. His loathing for me shows in his every glance, but for her own sake I will NEVER, NEVER relent.

'Local gossip suggests that his employer is secretly engaged in some evil commerce and is frequently away from his office while Rodgers swears that he is busily engaged within and must not be disturbed on any account. None of the clerks dare put this to the test.'

The next sentence in the diary ended as if in a more hurried hand:

'I do believe I can hear Rodgers downstairs—he climbs the stair ... I am afraid.'

Nothing but blank pages followed.

Jepson took the book and carefully closing it, said:

'I think this proves conclusively that Pritchard was not the murderer and suggests that Vance-Quebec would not have hesitated to give Rodgers a false alibi as a cover for his own activities.

'Yvonne herself must have dropped the piece of jewellery whose stone became attached to Pritchard's boot when he visited her. Maybe he had heard of the murder before the police approached him, and denied meeting her fearing that he would be an obvious suspect because of his record of violence.

'I'll show this journal to the magistrate I met the other day, so that the record may be put right even after all these years, and then perhaps your poor visitant will be able to rest at last, Alec.'

As the little group stood in silence around the harpsichord a muted whispering seemed to brush its strings for a moment ... perhaps it was caused by a slight settling of the cabinet.

Hudson thought the faintest hint of violets hung in the air for a moment, then was gone.

L. P. HARTLEY

The Stain on the Chair

Patience Castaway had been in love with her husband when she married him: at least she often told herself so when she had ceased to be in love with him and wasn't quite certain if she loved him. What a difficult transition that is, and how many imponderables play a part in it. There were still times when she saw Hector as she had first seen him, with a racket under his arm and a faint sprinkling of dew on his blond brow—the pride of the local tennis court! And when it so turned out that they were to play together in some friendly game, or even in some tournament, what bliss! Did it matter if they lost? Returning perhaps, arm-in-arm, or (even) racket to racket from the tennis court, they had the sense of solidarity which comes from a common aim, even if that aim has missed its mark.

Hector sometimes frowned if Patience fluffed a shot, but she was tolerant, even secretly delighted when his ball, with all his strength behind it, and the gleam of triumph in his eye, went out of bounds. She was content with her defensive tactics on the back line, and watching Hector's dashing and smashing operations at the net. She couldn't fail to notice that when a gentle lob from her won the set, often Hector's heroic exertions at the net, such skyward leaps, such threatened pulverisation of the opponents and all their balls, ended in a cry from the umpire: 'Out!'

How crestfallen Hector would look as he collected his tennis balls to resume the set, and how sorry Patience felt for him, as he clinked them together in his large, sun-burnt, but not really tennis-adept hands, before he, a little grudgingly, gave one to her, supposing they were partners.

Of course their lives didn't consist in tennis—few people's lives do or even want to. Besides, as Hector's figure grew more rotund, he avoided the courts, though he was still a vice-president where he and Patience had won their victories and suffered their defeats. But she remembered the old days with happiness and tried to persuade Hector to return to his old haunts, and play with her on his days off—Thursdays and week-ends. She could, of course, find other partners, but she had always preferred to play with him, and if he lost his temper, and the game, especially if it was through a fault of hers, she liked him the better, for wasn't that the way a real man should behave?

Meanwhile Hector, when in need of exercise, took to golf. He was not very good at it, except at the 19th hole, and Patience, patient as she was, really disliked it. She hated being told her faults, which were many and various, especially the defects of her *swing*, which was never quite right—nor was Hector's, however often he practised on the lawn in front of their house, protected by a thick net from passing motorists.

Patience watched him go through these solemn gestures in his spare time. Hector will never make a golfer, she thought, however hard he tries. If only he would stop taking it seriously—as Hector took his beyond the thick net behind the garden wall.

It was, of course, the solitariness and self-sufficiency of him that she minded. A hundred, perhaps two hundred balls, given what he believed to be the right swing, but seldom giving him *real* satisfaction, would have given them a real game of tennis, with the laughter and chaffing that goes with it, and the slowly-sinking sun that makes further play impossible.

But Hector was, or had become, like the cat that walks by itself. His solitary engagement with himself meant more to him than a large and cheerful party he had been invited to; but if he had accepted it, he must go.

Patience was socially inclined and didn't know that he was not, and urged him to accept invitations. She was a rather obtuse but very kindly woman, and it didn't occur to her that Hector was growing tired of social life.

What he wanted instead, what was at the back of his mind, he couldn't have told himself; but he found a mild game of squash-rackets, in which, for some reason of sex, his wife couldn't join, more exhilarating and less responsible, *vis-à-vis* one's partner, if one had one, than lawn tennis or golf, where every mistake was as culpable as a wrong lead in bridge.

So Patience went on playing tennis with anyone who would play with her (and there were quite a number), while Hector now retired to the squash court.

He wasn't specially good at squash, which is an exacting game, especially for a middle-aged man, and he often went into the changing-room dripping with perspiration. When his younger opponents, noticing his distress as he banged against the wall in an effort to get his ball above the line, said: 'Don't bother, Hector. You'll live to fight another day,' he was reminded painfully of his age, and sometimes threw his racket on the floor, as though the racket was to blame.

Then the shower, so soothing, but still leaving behind

the streaks of sweat on his darkening hair. Whereas Patience, taking tea with her friends at the tennis club, wiped away a rather becoming drop of moisture from her brow.

One day she said to Hector: 'Wouldn't it be rather nice if we had a game of tennis? It's so long since we had one. Not at all strenuous. You could always beat me with your back hand. I've got out of practice with those nice girls at Forest Hill. They're at it all the time. Such services and such *drives*! Your poor old Patience can't get within a mile of them.

'So how about a gentle game at Forest Hill? Nothing competitive, a few lobs that we needn't chase. Just to show the enthusiastic youngsters that they needn't take the game too seriously.'

Hector's brow darkened. 'I like to play with you, as you know. We often have, haven't we? But it's this wretched sweating. You come out as fair as a flower, while I, as far as I have any hair left'—he tugged at the scanty remnants, ill-fitting on his head—'I look a sight. I know I do. Besides, when I was once blond, as I believe I was—it now looks like a scalp streaked with black.'

'You could wear a skull-cap,' Patience said, half-laughing. 'Isn't it usual to sweat, or perspire, to use a more elegant word, at squash? I've always understood it was a very fast game.'

'So it is,' said Hector, 'and I'm getting too old for it. My hair,' of which he had once been proud, 'looks ridiculous now, all bald streaks and funny-looking patches. You wouldn't understand, Patience. You have kept your hair. Most women do,' he added, rather bitterly.

They were sitting in front of the large looking-glass in the sitting-room. Although Hector was several years older than Patience, there was a striking difference in their looks. And above all in their hair; hers had retained its fairness, while his, was streaked with black and grey and intermediate colours, not excluding pink.

'Yes, let's have a game of tennis,' he said. 'I'll probably have to give you thirty.'

As it happened, he didn't, for he wanted to win, nor was she unwilling to lose.

They returned to their flat, Patience, not having over-exerted herself, cool as a cucumber; Hector panting, though victorious, mopping his brow. 'I wish people didn't see me looking like this,' he said.

She brought out a pocket handkerchief—indeed, she brought out two—and began to swab his overheated brow, and his hair, once so bright and thick and plentiful, now a shadow of its former self.

'You still look very hot,' she said. 'Well, we're at home now. No one to look at you. Have a rest in your favourite chair, then I'll make a cup of tea—but not before it's time.'

'When will it be time?' asked Hector pettishly.

'Usual time. About an hour before dinner.'

'Don't make it any sooner. I must have a bath and make myself presentable. Is there any hot water?'

'Yes, plenty.'

'I need rather a lot, you know. I've been putting on weight.'

'Yes, I've noticed,' she said, with a dryness in her voice that he had not noticed before.

'Of course, it doesn't matter, at my age.'

'No, don't say that.'

'Perhaps we could have the water supply heated up a bit more.'

'As you like. You can have the water as hot as you like, until you look like a lobster.'

She glanced at him. He did look very hot still. Not

hot for a young man, as when he married her, but hot for a man of his age. All those streaks of dilapidation on his well-shaped head—dark brown where the gold had glittered—and those streaks of greasy grey between them, precursors of oncoming age.

All at once she felt sorry for him, as one does for someone who is leaving youth behind, yet she said, rather brutally:

'If you don't like your present *chevelure*, why don't you get a new one from a shop?'

Horrified, he said: 'Oh, I couldn't do that!'

'Why not, darling?'

He left her there and studied his face closely in the mirror. What an old face. He gave it all his attention. The up-strokes, the down-strokes, the side-strokes, marked with a soft but not unnatural feathering which had once been his pride. Young men had worn whiskers, curving down from their shaven cheeks, whiskers which would have horrified the officers and men of the 1914 war. How to make himself look manly again? And how, too, to have oneself tattooed, in the Waterloo Road, so as to make oneself irresistible to women? Or to men?

A great many servicemen, perhaps the majority, had tried this way of exhibiting their personal charms: sleeve rolled up to the elbow, and perhaps a snake devouring a sword, was enough to make a woman, or perhaps a man, feel that she or he had met the one they wanted to meet.

The King of Denmark was said to have been tattooed by a well-known expert in the Waterloo Road. But many servicemen had regretted the experiment, for it had been painful in the doing: and afterwards, should they get into trouble, it was helpful to the police.

Yet how many men, well aware of the disadvantage, have, at great personal discomfort, blistered their skins with gun-powder! Perhaps more men in England than anywhere else—because we feel the flesh is not enough by itself, but must have some kind of dynamite behind it. I have never seen a tattooed Italian. It is the Englishman who feels that his flesh is not enough by itself, needs the extra dynamite. Yet women are satisfied with the purity of their skins.

Patience did not again persuade Hector to join her on the tennis court. Grimly he kept on with squash and golf. She tried to tell him it was too much for him. He didn't take it well. He had some pals on the links and if he couldn't beat them, for most of them were younger than he, he came home in a bad temper, and always sweating, sweating.

'Dearest, please,' she said, noticing, as it was impossible not to notice, the runnels of sweat reaching down from forehead to chin, and from chin to throat, and from throat to a tangle of hair, 'aren't you taking too much out of yourself? My advice is for you to relax—a little badminton perhaps, if you *must* have exercise—and then a good lean-back in your favourite chair.' She indicated it. 'Then you'll feel much fitter.'

'You may be right,' he said. 'You may be right,' and, still sweating, he sank down into the chair, whose ample folds enfolded his ample folds. His head fell backwards.

'But let me tell you this,' he said. 'My life is my own and I don't want it tampered with. Can you remember that?' he added in a nasty tone.

Before she could answer, he had fallen asleep, the sweat still oozing from his temples on to the chair-back.

Day after day, some such episode occurred, and day after day Patience tried *her* patience to the utmost, and half-believed that he would have the sense to leave the

squash court and the golf links one day soon and return
to her and the tennis court.

But it was not to be. On his days off, he resumed the
self-torture and afterwards fell back in his chair and let
the sweat roll off him, soaking its cover.

Patience, as many women would have, put up with it
all, including his rudeness. She even set aside her preference for the tennis court to spend tedious (for her) hours
with him at the golf links ... considerably lengthened
by lectures on how she should improve her 'swing' etc.
Sometimes she nearly cried when he had told her to
alter her 'swing' at least twenty times.

Embarrassed, his friends stood round the tee, noting
his admonitions to her. ('Mind your left foot. You haven't
got it right.') Sorry for her, and eager to get on with the
game.

When he came home after a time on the links without
her, four or five down and black with rage and the rubs
of the green, he would hardly speak to her. Scanning his
card, he would tell her how unlucky he had been at this
or that hole. The 'Everest' along the banks of the sea-
shore was a famous trap for golfers. A drive of 250 or
300 yards might clear it. Hector was too old for it. When
waiting his turn with his juniors, hunching their shoulders and confidently stretching their legs, he was aware
of their politely waiting for him to take his place.

'Well hit!'

But his ball never reached 'Mount Everest', and his
caddie pushed along the curious perambulator which
contained clubs which Hector had never used.

The boy, eager to please, and thinking of his tip at
the end of the famous golf course, handed him one club
after another.

'This one, sir!'

'This one' was a cleek, an ancient instrument, liable

to carry too far or not far enough, according to the strength or skill of the player.

'No, I think Number 5 iron.'

Number 5 iron proved a failure as the caddie knew it would; and Hector returned to the club-house, and later to his home, five down.

It doesn't matter,' Patience said, with more anxiety than she cared to show. 'You'll do much better next time.'

'Who knows?' cried Hector, as if next time might be the last time in his life. 'I've never been five down before, since—since—' He tried to think when.

'Don't worry,' his wife said. 'The best of golfers have their off-days.'

'Thank you for that,' he said, not very kindly, for his soul was still smarting with defeat.

'Lean back for a bit,' she said, indicating his easy chair, 'and you'll feel better. What's a game of golf after all?'

Stupid woman, he thought.

Yet she tried so hard. She was a faithful wife to him, although day after day she lost her love, her affection, every scrap of regard for him.

Even so, it was still a shock to her when she came home one evening to find him sitting in his big chair, head leaning back on its rim, eyes closed, and she said: 'Dinner's almost ready. Just close your eyes' (an unnecessary admonition) 'and forget that there ever was such a game as golf.' And he seemed, momentarily, to hear her. But he couldn't have. His head still lolled helplessly back against the chair. He was dead.

Time went by, and the memory of Hector went by, but his chair remained, a perpetual reminder of what he had been and had ceased to be.

Patience was superstitious about it. She would sometimes go and look at it, in case there were drops of sweat
to be wiped away. But time was short. She was not an
impractical woman. The chair was a good and valuable
French chair and now that its occupant was gone, it
must be sent with all speed to the cleaners.

It was sent, and in due time it returned, much restored,
but for one thing: where the head used to lie, there was
a dirty patch. Much against her will, Patience bent down
over the eighteenth-century chair-cover, so beautiful
still.

At the top, round the edge, there were marks, dripping
forwards, which hadn't come out in the wash. They still,
she felt, had something *animal* about them—but could
they have?

She sent the chair-cover back to the cleaners. It was
returned again, with these spots, or whatever they were,
still clearly marked. She sent it back a third time, asking
the cleaners to pay special attention to the spots, but the
firm replied that the marks were ineradicable.

Patience had to take their word for it.

One day a friend came to see her.

'Remember that chair *he* used to use?' she asked her
friend.

'Well, yes. What of it?'

'I can't get its cover clean.'

'Why not?'

'They say the dirt won't come off the neck part. It was
where he used to put his neck when he came back from
wherever it was.'

'But this is too silly. Let me look at it, Patience.'

She showed him.

The outline of her husband's head and neck was clearly

marked against the chair-cover.

'It's like a sort of—drawing,' she said.

'Yes, it is quite like him. But then things do get marked, when people have used them for a long time.'

'Turn the cover round and look at the *back* of his neck. There's something there—'

'Yes, I do see what you mean'.

'It's something the cleaners can't get out. I've had it cleaned three times. But it's just as—as dirty—as ever. He put his neck there, you see, just in that place. He was a man who sweated a lot. Can you see anything else?'

Rather reluctantly, her friend bent down and saw what looked like a broken row of spots. 'A sort of rash?'

'I don't think so,' said Patience. 'It's something else—something odd that I don't understand—if it was just ordinary, the marks would have come out in the wash. As I told you, he was a man who sweated a lot—much more at golf and squash than at tennis—I never really understood him—I wish I had— Oh, if he was with us now—'

'But I *am* with you now,' a voice said.

KAY BATCHELOR

The Spirit Was Willing

Eve was young and inexperienced; otherwise she would have known that she got the job at Huntley Manor too easily. After all, vacancies in her particular profession were pretty hard to find, and there were more applicants every year, of course. It came as a shock, though, when it dawned on her just what she had taken on. She had always been told that the older a place was, the better for her sort of work; and that naturally no good English family existed without some distinctly questionable, if not bloody, episodes in its past. 'The best people,' they always told her, 'are bound to be bastards.'

Yet there it was. Eve found out almost at once that the Huntleys had been an appallingly respectable lot, and they had characteristically chosen to build their ancestral home in a flat unattractive part of the country, well off the tourist track. Huntley Manor was, in fact, an outstandingly ugly, lumpy, sprawling house, without a single secret panel, trap door or spook hole in any of its undistinguished rooms or corridors. In all its three hundred years, no one remotely interesting had ever slept there; there had never been a murder, a madman, or even a walled-up skeleton to brighten up the family's uneventful history; there was not the shadow of an ancient scandal, everyone had been born, boringly enough, on the right side of the blanket; there were no chains to rattle, no moat to drown in. Nothing.

And it didn't take Eve long to realise bitterly that—for a departed spirit with a stint to do—all this was going to make things practically impossible.

'Even if anyone did come near the place,' she moaned to herself as she drifted along the empty galleries one dull September evening, 'there's absolutely no atmosphere, no *tone* about the place. Of course,' she paused moodily by a mullioned window, 'I'd never have got landed with a hopeless place like this if I'd known the right people. Oh, it's always the same, here or there—it isn't what you are that counts, it's who you know.'

She was getting bitter, but she couldn't seem to stop herself even though she knew quite well that it only diminished her spectral potential—as they put it at headquarters when she was on the usual short course in metaphysics. In her job, they impressed on her, you could be angry, voluptuous, even murderous—anything passionate you liked—but never acid or mean or bitter. That got you nowhere, and in the end reduced you to a mere draught under the door.

Shrinking at the thought, Eve was staring down the dark deserted drive, wishing to goodness she had something—anything—to be passionate *about*, when she gradually became aware of something different in the air outside. Hardly daring to hope, she waited tensely, every extra sense tingling. Seconds passed; then a shadow suddenly crossed the path below. Eve expanded with delight, for not only was a live human being walking up to the very door of the Manor at last, but her sixth sense told her it already believed in spirits. All the traditional poltergeist fury rose in her at the thought.

'How dare you, dare you!' she screeched joyously,

whirling herself into a terrible cloud of dust, and echoing downstairs.

Out in the drive, Charles Turner hesitated as he heard the unearthly hooting. It was one of those tangibly dark autumn nights, and the wind was rustling too realistically through the dying leaves for his liking. Glancing up uneasily at the shadowy, unmistakably deserted old house, Charles shivered slightly. There was something queer about the place, one did not have to be especially psychic to feel that. However, his car was down there in the lane, front wheels deep in a ditch; he was still a long way from home, it was late, and there wasn't a village in miles. He was going to have to shelter in this house till morning, whatever happened.

Tentatively, he tried the great front door. It did not move. He pushed it hard with both hands. Nothing happened. Feeling some spots of rain, Charles wedged his shoulder to the panels and shoved more urgently. It did not yield an inch. Determined now to get in at all costs, he turned to make a short run at the door.

As he charged, Eve instinctively wrenched the heavy door back on its hinges, and before he could stop himself, Charles rushed through into the vast entrance hall. With a marvellously fiendish shriek, Eve slammed the door shut, and fell on him, all the months of pent-up rage and frustration breaking loose. She whirled round him in choking clouds of dust, whooping and screeching and bombarding him with stones. Closing in, she shook him, tore his hair, twisted his ears. She pushed, she pulled, she hurled him to the floor. In fact, she overdid it; and was eventually forced to shrink a bit and rest herself.

Dust settled slowly in the silence, and for a few moments neither of them moved. Then, very cautiously, Charles raised himself on his elbows. Nothing happened; so, slowly and painfully, he got to his feet. Eve moved close, positively throbbing with pleasure; and Charles had the exceedingly unpleasant feeling that he was being watched. A few minutes passed and, growing more confident, he put out a groping hand in the absolute darkness.

'Naughty, naughty,' chuckled Eve, idly flipping a loose stone at him.

Unfortunately for her, it caught him rather hard on the side of his head; and when Charles put a hand to the place and felt the stickiness of blood, his fear evaporated abruptly.

'Now listen, whatever you are,' he roared furiously, thrashing the darkness round him, 'that's enough—any more rough stuff, and *you'll* get hurt!'

His last blind swing went through Eve with a nasty jolt. Astounded, she leapt back, accidentally dislodging some loose stones on him.

'Right!' Charles bellowed, blundering forward, 'you asked for it.'

Vainly, Eve tried to whoop, whirl up dust, feel fierce. In face of his solid determined swiping, her splendid rage was dwindling, her very density diminishing. And when, unknowingly, he had her pinned against a wall between his outstretched arms, Eve was reduced to the same ineffectual, miserable, intangible self she had been ever since she got to the Manor. She moaned weakly.

'And now, my invisible friend,' said Charles firmly, feeling agreeably strong and confident, 'we'd better come to terms. Though this may be, technically speaking, *your* house, I'm going to stay here tonight, whether you like it or not.'

Overcome by the unfairness, the impropriety, the outrageous reversal of the usual situation, Eve began to cry helplessly. Hearing the unmistakable sobs, something slowly dawned on Charles.

'There, there, dear,' he said more gently, slipping automatically into the formula he found infallible with more tangible feminine tears, 'can't we sit down somewhere and talk this over?— can't see a thing in this infernal darkness, you know,' and he held out a practised, confiding hand.

Eve, who had died rather young to know much about this sort of approach, was at once softened by his sympathy and warmed by his apparent helplessness. Sniffing back her tears, she took his hand trustingly and led him into what had been the long drawing-room. Charles, aware only of a soft pressure on his hand, stumbled across the bare floor and nearly fell over the ancient sofa to which she brought him.

He sat down carefully, and was immediately aware of the springs creaking beside him. He smiled ironically to himself; this was rather different from the usual situation, but he could always try something of the usual technique. It did not help him, of course, that in this case he could not see the girl. But she had an undeniably sweet young presence, so he extended his arm tentatively along the back of the sofa, and hoped he was encircling her.

'Now, my sweet,' he said, with a nice mixture of tenderness and exasperation, 'suppose you tell me all about it.'

Eve was enchanted; and, bursting luxuriously into tears again, she flung herself impulsively into his arms. Off his guard, Charles warmed suddenly with genuine feeling; there was something peculiarly moving about the sobbing little spirit, whose intangible presence lay soft and real against him.

'There, there,' he murmured soothingly, as the sobs grew quieter, 'what's the matter, eh?'

'No one ever comes here,' Eve's sad whisper was no louder than the faintly rustling trees outside the window, 'and if I can't haunt someone soon, I shall be punished.'

'Poor little thing,' said Charles sympathetically, not sure whether or not he was really hearing either words or a voice, 'so there was no one to frighten till I came?'

'No,' moaned Eve faintly, 'you're the first person I've ever had—and *look* what's happened. It shouldn't be like this, not a bit like this—I oughtn't to be here—with you—and everything.'

She was growing agreeably excited. Charles tried to tighten his arm round her.

'Do you mind?' he asked, deliberately tender.

'Yes—no—of course I do!' she cried. 'This may be my last chance, and then...'

'But how can you be punished—er—now?'

'Oh,' Eve wailed, 'you don't understand—it's awful—you have to—to—' she choked, 'you have to *come back to life again!*'

'I see,' said Charles, considerably taken aback.

They sat silent for a while after that, each comfortably and pleasantly aware of the other's presence, without feeling the need for further communication. For her part, Eve was feeling deliciously refreshed for having a good cry, and strangely cheerful in spite of herself. As for Charles, he found he was unbelievably content to be sitting on a dusty sofa in a deserted old house late on a rainy night, comforting a gentle distressed spirit. Neither he nor Eve felt any inclination to move, and presently Charles fell peacefully asleep.

Bright sunlight was streaming in through the dusty windows when he woke; and he lay for a moment, frowning uncertainly round the unfamiliar uncarpeted room, and down at the tattered brocade of the sofa on which he had apparently slept the night. He thought back:

he had had an accident, had left his car, and had found an empty old house to shelter in; that much he remembered. But what on earth had happened after that? A strange happiness seemed to be fading as he sat up, shaking his head and struggling to remember.

'One of those dreams, I suppose,' he sighed at last, swinging his legs stiffly to the floor, 'gone as soon as you try to catch them. Ah well,' he stood up, yawning and straightening his crumpled clothes, 'I'd better get going, the nearest phone must be a long...'

'Good morning,' breathed a timid feminine voice behind him.

'Hello!' cried Charles delightedly, spinning round as he remembered everything, 'and how are *you* this fine morning?'

There was a swift rustling, and he felt a warmth trembling in his hand. He smiled unseeingly.

'I'm awfully glad you came to see me,' he said. 'I wouldn't have wanted to leave without saying goodbye.'

The pressure on his hand was removed abruptly, and Charles sensed very keenly that he had said the wrong thing. Eve was, indeed, absolutely furious. The moment she knew he was awake, she had rushed to him in a delicious tumult of new emotions. And here he was, hateful creature, calmly tidying himself and getting ready to leave as if nothing had happened.

'Well—of course—this isn't really goodbye,' Charles began heartily, aware of an atmosphere of gloom and anger creeping slowly over the sunlit room, 'we shall keep in touch—as it were—and someday maybe...'

He faltered as the long iron shutters suddenly clanged shut across the windows.

'You must understand, surely,' he began, backing awkwardly into the hall, 'I've got a job—and I—there's my car—I couldn't stay...'

Aware suddenly of Eve passing him like the wind, he flung himself forward desperately. But the great front door creaked rustily shut and, as he fell against it fumbling wildly for the handle, the huge iron bolts grated across high above his head. Eve stood back, grinning maliciously, as he struggled ineffectually to open the door.

'Now look here!' Charles sensed crossly that he was being laughed at, 'you can't do this to me, you know. Someone's bound to miss me, and sooner or later they're going to find me.'

Even as he said it, Charles realised that this could be just what Eve needed. And in fact she was whirling round, echoing with delighted laughter as he spoke. This was unexpected gilt on the gingerbread indeed; to be able to do what she really wanted, and find that it was positively good for her reputation as well—what more could a girl want? Eve flung herself rapturously into Charles's arms.

'L-look here,' he began unconvincingly; and surrendered without a struggle to her exquisitely soft embrace.

It was not until much later, when they were sitting together on the sofa, that Charles suddenly realised that he had not eaten anything since the afternoon of the day before.

'You're hungry,' said Eve, before he could speak. 'I'll get you something to eat.'

Charles sighed contentedly. 'That's the most wonderful thing about you,' he said, 'I don't have to say anything, you just understand.'

He winced a little as he recognised a weary cliché, but comforted himself that this time at any rate it happened to be absolutely true. He was already finding it less and less necessary to say anything; Eve sensed everything first.

'But I say!' he sat up abruptly, 'there can't be any food here—I mean—you don't—that is . . .'

'Of course there isn't, and I don't,' Eve laughed softly, 'but it won't take me a moment to get some, just the same.'

And Charles, whose own senses were sharpening already, knew after a moment that she had left him. He was beginning to accept Eve's limitless, timeless world; and when she returned almost at once with a steak done exactly how he most liked it, and a glass of good red wine, he did not even bother to ask her how or where she had obtained it. He simply ate with great enjoyment, conscious of her happiness glowing beside him. And afterwards, as he sat back with a sigh, Eve settled into his arms.

A week or so passed in happiness and tranquillity. A strange tenderness grew between them. Charles found Eve elusively charming and delicately different from any girl on earth; while Eve found in Charles the strength and solidity which the men of her world seemed to lack.

They were not, however, left in such peace for long. Two of Charles's friends, searching the countryside conscientiously for him, had finally found his car near the Manor gates. It was not long, of course, before they penetrated the overgrown drive to the house itself. They might never have found Charles even then, if he and Eve had been inside the Manor. But it was such a soft sunny autumn day that Charles unfortunately happened to be sitting out under his favourite mulberry tree on the grass in front of the Manor. Eve was rustling about in the gnarled branches above his head, looking for ripe mulberries.

'Open your mouth, darling,' she whispered, 'here comes a beauty.' As Charles tilted his head back, he suddenly caught sight of the two figures coming slowly up the drive.

'Quick!' he roared, leaping to his feet, 'into the house.'

But it was too late. The two figures began to run towards him, shouting 'Hi, Charles, it's us—Tom and Dick—hi!'

There was nothing for it, and with a sigh Charles turned at the top of the steps and waited for them. Panting and laughing, the two men stopped short when they got close, and their smiles faded as they looked up at him. They had known Charles Turner as a seemingly normal, good-looking, well-groomed young man; very different indeed from the dishevelled strange-eyed man who stood wiping mulberry juice off his lips and beard with the back of his hand, and watching them silently.

'Charles?' one of them faltered. 'It *is* you, Charles, isn't it?' Charles nodded mutely. He had almost forgotten how to talk out loud.

'We felt sure you must have had an accident,' said the other, trying to sound jovial. 'It's not like you to be out of circulation for so long!'

'That's right,' chimed in the first, over-eagerly, 'and when we found your old car down there in such bad shape, we were afraid you might have been hurt—but now . . .' he hesitated.

'Now we've found you,' said the second, hurriedly, 'we'll take you right home—we left our car down there by the gates—we'll have you back in civilisation in no time!'

They fell silent, staring up at Charles, uncertain smiles on their pleasant unsuspecting faces.

'I—won't—come,' Charles blurted out finally, awkwardly framing words he no longer had to use. 'I'm—staying—here.'

His friends looked significantly at each other.

'Nasty concussion, obviously,' murmured Tom.

'Better persuade him gently,' suggested Dick.

They came towards him, smiling nervously, their hands outstretched. They were reckoning, of course, without Eve. She had been close to Charles's side, watching them with growing suspicion.

'If they so much as lay a finger on you, darling!' she breathed.

'We're a match for them, my sweet,' Charles said firmly.

Tom and Dick hesitated, not sure whether or not they had heard anyone speaking. The whole place seemed full of whisperings and rustlings, it seemed to be growing dark, and altogether they began to feel they were taking on more than they could handle. However, being men of kindly intentions and not without a certain stupid courage, they made one last try.

'We are your friends,' they said distinctly, trying to take his arms. 'We've come to take you home, old man— you're not well.'

The instant they touched Charles, Eve fell on them with a shriek of rage. Whirled into what Charles noticed with pleasure was one of her best dust storms, the two men were bundled, choking and breathless, down the steps. They picked themselves up, looked hurriedly back at the Manor, and set off down the drive as fast as they could.

'I think that's the last we'll see of them,' Charles grinned, as he and Eve went in and closed the great door behind them.

But he underestimated his friends. They were resolutely determined now to save him from what they regarded as the dangerous after-effects of his car accident. Accordingly, they came back again, several times. They brought other people with them in the hope that fresh voices might penetrate what appeared to be his deranged mind. All this was splendid for Eve; whatever people thought of Charles's condition, her psychic manifestations were regarded with the most satisfying mixture of fear, admiration and interest. 'Haunted Huntley Manor' caught the public imagination; for a couple of days the newspapers were full of it, and people came in droves to be frightened to death. Eve's spiritual reputation was made; and she and Charles had a marvellous time devising new and terrifying performances for her to put on.

One day, however, Tom and Dick arrived once more, during a lull. This time they brought Charles's girl-friend, Julia.

'What's that *woman* doing here?' Eve hissed in Charles's ear, as the trio emerged from their car and hesitantly approached the house.

'I—I don't know, my sweet. I can't think why Tom and Dick should have brought her...'

A familiar atmosphere of gloom and anger grew thick about him as he spoke.

'Eve, darling, my pet, do listen—she's nothing—just a girl I used to know—really...'

The air went on thickening ominously.

'Please—darling—you must believe me.' Charles felt himself impelled firmly towards the door. 'All right, all right, I'm going—I'll tell them to take her away.' The compulsion grew stronger. 'That is, I'll tell *her* to go away myself.'

Immediately he said that, the pressure slackened, the atmosphere lifted; and as he went out on the steps, Eve's incredibly light kisses brushed his neck.

'Minx,' he murmured delightedly, as the two men with Julia between them reached the bottom of the steps. Noticing the smile, Tom and Dick nodded encouragingly at Julia.

'There you are, he's pleased to see *you* at any rate,' they whispered, 'you always could handle him, dear—you go on and get him.'

Ignobly they pushed Julia forward alone to speak to

Charles. Eve, however, had other ideas.

'Don't, *don't*,' squealed Julia, as the first stones hit her. 'Tom—Dick—help!'

As the two men ran up the steps to drag her out of range, Charles turned sternly to Eve.

'If you throw so much as one more little pebble, my talented hot-tempered spirit, I shall get in that car and go back with them—I'm warning you!'

'But she's so ugly,' Eve wailed.

'Not at all,' Charles was unusually tactless.

'She is, she is,' screamed Eve.

'Put that beam down at once.' Charles was really alarmed. 'Do you want to get *me* hung for a murder *you* do?'

Slowly the rafter was replaced on the floor.

'That's better. Now come out here and stand by me.' Charles felt a warmth pressing into his side. 'Good girl —now we'll see them together and tell them politely, once and for all,' he was nudged sharply, 'yes, Julia as well—to go away and stay away!'

During the lull, and feeling safe to come forward again, the trio began climbing the steps to the great front door.

'Er—hullo, Julia.' Charles winced as something sharp nipped his arm. 'And Tom and Dick, of course—won't you all come in?'

'Oh, Charlie!' Julia cried, when they were all settled more or less comfortably in the drawing-room.

'Charlie—arlie—arlie,' mocked an echo in the vaulted ceiling.

Everyone looked up startled; and Charles suppressed a grin. This was a talent Eve had not shown him before.

'Amazing places, these old houses, don't you think?' he mumbled idiotically.

'Charles, you might have the decency to listen to Julia,' said Tom pompously.

'But—I am—trying—to listen,' protested Charles awkwardly, his ears filled with flutterings and flutings. 'Stop it, will you?' he breathed aside. 'You're not helping things.'

'She's fat, too fat,' whispered Eve.

'Oh, I don't know that I would say *that*.' Charles looked Julia up and down reflectively.

'I've missed you, Charlie darling,' Julia cooed, leaning forward uneasily.

There was a crash and a scream; and a cloud of dust grew suspiciously thick as all three men rushed forward to haul the moaning Julia out of the ruins of her chair.

'Charlie dear,' Julia cried, clinging frantically to Charles's hand, 'don't you love me any more?'

'I—ouch,' gasped Charles, doubling up over what felt like a terrible punch in the stomach.

Mistaking his movement towards her, Julia closed her eyes and pursed her lips expectantly. 'Oh, darling,' she breathed unconvincingly.

As the vast echo of a succulent illusory kiss faded round the room, Julia opened her eyes furiously to see Charles being helped to a chair.

'He's winded,' said Tom.

'Must have hit himself on the chair,' said Dick.

'Are you trying to make a fool of me?' Julia spat out.

'Can't make her what she is already,' breathed Eve, tweaking Charles's nose hard, and viciously jabbing the two other men at the same time.

'What the...' shouted Dick.

'Who the...' bawled Tom.

'Charlie,' cried Julia, closing in again, 'kiss me, Charlie.'

As she wound herself resolutely round his neck, there was a fearful tearing sound above their heads. The great pendant chandelier hovered for an instant and, as Charles felt himself plucked backwards, it fell. Full on Julia.

'Good Lord!' said Tom, as they laid her gently on the sofa, 'she's out cold.'

'Look here, old man,' said Dick, sombrely, 'this has gone far enough.'

'Too far, much too far,' groaned Charles, nursing his ear which had been grazed as the chandelier crashed on Julia. '*Now* will you believe I'm not leaving here? For goodness' sake, go away—and take her with you, before she's killed!'

Carrying Julia's limp body carefully between them, the two men went back to their car. And presently the sound of its engine faded away down the drive.

'Oh darling, petling, angel,' crooned Eve extravagantly, before Charles had time to recover. 'I'm terribly sorry, truly I am, and I wouldn't have hurt your ear for *any-thing*.' She kissed it passionately. 'But I just couldn't bear to see that ugly fat stupid woman near you!'

'I don't know!' sighed Charles, grinning in spite of himself as she produced a bottle of his favourite beer, a glass, and a bottle-opener. 'I never had a chance, had I?'

But the episode brought things to a head. So much publicity was now gathering round Haunted Huntley Manor that Julia's injuries, though amazingly slight, could not have been hushed up for long. In any case, Julia made them the centre of a long dramatic tale in which, not unnaturally, Tom and Dick showed up rather badly, and Charles emerged as a dangerous lunatic. As matters were, there was nothing for it but to get the appropriate medical authorities to help remove the deranged man to a place of safety and cure.

So it happened that one morning, when Eve and Charles had climbed high out on the roof-walk to be as far as possible from expected trouble, they saw a number of white-coated men climb out of an ambulance and start walking in a resolute manner up the drive. The moment had arrived; and instinctively Eve and Charles drew closer together as they watched the procession approaching the front door far below. Then Eve sighed, and sadly withdrew from her lover's side. She knew what she must do. His coming had solved all her problems, her haunting record was now one of the best in the country, and there was only one thing more she wanted.

'This won't hurt, my love,' she murmured, as she pushed him over the edge of the roof, 'and in a moment you'll be back with me—forever.'

ROSEMARY TIMPERLEY

Sister Varden

'Will you do something for me?' she asked.

'Of course, Sister. What is it?'

'Come with me to James's house this evening.'

'Why, certainly. I'll be glad to.'

'Thank you. It won't take more than five minutes.' She smiled and went into her office, leaving me to wheel the trolley of tea-things into the ward.

I came to this hospital as a voluntary worker every Sunday afternoon to help serve tea and supper, then left at eight when the day staff went off duty. Nina Varden, the ward sister, had been friendly towards me from the start and now we knew each other quite well. She was a wonderful nurse and I admired her as much as I liked her. She was always so calm and self-controlled. Whatever happened on the ward, she never flapped. She was supremely well balanced, mistress of herself.

Compared with her busy and peopled day at the hospital, her private life was lonely. She had never married, although she was attractive and must have had chances. According to hospital gossip she'd had a long drawn out love affair with a married man and it had fizzled out in the end, leaving her stranded. But that was merely what

I'd heard—she never discussed personal matters with me.

The only friend she'd mentioned to me was James, her cousin. He was also unmarried and in his forties now, like Nina. He'd been living with his widowed mother, who had died a year or so back, so now he was by himself in the large house which she had owned. He was a biologist, dividing his time between university lecturing and research, and the latter involved frequent trips abroad. He was particularly interested in marine biology and at the moment was on an expedition in the Seychelles.

James and Nina had always been friends and since his mother's death they had drawn even closer together. I'd seen him at the hospital once or twice when he'd dropped in for a chat and then taken Nina out to supper afterwards. She was immensely fond of him, glad to do anything for him, and when he was abroad she made it her business to visit his empty house regularly to see that all was well.

She performed this small labour of love on Sunday evenings. When we went off duty she would give me a lift to the bus-stop, then drive on to James's house before returning to her own flat.

She had never before asked me to go to the house with her, so although I was pleased that she wanted my company, I was also puzzled. I'd have thought that the last thing she wanted when she went to James's house was the intrusion of any other presence. For I knew she was in love with him really although, being middle-aged and proud, she wouldn't have confessed it to anyone.

At eight o'clock that Sunday evening we set out together in her car. We passed the bus-stop and, about ten minutes later, reached James's house. I had never been there before.

It was a large detached house with two sets of front gates and a semi-circular drive. The semi-circle was filled in with tall, thick trees which tonight were waving wildly in a high wind and making a rushing, rustling, hissing sound which was slightly sinister. In fact, as we walked up the drive I felt unexpectedly nervous. Nina too was unusually tense. Why? And why had she asked me to come with her?

She let us into the house. It was utterly silent but for the rustling of the trees outside. She turned on lights as we crossed the hall.

'That's the living-room,' she said, indicating a well-furnished room on the right. 'The breakfast-room and kitchen are along here.'

'Breakfast-room? How posh,' I said foolishly, trying to cover my unease with light chat.

We went through the small room with its table set against the window and into the kitchen, where Nina was keeping a boiler going so that the house wouldn't freeze up in the cold weather. While she was dealing with this, I looked around and chattered for chattering's sake. When I stopped the silence seemed to descend on us even more oppressively.

Suddenly, without thinking first, I exclaimed: 'Isn't it creepy!'

Nina didn't say anything but turned to look at me.

And her eyes were full of fear.

With anyone else I think I'd have said: 'What's the matter? Why didn't you want to come here alone?' but she was so reserved that I'm sure she wouldn't have answered me.

Nothing happened after that. We just left together, then she took me to the next bus-stop on my route, said: 'Goodbye. Thanks for coming with me. See you next Sunday,' and drove away.

It was such a small, apparently trivial episode, yet I couldn't forget it. I kept seeing her frightened face in my mind's eye. I had never seen Nina Varden look like that before. And she was not a foolishly nervous person to be made uneasy by an empty house. Why *had* she been so afraid?

As Nina and I had so little to do with each other's everyday lives, I rarely contacted her during the week, but this time, as I felt so concerned, I did ring her on the Wednesday evening.

When she answered, I knew that my disquiet had not been groundless. Her voice sounded different, slow and curiously broken.

'What did you ring for?' she asked.

'Nothing special. I only wondered how you were.'

There was a little pause, then she said: 'I've had a great tragedy in my life.'

Dramatic words, all the more striking when spoken in the voice of a woman who did not normally use emotional language.

'What's happened?'

'James is dead. He was drowned off the coast of one of the Seychelle islands. He was swimming under water to study the fauna there and never came back to the surface.'

'Oh, my God, how awful. When did you hear?'

'This morning.'

'And when—when did it actually happen?'

'On Sunday.'

'You knew something had happened! You knew then!'

'No. But I felt—doomed.' She caught her breath then continued calmly: 'I shall be very busy now. There's only me to handle everything. He's going to be buried out there.'

'Are you taking time off from work?'

'I have some leave due to me so I shall take two weeks from next Monday. I'll see you on Sunday.'

'Yes. Oh, God, Nina, I'm so *sorry*.'

'Thank you.' She rang off.

When I saw her on the following Sunday, she looked and sounded the same as usual. No stranger would have guessed that anything had happened. Staff and patients who knew that her cousin had died had no notion of how stricken she was. Even I was almost deceived by her serene manner. We had no personal talk during the afternoon, but when eight o'clock came and we walked to her car, she said: 'I'll have to go to the house.'

'Why?'

'To see to the boiler. He wouldn't want me to neglect his property just because he's not there.'

'May I come with you?'

She hesitated. 'If you'd like to.'

'I'd like to very much,' I said firmly, knowing that she didn't really want me around this time but was too kind to rebuff me. Sister Varden would sooner suffer an inconvenience than hurt anyone's feelings. Of course I didn't want to go to that house at all but nor did I like the idea of her going there alone.

We reached the house and it looked as before, with the trees dashing blackly against the night sky and whispering, whispering. But when we went inside I didn't feel as nervous as I had last time. I think I know why. My previous fear had been an infection of what she was feeling. That sense of impending doom. She'd had an inner certainty then that something terrible had happened to James. Because she'd had no logical reason for feeling thus, she'd been torn with doubts. Uncertainty was a rare emotion for her. She hadn't understood it. That was why she couldn't face the empty house alone—although of course she would have done if I'd been unable to accompany her. Now there was no more doubt, so she was not afraid. When what you most feared has happened, there is nothing to fear any more. Nothing at all any more.

We went into the kitchen and she fixed the boiler. She made a comment on the quality of the coke; it was better than the last lot because James had complained to the coal merchant. Her glance lighted on a row of jars of marmalade on a shelf. 'He was very fond of marmalade,' she said. 'I made that lot specially for him.'

'You made it? How clever of you.'

'Not at all. One merely buys the right quantity of everything then follows instructions in a book. Would you like a jar? Yes, do have one.'

'Well—thank you.' I stood there uselessly, the jar of marmalade in my hands. I felt that for two pins I'd burst into tears. That must *not* happen. It would be too idiotic. I'd hardly known James at all. I felt nothing really about his death, except vicarious sorrow for Nina. Indeed secretly I thought he was lucky to die like that, in his forties, while doing the work he enjoyed. Not for him the long drag along the road to old age, the encroachment of feebleness and pains, the geriatric ward, the slow dying. Lucky James. But poor Nina. Poor, poor Nina!

She saw my eyes fill with tears. 'You shouldn't have come,' she said gently. 'It was very sweet of you and you came for my sake, I know, but it's upsetting you.'

'Never mind about *me*. What about *you*?'

'I'm not upset,' she said. 'I don't think I shall ever feel anything again.'

We returned to the car. 'I'll drive you home,' she said.

'No, Nina. It's too far. Put me down at the bus-stop as usual.'

'But I'd like to drive you home. It's not much considering what you've done for me.'

'I've done nothing for you—and you gave me the marmalade.' That made me nearly weep again.

'You've done more than you realise,' she said. 'I couldn't have asked anyone else to come with me last Sunday. They'd have asked questions. You didn't. You just came, as I'd known you would.'

I felt a bit guilty at that as I had wanted to ask questions. Thank goodness I hadn't!

'Nina, please just drop me at the bus-stop. You must be tired out and I don't like the thought of your driving all the way back, alone in the dark.'

'Alone in the dark? That's where I live now.'

She drove on past the stop. We didn't talk any more. Usually I am rather frightened when being driven in a car at night. All the lights coming from cars travelling in the opposite direction seem to be making a bee line for me and each few seconds I close my eyes and steel myself for the crash ... But this time I gave no thought to such self-induced fear. My thoughts were taken up with James's death and Nina's grief. She had loved him more deeply than I ever knew, and certainly more deeply than I'd ever loved anyone myself.

Just before we arrived, she said: 'One of the staff nurses will be in charge next Sunday and the one after. You'll be going there as usual, won't you? Keep an eye on my patients for me.'

'Yes, Sister.' I did call her 'Sister' instead of 'Nina' sometimes. I had to on the ward because everyone else did, and whenever she spoke of her work she *was* Sister. One could almost forget the woman behind the image. But now it was the woman who was in distress. She wouldn't even have the protection of her uniform for the next fortnight.

'Nina, can I do anything for you? Anything at all?'

'Nothing, my dear. I shall be coping with solicitors, writing letters, arranging for the burial over there and the memorial service here. Nobody but me can do it and it's what James would have wished. We had no one but each other.'

'Has he left a will?'

'Yes. He's bequeathed everything to me—his money, income from various stocks and shares, and the house.'

'What shall you do with the house?'

'Live in it.'

She said it so sadly. Some people would have been delighted to inherit a handsome house, especially at a time when to buy such a house at all was beyond the means of all but the affluent, but I knew that the financial benefit was no compensation to her. She'd never had much money because of her profession and was indifferent to material luxury. And somehow I didn't like the idea of her going to live in James's house. How would she ever get over his loss if she was surrounded by his property all the time? Every step she took, every item she touched in that house would remind her of him.

In the fortnight that followed, I didn't contact Nina Varden at all. Often I wanted to telephone her, but refrained because I knew that most of her calls would be in connection with the death and there was no kindness in unnecessary interruptions. I was only an acquaintance on the outskirts of her life so the best thing I could do for the moment was to keep out of her way.

So I didn't see her again until her first Sunday back at work. Then I was almost afraid of seeing her, in case she looked ill and devastated. But, to my astonishment, the very opposite had happened—she looked radiant. There was a glow about her, as if something wonderful had happened and she was hugging it to herself but couldn't help letting her happiness show. They say *Love and a red nose can't be hid*. Had she fallen in love again? As in that pretty, popular song, the look of love was on her face. She looked younger, and beautiful. Perhaps she'd met someone special at the memorial service, one of James's friends or colleagues. This seemed quite likely. In her working life she didn't meet many men, only visiting consultants and husbands of patients, but James's death would have introduced her to new people, men of intellect like himself and of a similar age group. How glad I would be if something like that had happened—and *something* certainly had. I wouldn't ask anything, of course, but would she tell me?

The work-filled afternoon passed quickly. The atmosphere was good as Sister's gaiety made the patients and visitors cheerful. I had never heard her laugh so often. Then, when we went off duty and were in her car, she told me about the memorial service and mentioned various distinguished people who had attended.

'I knew he was liked and admired,' she said, 'but I'd never realised how much. Such a *lot* of people came. He was so pleased!'

'Who was?'

'James, of course. He's so modest that he hadn't dreamed that so many people cared about him.'

That struck me temporarily dumb. She was talking as if he were alive.

'I moved into the house straight away,' she told me. 'I always wanted to live there, you know, but I was afraid there'd be gossip if I went before. You know how it is when a man and a woman live together without being married, and hospital nurses are expected to appear respectable if they can. But now no one can gossip at all as they think I'm there by myself.'

'But you—you *are* there by yourself, Nina.'

She gave me a surprised look. 'I wouldn't have anticipated that remark from you.'

'Why not?' I'd gone chilly and goosefleshy.

'Because you've always had this awareness of other
worlds, much more than I have. He wasn't there at first,
mind you. When I went to the house to clear things up,
it was heart-breakingly empty but as soon as I moved in
and started living there, I knew he was there too. We've
been chattering away together ever since.'

My God, did she walk around that house talking to
herself? Sister Varden, of all people!

'I don't mean I speak aloud,' she went on. 'There's no
need. There are silent voices. I frame the words silently
in my head and I hear him answer—hear with some
mysterious inner ear. I've got a photograph of his grave
in the Seychelles. Would you like to come back with me
and see it? He won't mind—he likes you.'

She was so matter-of-fact about it that I responded in
the same prosaic tone: 'Sure. I'd love to come.' But I
felt unreal as we approached the house. This was like a
dream. Here was practical, sensible Sister Varden believ-
ing that she was living with the spirit of her dead cousin,
and finding it more suitable than if she'd lived with
him when he was alive. With any of my more tempera-
mental friends I'd have thought it was a case of mental
breakdown, but Nina was so *sane* ... a damned sight
saner than I've ever been. It was her sanity that had
always attracted me to her, me with my quick emotions
and irrational fears. She had been an anchor of calm and
commonsense.

Now what would happen when I went into that house
with her? Would I too sense James's presence? And if I
did, would I accept it with equanimity or run out screaming? For although I had played with the idea of ghosts
often enough, I had never had anything to do with any.

She opened the door and we went in. The place was warm, cosy, homelike, with no hint of the uncanniness I had felt before. I was both pleased and relieved. Had she by any chance been pulling my leg? No, not Nina. And yet she had been more gay and mischievous today than I'd ever known her.

'How pleasant it is,' I said. 'You must have worked like the devil to get everything so nice in such a short time.'

'I have worked hard, but we nurses are strong as horses, you know. We have to be or we'd crack up. Anyway, it was all fun as I had James for company. He kept laughing and saying he wished he could lend a hand but was so glad he couldn't.'

Talkative and vivacious, she showed me all over the house. She was like a proud young bride before the gilt has worn off the marriage gingerbread. I found myself infected by her happiness, delighted by her delight, and only now and then did I glance over my shoulder after catching imaginary glimpses of indefinable movement out of the corner of my eye. But the main impression was not of a haunted house but a happily lived in house. To bachelor James it must have been little more than a tent offering him shelter after his day's work. Now it was a home.

Nina made coffee and brought it into the living-room. As we sat side by side on the couch and drank it, she showed me the photograph of James's grave. The ground in front of the gravestone was decorated with a profusion of flowers and intricate patterns of sea-shells.

'It's lovely,' I said.

'I knew you'd think so. I arranged for a press photographer out there to take it for me, and now I can hardly wait to go and see it and take pictures of it myself. James has seen it, of course. He can see anything he wants to see, bless him. I still have to pay fares and climb into aeroplanes to get anywhere,' and she laughed.

'Do you see him?' I asked bluntly.

'No. Well, one could hardly see a soul, could one? The whole point of leaving the body behind is that you can move around without it so there's nothing to see—not with our earthbound eyes anyway.'

'But if he did become visible to you—'

'How could he? There's no visible form which could *be* James. If there was, it would be a mixture of baby, boy, young man, older man—an impossible conglomeration.'

A horrifying conglomeration, I thought. It would be a monster.

'You're not afraid, are you?' she asked me suddenly.

'I can't help being a bit afraid of what I don't understand.'

'That's just silly,' said Nina. 'We understand nothing about life really, yet I'm sure we aren't meant to feel afraid all the time. We must learn to accept mystery and be grateful when it's good. I'm so grateful.' She stopped and listened, then said: 'James says you're too timid about things which mystify you.'

'Perhaps I am.'

She listened again. 'He says you think I've gone mad and are too tactful to say so.' She laughed with great amusement and I tried to be amused too.

'Foolish thing,' she said, touching my shoulder gently as if I were a nervous patient. 'You know how balanced I am. My working life has trained me that way. Before this happened to me, I admit I wouldn't have believed it could happen. I'd never have *imagined* living here with James. I'm not an imaginative type, like you. But it's quite simply happened, and I've never been so contented before. Never! I used to have moments of ecstatic happiness when I was younger, and there was someone I was in love with, but those moments were always cancelled out by the misery that followed—as if they had to be paid for because they were guilty. He was married, you see.'

'Yes.'

'You knew about that?'

'Nothing definite. The merest whisper.'

'I know. Grapevine stuff. No escape from it. It's horrible to be gossiped about. That was why I was so careful when I grew to love James.'

'Why didn't you and he get married?'

'Because apparently it's only since his death that he's known how much I care for him. I rather hid my feelings before in case he didn't respond. He's told me since that he was afraid to ask me in case I refused, and then our friendship would have been spoiled. Aside from that, we're neither of us the marrying kind. Living as we do now, we have complete freedom, yet we're together all the time—together inside. It's like a miracle.'

'It *is* a miracle if—' But I didn't go on to say: '—if it's not a delusion.'

After one of her listening pauses, Nina said: 'James wants you to know that it isn't a delusion. Oh, please don't be sceptical and make me sorry I confided in you.'

'No, no, I'm glad you did. As long as you're happy, that's all that matters. Forgive me if I'm being—limited.'

She nodded. 'Yes. The way I used to be.'

I left shortly afterwards and as the front door closed behind me, I heard her laugh—a long, sweet, free ripple of laughter, as if someone had just made a joke. James perhaps? But once removed from Nina's presence, and sitting on the top deck of an ordinary bus, I sank right back into a mood of doubt and fear. I couldn't believe that James's spirit was really in that house. Nina was hallucinating like mad. Maybe the illusion was making her happy now, but how would she feel when it passed? Then it would be as if James had died twice, and the second time would be worse than the first. If she was mad, she'd be better off continuing to be mad, as long as it didn't affect her work. But schizophrenia, with its attendant hallucinations, doesn't usually last for ever. It most often dies away again, like influenza, an equally incalculable 'influence'. Having been alarmed by the fact that Nina was haunted, I now found myself more alarmed that she would get unhaunted again—find herself deserted in that empty house—listening for a silent voice which never spoke—seeking an intangible presence which had vanished of its own accord.

For the next few Sundays I went to the hospital as usual, and Nina still seemed well and happy, but she kept off personal topics when we were together and didn't invite me back to the house. I'm afraid she thought that she'd overrated my capacity for understanding her situation, so it would be better for me not to be bothered with it any more.

Then one Sunday when I was washing up in the ward kitchen I heard a couple of the nurses talking about Sister Varden as they sipped illicit cups of tea.

One of them said: 'I've never known anyone change so much. She used to be so quiet and reserved, and sort of sad underneath, but now she laughs and talks all the time and seems to be on top of the world.'

'So would I be if a cousin died and left me a super house and all his lolly,' said the other nurse, 'but all the same you'd think she'd be a bit more sad about his death instead of acting as if she'd won the Pools. I don't think she's quite as good on the ward as she used to be. She doesn't seem to care about the patients so much.'

Then there was dead silence as they suddenly realised

that 'Sister's friend' was working at the sink with her ears pricked up. Washers-up do hear a lot as people forget they're there. But the girls needn't have worried about me. That was the last sort of talk I'd pass on to Sister. All the same, I wondered whether it was true that she was paying a little less attention to her patients and, if so, whether she was aware of it herself.

I was to find the answer to that on the same evening, for when she was driving me to the bus-stop she said: 'Will you come back and have some coffee with us—with me?'

'Thank you, Nina. I'd like to.'

When we were in the living-room and she'd made the coffee, she said: 'I had a reason for inviting you. It's to say goodbye.'

'What?'

'Yes. Today was my last Sunday on duty. I'm leaving at the end of the week.'

'Leaving the hospital? Oh, no!'

'It's the best thing to do. I'm old enough to retire now if I want to. I was going to continue working until I *had* to retire, because my work was my life, but James is my life now and I need more free time with him. I haven't been concentrating as well on the patients as I used to, and I don't want to turn into the sort of nurse who simply doles out drugs and writes reports without her heart being in it. My heart just isn't in the ward any longer.'

'But Nina, you should keep the ward there for—for when maybe your heart is free for it again. Don't burn your boats.'

She laughed. 'There was a time when you were the reckless one and I was the sobersides. We seem to have changed roles. No, I've got enough money not to have to work any more, so why should I go on slaving away?

I've served society for a pittance for long enough. Now I'm going to travel the world with James. Seychelles first stop.'

'And then?'

'Anywhere the fancy takes us. James can decide.'

'But—how can you be sure that he—that he'll be with you still when you leave his house?'

'Don't be ridiculous. He's not housebound. Souls don't have agoraphobia.' She listened alertly. 'No, James says they certainly don't and he'll be wherever I am.'

'Oh, Nina, stop this!' The words broke out of me harshly, shockingly, ending in an hysterical wail.

'What on earth's the matter with you?'

'Not me—you. You're making yourself worse—you're encouraging yourself in this—this—'

'Delusion?'

'Yes! You mustn't let this mad dream take you away from your work, which is your real life, your—your security of spirit. You'd hate just wandering round the world like a rich tourist—you'd feel idle and wasted and miss the rewards of your vocation—and then when this dream passes, you wouldn't even have your work to go back to—'

'Control yourself,' said Sister Varden.

Ashamed now, I controlled myself. 'I'd better go. I'm sorry.'

'Never mind. You just don't understand. You really are limited, but you can't help it. Goodbye, my dear. Thanks for all your help on the ward. I'll write to you from the Seychelles and you must write back and regale me with all the hospital gossip. Will you do that?' Sweet voice. Nurse to patient.

'Yes, Sister. I shall miss you on Sundays.'

'I shall miss you too,' she said kindly, indifferently.

'You're going alone, I suppose.'

'Now don't start that again. You know I'm not going alone. I'm going with James. He looks after me.'

He looks after me. I found the words unbearably touching coming from Sister Varden, who had spent her life in looking after other people and must all the time, deep down, have wanted to be looked after herself.

She laughed a little. 'When I'm setting off to enjoy myself on my travels, I wish you wouldn't look as if I'm going to my doom.'

'Oh, I'm sorry. I hope you have a wonderful time, and that it lasts for ever.'

'Thank you, and I hope you'll be happy one day too.'

We embraced. I kissed her on the cheek. And then I got out of the place quickly because I felt weepy. Partings are always awful and this one was particularly distressing. I was so afraid for Nina Varden and felt almost certain that I would never hear from her again. The episode, and the fragile friendship, were finished.

And it turned out that I was right in that feeling. I didn't hear from Nina again, but I did hear *of* her. This happened because one of the doctors who attended the hospital had a friend and colleague in the Seychelles. He heard that Sister Varden was going there to see her cousin's grave, so wrote to his friend to get in touch with her, as she was travelling alone. Several weeks later, this doctor friend wrote back and told him of the events which had passed. He in turn told me, when he came one Sunday to see a patient and I was there. He knew that Nina and I had been friends and that I hadn't heard from her.

He said that on her arrival Nina had booked into an hotel, then visited James's grave and taken photographs of it. She had been in good spirits, extremely gay and elated, but within a week that elation had evaporated. She had seemed to grow much older and sank into deep depression. She wandered about looking, listening, hardly speaking, as if she were searching for something she couldn't find. Then she had gone down with some mysterious fever and was transferred to hospital.

She talked ceaselessly in delirium, repeating and repeating sentences on the lines of 'Please speak to me. Where are you? Why won't you talk to me any more? What have I done? Are you angry with me? If you are, tell me what it is and I'll do anything—anything—please come back— Oh, come back, come back—speak to me, darling, please—please—if you can't come to me, tell me why—just tell me why—shall I come to you? Is that what you want? Just *tell* me what you want. *Tell* me!'

Then one day when she'd been left alone, she crept unseen out of the hospital and went down to the shore. She stripped off her dressing-gown and nightdress and walked naked into the water. A native on the beach had seen her, without knowing who she was, but he was accustomed to the eccentricities of tourists so paid scant attention. When he realised that she had walked right out to sea and was not returning, he gave the alarm. But it was too late. By the time a boat reached her, she had died by drowning.

She was buried in a grave alongside James's grave, amid a profusion of bright flowers and intricate patterns of sea-shells. The doctor showed me a coloured photograph of the two graves side by side. His friend had sent it to him.

'Did your friend take the photograph?' I asked, just for something ordinary to say.

'No,' the doctor answered. 'No one knows who took it. It was the last film on a roll in her own camera. All the other pictures are simply of the cousin's grave, and this last one—well, your guess is as good as mine. It was noticed, when her effects were gathered together, that there was one unused film in the roll, so one can only suppose that someone borrowed the camera for a while, took the final picture after she'd been buried, and then when my friend took the roll to be developed, this picture came to light.'

'He didn't notice when he took it to the shop that the last film had been used?'

'In his letter, he says he didn't think it had, but that he must have been wrong. Well, he must have been. There's no other explanation for it, is there?'

'No,' I said. 'No other explanation at all.'

JOHN HYNAM

One For My Baby

Dear Mr Sinatra:

I am writing this to you because it is the only hope left for me. In a way, its a begging letter, but not for money; I know that you are generous, because I heard about them concerts you did in London for charity, and how you helped Buddy Rich start his new band. I like his band, but I reckon you should ask him to play more tunes what people link up with you.

I dont even know if this letter will ever get to you. If it does then you will see that my writing is pretty lousy, and I dint have much education. I dont have no good looks and I dont have no talent for anything much, but Im strong and I can drive a truck.

Im not asking you for no job neither. This is so hard for me I got to do it my own way, and I hope you dont mind reading on because you are my only hope and thats the truth.

Boys like me what grow into men like me have a hard time, and some of us have it so dam hard it aint easy to tell about. Me I never had no parents, no family. Old McFee and his wife took me on as a foster boy so as they'd have more money for booze, I reckon; they kicked me and hurt me so hard that I always had bruises.

I stole food to stay alive, and that was the first time I got
picked up by the police, and you shoulda heard the way
them two went on, how theyd looked after me and give
me the best of everything and when I shouted liar I was
told to shut up.

I got sent to a reformatory school what dint do me no
good because there was guys what liked to play about
dirty. Men what run that school was no better than the
McFees. After the reformatory school they took me back,
but things was worse nor ever; I dint have no money
and no hope. Old McFee was like the devil to me, and I
started to pray for him to die, and the harder the better,
and this feeling of what oughter happen got sort of fixed
in me, like a kind of thick aching pain what seemed to
stay inside me and went all the way from my throat right
down to my stomach. I knew I had to do something
about the old swine, because hed cast me aside in his
mind like I was of no account, and nobody likes to be of
no account, do they, Mr Sinatra? I mean that you are
real top of the heap, and Ive heard so much about what
an understanding guy you are, and I feel sure youll be
understanding me now, because this is really all
about you, and what you could do for me if you said
OK.

One Satday night I waited for old McFee to come back,
pissing drunk. He had to come down the dirt road and
make his way along the side of a picket fence. He had a
bottle in his hand; stopped to drink of it, singing that
daft song about boiled beef and carrots, and I upped
and grabbed the bottle and swung it at his head, and
down he went. He lay still. I figured like he was dead.
So I put the bottle in the old swine's hand and when I
come by the shed against the house I threw in the gardening gloves I'd borrowed, and then I went and slept real
peaceful, cause I knew that even if he did come back

from the dead he wunt know who hit him, and if he dint come back that was all right with me. They couldnt check anything from the old hag because she was near stone deaf. I sort of laughed to myself.

When the police came next morning I heard them say that the old man died of natural causes, they reckoned. It was a heart attack that fixed him, and his drinking helped to kill him. When the old hag screamed and moaned I went back to the pigs; I was real pleased to see them pigs.

Well, the old hag couldnt hit me like her old man used to; Id growed real big by this time anyway. She got around to the idea that I ought to be paid wages, and I thought that was a bit better. But one Friday when she paid me I saw the big roll of notes she got; must of been round three hundred notes in that roll, and I got thinking and wondering why she and her old man went on like they did when there was all that money.

Well, I stayed and worked at the farm, but I dint feel right about things. When you've had the life Ive had, its real hard to feel that you are right. I did feel a lot better, for a time, after the old man died, but that feeling dint last. I dont mean just money; theres other things, like women. I got used to seeing old MacFees ghost, and that proved he was dead for sure. And when I saw him walk in through the wall he was humming that song about boiled beef and carrots. I never told the old woman about it, how the old man showed hisself. Sometimes he wunt be humming or singing the song, but I knew that was what made him show; when that tune was being played or sung, anywhere, up hed come.

It was a real good day for me when I got myself a suit. Maybe you can remember how good it is for a boy when he gets his first real suit? The man what sold it to me give me some money back off the marked price, because he said hed had it some time, and big fellers like me dint come in very often, so he was ready to sell it cheaper to the first real big feller what come in.

Well then I had some beer, and after that I went along to the discotake what you could hear all the way from the street junction. I paid and went in and it was smart with nice-coloured lights and the speakers making the place fizzle with sound, they was so loud. There was some girls there and that made me breathe a bit hard because I hant never had a girl but I knew I would now that I was dressed smart.

Then there was some fellers about my age, but not so big like me, and they was laughing at somebody. And one said: 'Looka that suit. Aint it enough to blow your mind?'

And another said: 'Yeah. Come to that, look at the swede what's in it.'

Another came closer and said: 'Did you buy it or did the man pay you to take it away?'

And then I saw it real quick they was laughin at me. So I sized these guys up and I come closer and I said: 'What you laughin at?' There was five or six of them and they gathered round and they laughed like I was a sideshow at a fair or something. One of them come close and said: 'Why, its Joey Roll from old MacFees! You come to get yourself a girl, Joey Boy?'

Then I hit him. People always think a big feller will be slow, but I want slow and I hit him right in the mouth and I felt his front teeth go and there was a bit of a crack and I reckoned that was his jaw. Then they all had a try and I laid out three of them real horizontal and there was blood everywhere, and then the bouncers come and held me. They phoned the police and the police come and they wouldnt let me speak cause they was listening to this little runt of a manager, and not to me.

And then there come this girl. She was nice—not like Jane Fonda or anything like that, but nice—and she spoke up for me. She said: 'This big guy want harming nobody, and these others was settin on him and being insulting. They was six to one and he laid out four of them, in self defence.'

Well, Mr Sinatra, it ended with the police taking away all six guys, and four of them Id laid out and the other two went real quiet. But when I looked round for that girl she'd gone, and I couldn't find her and I guess I got real mad; Id think a real nice girl like that would stay a bit, if only to let me thank her.

I was walking up the dirt road to the farm, and just as I was going to go over the stream bridge there was old Mrs McFee, leaning over the rail with a bottle in her hand, and being sick. So I just walked up, took hold of her legs and hoisted her over, and the splash she made sounded real good; I felt better this time. I went into the house and found the money and then I got back to my bunk and I slept good for a bit, but then I found I was woke up and thinking about that girl.

When they fished the old woman outer the stream nobody asked me much because they said they knew about her, and she must of leaned over the rail and been sick and fell in, and I thought them cops was pretty smart because thats what did happen. And they told me after the inquest that Id better stay there at the farm and look after it while the lawyers got the affairs straightened out. So that left me on my own, and suddenlike I got the idea that they would give me the farm. I never heard tell of no relatives what the McFees had, and if the relatives dont show up theyd give the farm to me. I was so happy now that I just dint take notice of when either of the ghosts turned up. Sometimes I heard the man humming that boiled beef and carrots song, sometimes the woman muttered some tune what I couldn't make out nohow. It dint worry me none.

When I sold a couple of pigs what Id reared I felt real good all through. There was this guy at the market who tried to put a false note in with the others, but I just took him quiet like by the throat and showed him how wrong he was, and he paid up real nice and pleasant, no fuss. I dont like fuss. Then I got me a real new suit, one that was really right, with all the fixings and the right kind of shirt and shoes and that, and I knew my suit was OK because I seen one like it in a big book at the tailors what had got in it dozens of guys in the pictures what was wearing a suit cut like mine.

When it was evening, I went to the discotake, what was just starting up. I wanted to be there to find that girl what spoke up for me; I wanted to meet her and thank her and maybe buy her a drink and be real nice to her. I was standing and just looking round when another girl come up. She looked slicker, and she wore big earrings and big tits all pushed up like, the way her dress was made, and she smiled real pleasant and said would I like to dance? I guessed that she was a whore, but I thought it would pass the time, so we danced. It was all sorta easy, because this jigjig kinda dancing is easy, but when there was a waltz tune she danced real close, and that give me a hard what made me pant, cause I rouse quick and easy. She said: 'Why not come and see my flat baby?' and I was near on the point of doing that when I see this girl what spoke up for me, and I just left this whore standing there and her yelling at me and nobody taking notice and sure I dint because there was this girl standing in front of me and smiling.

I felt my face smile big. 'Hello.'

She said: 'Hello to you.' Her voice was gentle, and just a bit husky sounding.

'I was hoping to see you again,' I said, 'because of what you done that time when the guys tried to hustle me a little, and I did a bit of hustling back.'

'It was right, wasnt it?'

'It sure was,' I said, 'and whats your name?'

'Nina. Whats yours?'

'Joe.'

'Hello Joe.'

'Hello Nina.'

Then we both laughed because it was all friendly. We shook hands.

'Like to buy you a drink,' I said.

And she said: 'I dont go much on the likker. How about an ice cream?'

So ice cream it was, the biggest on the list, two Golden Glories what cost one fifty each, and we took a long time eating them and I guess I just talked and talked and she followed every word I said. It was good. I felt like a wreckling plant what had grown miserable like under a stone, and then somebody lifted the stone and let the plant grow straight and tall in the sun, like it should of done all along. By the time the dance was over we knew a lot about each other, and she was a typist in a office, and she was real interested in hearing about the farm, though mind I did play fair and dint say it was my farm. Then I walked part way home with her, and she said yes shed like to meet me again, and I got the bus at the station and got off at the place where the dirt road joined the highway. I was so happy the way things was going.

I got two free ghost shows on the way to the farm. There was me cracking old McFee with the bottle, and the other was when I saw me help the old hag over the rail of the bridge, and that made me feel real good and I slept like a babe.

Please, Mr Sinatra, dont leave off reading now. There aint but one way I can tell you what you need to know before I ask you the question what I got to ask; I got to do it my way. Please be kind. If I dint know you was a kind man, I wouldnt be writing to you, would I?

As the weeks went on I worked hard at the farm and got it working right as well as looking right, and I got white paint and whitewash and roofing felt and tar and I did the whole outside of the place up and it looked like it was worth ten thousand dollars. I worked on sanitation, and piping and feed boxes; it was real good, Mr Sinatra; all the happy songs you ever made on records seemed right for me at that time, like French Foreign Legion and High Hopes and Come Fly With Me and lotsa others. The farm inspector come and he said I was a good farmer and that things was being done right. I showed him my account of the money in and out, and he was a bit surprised at that. What Id written down was rough, but he said he could understand it and he said: 'Well, that looks all right to me; better pay you three hundred dollars now.'

And that made me happy and I told him about Nina and he said if she was half as nice as I said she was, I was real lucky, and I said that was what I thought, too. But I never told him about the ghosts of the old man and the old woman. There want no reason to do it; they only come along when them two silly songs was being played or sung some place.

*　　　*　　　*

Nina and me, we was always out together now. And one time I bought her some candy, and another time some flowers, and she must of knew how fond I was of her. You only got to see her, with that neat little figger, and that corn-coloured hair and the eyes I never could tell for certain if they was blue or grey, and youd understand how I was feeling. It want all happiness, though. It was tough about her family; she wunt let me come home with her because she said that it was such a poor home, with her father out of work and her mother lame and her little brother who had some disease like dissem—something or other—slerosis, they was in a bad way. So one time, when Id sold a coupla pigs, and she was being sad about her troubles, I give her this twenty dollars and I said I hoped that might help. She cried and said she couldnt accept it, but I was gentle and I made her change her mind, and then she cried some more and said I was a truly good man.

So after that I used to give what I could to help that poor family out. Sometimes it was ten dollars, sometimes twenty, and once it was a thirty. By this time I knowd I loved her, and she said that she loved me. Then I said: 'Look, Nina. Ifn we going to get married, its got to be all cards on the table. You come and see the farm, and Ill come and meet your people. Yeah?'

She agreed. She said: 'But Joe, I dont know when.'

'Sooner the better,' I said.

We was sitting in the park, this Sunday when this happened, and I remember it clear because somebody had a little radio and it was playing your record One for My Baby what you sorta act the words in and it all sounds good and real. She said: 'Want that wonderful?

A friend of mine got twenty lp records of him. Listen, and he can teach you things.'

'Whats your favourite Sinatra tune, Nina?'

And she said: 'That one. One for My Baby. This friend of mine has nearly wore out the track on the record where that one comes.'

I said: 'I reckon the whole world plays it, all the time. The money that guy makes. But Id sooner have you, Nina, than all that money.'

She stayed quite still for a minute, and then she started to cry, although she hardly made a sound.

'Whats the matter, Nina? What is it?' Oh, I was real tender.

She said: 'Theres nothing you can do, Joe. Ive no right to burden you with any more trouble. I musnt do that. Theres no way out.'

Bit by bit, I got it out of her. It was about her little brother, and this muscular disease thing.

'If we could get him to this clinic for about three weeks, the doctor says he might stand a chance, with all the clever people they got there. And we could get a state grant for the money, but that leaves us three hundred dollars short of what we need.'

Then she sobbed, very quietly, and I thought a long time, and then I made a suggestion. 'Well, look. I got three hundred dollars. If thatll help—well, its really farm money, see—? But you have it. Here.'

She stared, and burst into tears, and clung hold of me and said I was wonderful, and shed marry me when things got a bit more settled. Well, then she said she have to go and telephone the doctor and tell him that now they could manage to send the crippled boy to the clinic. She said to see me later, and to come out to the farm by bus and tell me how the boy was getting on. And it was all warm and loving, and I was as pleased and proud as I could be; I reckoned Id got the right.

I saw her on the bus and then I went back through the park and I passed by where we had been sittin, and there was a screwed up handkerchief there, with most of an envelope inside it. The letter was addressed to 'Miss N. Davenport, 44 Vicksburgh Avenue.' Just an envelope. I thought it want hers, she being Nina Dalton.

I decided I might take both items back. I got on a bus and got off at Vicksburgh Avenue, where I walked down until I found the number. I rung the bell and a sharp sort of woman opened the door. I told her, and showed the handkerchief.

'No,' she said, 'no Daltons here. But theres one named Gomez and another name of Davenport. Shes blonde and smallish and has blue eyes and works in an office, some place.'

I felt just struck solid. When the woman shut the door I still stood there. From somewhere nearby a radio was playing One For My Baby. All it did for me that time was to make me think that all I added up to was a lot of tears and misery and nohope. I felt like dropping down dead.

Next day I worked just enough to keep the animals fed and watered, and left the other jobs to look after thereselves. Old McFees ghost showed up for a coupla minutes, and he set and watched me a while, but it dint mean a thing to me. I drank some corn likker, and it hit hard; a couple more drinks seemed to help against the misery I was still feeling.

Evening time there was the sound of a car. I got up and went out. It was an oldish Dodge, and driving it was Nina Dalton—or maybe Nina Davenport.

I just stood and watched her coming.

She got out and came to me. She smelt beautiful as a beanfield in flower. 'Joe,' she said.

I never answered.

'Joe, thanks for returning my handkerchief.'

I let her go on.

'Its like this,' she said, 'I have to live in town because of my work, you see? I share that place in Vicksburg Avenue with a friend.'

She waited on me to speak, and I dint.

'It was necessary ... I send them all the money I can, dont you see?'

She tried to keep her face straight, sort of in control, but it want easy, I could see that. I pulled out an old envelope, and handed it to her. 'You write that address down for me, and then we can go and see your family, right this minute, in your car.' I watched her face very close.

'Joe––they wunt be expecting us.'

'Like I wasn't expecting to pick up that handkerchief and the envelope. Now, you got a car out there. Lets go and visit your folks right away, and then everything will be all right and I will love you and carry out all them promises we made. Thats the way to do it. Thatd be fine, wunt it?'

She stared; I thought she was beginning to look afraid.

'Nina, howd you get that car out there?'

'Hired it.'

'Oh, fine,' I said. 'Just for a little while I was thinking something else.' I kept real quiet. 'So show me the hire card.'

I was right; now she was looking scared.

'You aint got no hire card,' I told her.

She never spoke, but her face told me what I wanted

to know. I couldnt be tough with her, though. I asked: 'Nina,' I said, all soft, 'do you still love me?'

She started to breathe heavy, and then she laughed. It was nasty laughter, like from a tomb. There was a sorta madness in it. 'Love! Love you, you ignorant swede! Who needs you? Love you, marry you, you lout! Get wise to yourself! At first it was fun, then the cash made it better, but—marry you—marry—marry—'

There was a lot more of that nasty laughing, but now I felt that thick despair coming up inside me, and I took hold of her by the throat and begged her to stop laughing but she kept on, so I held her, shouting, pleading with her until her eyes seemed to pop and she went all limp, and I lowered her to the ground. It was right. The McFees was bad enough, but this one, she deserved what she got, because she took away hope.

Straight away I took her and buried her by the three oaks, real deep, and when that was done I felt better, and I thought about the corn likker, and I went into the house to get it.

She sat there, looking at me.

I took a drink, and still she looked at me. And this time, it hurt. It didnt matter about the other two, but this one I had told I loved, and I was deceived; what was more, I still loved her. After maybe ten minutes I started to shake, because she still sat there, looking at me. Through the day there was two or three times when she faded a bit for perhaps a minute at a time, but back she come. Shes there most of the time, now. She is watching me now as I try to write this, ten days after I buried her by the oaks. Ive tried to speak to her, to ask her to go away, but she wont, and I know she wont.

Mr Sinatra, can you imagine what this is doing to me? Pretty soon Ill be mad as a bee-stung bull, if she keeps this up. *Shes there all the time!* Thats the terrible thing,

I cant stand it, I really cant, and you gotta help me, Mr Sinatra, you just must help me.

Dont you see it? The old man and woman only turn up not very often, when them old songs they knew are being played somewhere in the world, but Ninas favourite was One For My Baby, and thats always being played, radio, phonograph or tv, all the time *somewhere* its playing. As long as it plays, for all them times, Ninas ghost is gonna be here, and if it goes on maybe I think Ill kill myself, which aint fair.

Please. Mr Sinatra, you can afford to do this to save a life. Have the word go out that you dont want that song played no more, no more, Mr Sinatra. Please, please, please have it stopped, so that I can get peace, and forget how much I love her.

Only you can do this. Please, Mr Sinatra.

Yours in hope,
Joe Roll.

JAMES TURNER

Love Me, Love My Car

She liked the car at once. It was absurd, of course, to say that she had a feeling that it was waiting for her, but its radiator grille, generally grinning and ready to bite, was slightly bent in the left hand corner. This gave the mouth, she thought, a pathetic look. It brought out all her compassion.

'I'm being anthropomorphic,' she said to herself, 'and it's damned silly over an old bit of iron and glass.' But she loved any chance to roll off her tongue such long words; to do so made her feel good and, God knows, being a librarian, she had every chance to indulge her love of words, never mind if people sometimes accused her of showing off.

The car was an Austin Countryman of about 1965, which meant that it just suited them for holidays, with being able to let down the back seat and make all that room inside. Ted, her husband, opened the door and got in. 'Don't make 'em any longer,' he said. 'That's why it's cheap. Bit of rust here and there, too, but that hardly matters. Do us for a year or so, I imagine.'

Actually he didn't tell her until they were packed up and on their way to Cornwall, that there was another reason for the low price. The car had been smashed up quite a bit in an accident in Rampart Street, Salisbury. It had been rebuilt.

'Oh, Ted,' she said, 'was it wise to buy it then?' Conscious in her own mind that she herself was half responsible for their owning it, she being in her silly mood when they went to the car dealer in the Camberwell Road, after seeing it advertised in the evening paper. 'It looks pathetic,' she had said when Ted asked her there, in the yard, whether she liked it. 'Uncared for, like an old dog.'

'Don't be bloody stupid,' Ted replied. 'Get in and see if you feel like driving in it.' And she had. At once she felt at home. The car seemed to respond to her.

Now Ted drew into a lay-by and, in answer to her question, produced an M.O.T. certificate of road-worthiness as well as a guarantee from the salesman. 'Can't do more than that, can you? And we only had £150, so we could hardly have gone to something more ambitious. And she does go well, there's no denying.'

'I suppose the bent radiator grille is part of the accident?' she asked, pulling out a thermos and some sandwiches. 'Let's have lunch now.'

It wasn't the ideal place, a lay-by with traffic whizzing past at high speed, but she knew that if Ted drove on he would be 'difficult' about finding a turning-off.

'I suppose so,' he said, happy that their first holiday as man and wife had begun. 'But I never noticed it.'

The weather that September was blazing. Summer had come suddenly and late. It was unbelievable. Only, of course, the nights were drawing in. They parked the car on a headland, out of St Agnes, amongst some gorse and heather, a sort of secret place.

The 'season' was almost over and there was no other

car in sight. In the heat of the afternoon they ran down the cliff path to the sea below, through the quickset hedges and the ling and gorse, laughing like two children (they were not much more). They undressed and positively flung themselves into the sea which seemed almost to be waiting for them, for their youth and happiness. Meg, born and bred in London, had never seen anything like it. The sea, smooth and opalescent, the mauve-grey rocks, the impossible beauty of sand-pools and the light created by the beneficent September sun were so beyond her expectations that she wanted to wriggle herself into the soft sand, become a part of it. The shells she picked up, ordinary to most people living here, were, to her, a wonder beyond belief. Above all she wanted to possess it so that the pictures, the feel of the seascape, the clouds and the sea itself, would never leave her. She was ecstatic and speechless and Ted, who was a Cornishman, born in Penzance, looked at her and loved her twice as much.

Meg kept to the shallow water near the pools where the small waves came in and washed the shells bright again. She wasn't, anyway, a brilliant swimmer. But Ted, who was, swam out into the bay, round a headland and out of her sight. The heat of the afternoon was terrific and she was beginning to be sun-burnt. The moment she began to be apprehensive for Ted's safety, he appeared round the headland rocks and swam in to her, lying gasping on the sand, pretending to be exhausted.

She ran to help him, uttering little cries. He caught her and pulled her down to the wet sand, laughing at her distress. He didn't understand her sudden anger, or the way she was slapping him in her relief.

'Don't ever do that again,' she said, her eyes blazing.

'What, darling?'

'Swim out of my sight and pretend to be half dead when you come in. I can't bear it. I won't bear it.' She picked up a length of wet seaweed and began lashing him with it as if he were a naughty child.

'Darling, darling,' he laughed, and clung to her in her fury, the seaweed stinging his back. 'I adore you. I promise never to play the fool again.' He picked her up and carried her to her place beside the deep rock pool. She was laughing happily now that she had him safe again. He threw her into the water and followed her. Neither of them had been so happy since the day they were married a year ago.

When they were drying themselves in the late afternoon sun Ted said: 'Tell you what. We won't try to find digs or an hotel. Let's stay with the car. There's plenty of food, isn't there?' She nodded sleepily, the sea soothing her, her whole body melting in the in-and-out sighing of the waves. 'And there'll be a moon. We can bathe by moonlight, like I used to when I was a kid.'

They stayed on the sand until they were hungry and then began the climb back to the cliff top and the car. When they emerged from the cliff path and the stretch of sward was between them and the car, Ted let out a yell and shouted. He began running, shouting, 'Get out of there! What the bloody hell...'

Meg, who had caught her dress on a whip of gorse and was bending over it to unloose it, was astonished to see and hear him. He seemed suddenly to have gone mad. Actually she began laughing at the picture of Ted running towards the car waving his arms and shouting at non-existent people. At least she could see no one. She released her dress with only a small tear, and ran across the grass to him.

'Whatever's the matter?' she panted out, coming up to

the dark car. 'What's all the fuss about? Sheep or something?'

'Sheep nothing,' Ted said shamefacedly.

'Well, why all the shouting and carry on? Do you want all Cornwall to know you're back in the land of your fathers?' She thrust her long hair out of her eyes, that hair which, in the deep pool, had made her imagine she was a mermaid. Suddenly, as she bent her head backwards, Ted could see the moon reflected in her eyes. 'Oh, it was nothing, I suppose. Some trick of the moonlight. Or the country. Or the sea.'

'Well, what trick? You must have thought something was up or you wouldn't have pulled the back of the car open.'

'It was lovers.'

'Lovers? What on earth do you mean?'

'In the back of the car.'

'Don't be silly. I saw nobody and I was right behind you. There was nobody. I don't suppose there's anybody for miles. You were dreaming. All that sun and sea water, that's what's the matter with you.'

'It was when I came off the cliff path. There was a light on in the car. Really, Meg, there was. You know, the inside light. A couple were in the back, making love. I heard them. Bloody cheek! In our car!'

'But, Ted, look. The back seat is still up in position. That only gives them, whoever it was, a tiny space. To make love you'd need that seat flat. That's the point of the car, isn't it?'

'I don't care how much space they had, they were there. I saw them, a girl with golden hair and a man with a beard. Right on top of her, he was. She was struggling and hitting him.'

'Well, where are they now? They couldn't have got far.' She laughed. Her laughter seemed to reflect off the dark sky. 'You've got love-making on the brain, like all men.'

'How the hell do I know where they are? They'd gone when I reached the car and the inside light was off.'

Meg began to busy herself with making supper. She stood beside the car. 'There isn't anyone for miles,' she said again, as if to convince herself and calm her fears. 'Here, have some coffee, do you good.'

They sat by the car (a haven of safety in the surrounding night) and listened to the sounds of silence, the insect noises in the grass, the movement of small animals in the gorse and bracken. Where the cliff edge began to drop down to the sea the light was mauve, the gorse tipped with yellow moonlight, the interior of the quick hedges black and still. A little knot of old man's beard, gone to seed, was like gossamer on the thick hedge. Someone might have left cotton wool about.

They put their arms round each other in the primal loneliness of the early night and let the sound of the sea come up to them, her small round face beside his. 'The quiet is bliss.' She was half asleep against the car and her husband. She was thinking and hearing in her head the sound of trains over a viaduct near their home in London. Suddenly she realised that tonight was the first time she was hearing them when they weren't there. So accustomed had she become to them. 'No trains,' she said dreamily. 'No trains at all.'

It was their first adventure together, there beside the car on the cliff top beyond the road, in their secret place, with the pineapple smell of the gorse about them and the winking light of a lighthouse miles away. Vaguely she heard Ted say, 'It'll be Trevose Head. Shouldn't think there'll be much danger with the sea so calm and the night so bright and warm.' Later he got up and stretched. 'I'm going down for a last dip,' he said. 'What about you?'

The moon was now huge in the mauve sky. The earth was giving off a heat which surrounded them like a blanket. The mouth of the path through the bracken and gorse was black with shadow and, in the field across the road behind the car, sheep were snuffling and pulling grass in the half-light.

'It's magical,' Meg said, falling sideways on to the grass, looking up at the moon, her mouth open with the pleasure of it. She had never been in the country at night in her life, to say nothing of being half in country and half in sea. Though she had often watched the moonlight over the London roofs from her bedroom in Streatham, it was nothing like this, nothing so pure as this. The light, soft as it was, almost hurt her in its purity and lack of dust. It was like a very highly polished mirror; she could almost see herself in it.

'You go down,' she said, completely unafraid. 'I'll get the car ready to sleep in. It will be chilly later on, you see. You'll be glad of it. We've a lot of coats and rugs and things. I'll make up a bed. For real lovers this time.' She watched him disappear into the gorse and heard him call back: 'Won't be long and I'll take care.' And then he was gone.

It was only then that the night, the dark unfamiliar places of the countryside created by the moon shadows, the cries of sea birds which she thought she heard and the distant winking of the lighthouse, made her suddenly afraid, suddenly aware that she was entirely alone and that if anyone were to come out of the dark headland scrub, Ted would be too far away to help her. Now they began whispering to her, the things of the night. Now the tiny sounds of insects were voices calling to her. An enormous, hard-shelled beetle zoomed almost into her hair and banged its way through the dark night as if, she thought, it had come for her. She held her breasts in her hand as if the cattle would come out of the night to drink her milk, or the great Cornish giant, Bedruthan, about which Ted had told her tales, was already striding in her direction, hollowing the earth with his huge footsteps. And the black hound slavering over the grass...

She opened the back of the 'Countryman', pulled the seat down to make the large space behind the driving seat, and crept in. She was safe under the tiny light of the car. It was like putting on armour. If things were moving in the dark gorse or across the sheep field, they could do her no harm here.

She hadn't realised that she was so sleepy. When she arranged the rugs and cushions they brought with them, she lay down, her feet out before her, pulled a raincoat over her shoulders and was fast asleep in a minute.

She must have been asleep an hour. She awoke with a start and felt herself pinned to the floor of the car.

'Ted,' she whispered dreamily. 'Darling, oh, darling,' and put up her arms to hold him, to love him. Sleepily she thought he must have come back and crept into the car, not wanting to disturb her. It was quite dark inside the car because the moon was directly overhead. She could sense Ted's face coming down on hers, holding her head firmly, and then the hot mouth and the feel of hair. When she realised that the hair was a beard, she shrieked and tried to get up in the enclosed space at the back of the car. She was pushed down again. She felt the hands of the man pulling up her dress and the feel of naked limbs on hers and the man going in between her legs. She screamed again, but the man's body bore down upon her and his words filled the car. 'Shut up, you little bitch. You've asked for it.'

'Ted!' she screamed again, flung out a hand towards the interior light and switched it on. For a second she saw him, a thin man with a beard, his lips wet, his mouth open, and then she was alone in the car. Now, when she looked out of the windows she could see the moonlight each side of the car, slices of yellow light stretching off into the country and out to sea. She shoved the back open and got out into the perfect night.

She was utterly alone. She was shivering with fright, her hands quivering in front of her, the bushes behind her full of menace and faces and obscene words. Yet there was nobody and, in her mind, she knew that no one was there in the flesh. Yet it had been so real, her attempted rape.

When Ted found her she was still standing beside the car, shivering and weeping. He took her into his arms.

'Come on,' he said, comforting her. 'It's not all that late. Somewhere will be open. We'll find somewhere. We can't stay here.'

She quickly recovered and helped him to fix up the car. They drove into the nearest village. They were lucky. Pubs in Cornwall are few and far between. But this one—only a mile from the headland—was still open and they had a double room.

Later they were in each other's arms in bed and laughing. They were young enough not to be disturbed for long.

'It was your man with a beard,' Meg said, returned to her level-headedness. 'What a brute! He nearly raped me, Ted, he did proper.'

'Get away with you,' Ted said jokingly, though he had not been deceived by the condition he found Meg in when he came back from his moonlight bathe. She was dead scared, no doubt of it. All he wanted to do, then, was to calm her fears, smoothe them away. 'I don't know, darling,' he said, 'I certainly did see those two making love in the car. And now you say—damn him, I'd like to get my hands on him.'

'You'll never do that, dear. Whoever it was, he's dead. Oh, God, Ted, I can't explain it any more than you can.'

'It's probably got something to do with the place we put the car. Damn it, hundreds of people must have made love at that spot, it's so secret. Some trace still left, perhaps?'

Meg looked up at the ceiling. She was warm now, happy, her fears dispelled. The countryside had been destroyed in the warmth of the pub and the bed. 'It was an incubus,' she said, conscious that she loved pronouncing the word. 'I know it was. I've read about them!'

'What in hell's that? You and your long words.'

'It's a spirit, a demon, which makes love to a woman. Just as a succubus is a spirit which makes love to a man.'

'Get away with you,' Ted said again, putting his arms round her in the big double bed. 'The things you know! I'll have to try sleeping in the car alone. Might be fun.'

'Don't you dare, Ted Baxter.' Meg propped herself on an elbow and looked down at him. 'And, as of now, my lad, you can just stop making jokes about spirit lovers. I know you, you'll go on forever about them, boring everyone.'

Ted kissed her and fondled her and loved her. 'God bless you, honey, I can't stay awake any longer. But call me if this incubus thing comes again. I'll know how to deal with him.'

'Funny thing was, Ted,' she teased him in her relief and happiness, 'when I got over my fright, I rather liked it. He wasn't bad.'

But Ted was asleep and never heard the remark.

She told herself, when the end came, that she should have realised what was going to happen. It was not that anything big, like her phantom lover, occurred again. Indeed, nothing marred the rest of their holiday. Yet a number of small things, the dog and the children and, idiotically, an old coat which she found in the car one day which didn't belong to either of them, should have warned her. In one sense they were part of the dark side of her experience and now, above all, on this wonderful holiday, she wanted light, of the sun, of the sea, of the spinning sea-gulls in the headland breezes. It was the absorption into this light which, she knew, was creating her, even perhaps creating their child within her.

Maybe the first time she heard the children she did try to talk to Ted about it. But he only treated the whole thing as a joke.

'We've got a haunted car on our hands, darling,' he said. 'Bet that's never happened before.' And they had gone off, arm in arm, to the local pub for pasties and the wrestling in a field behind. Not that she worried, the weather was so fine and the days too full for worry. The holiday was slipping away so quickly, and she had seen nothing but the immediate neighbourhood of the pub where, finally, they had agreed to stay.

The children hadn't been in the car, of course, not in the flesh anyway, she said to herself. Though when she first heard them and the noise they were making, she turned automatically, as if she were back in the library, and admonished them. A man's voice had said distinctly, 'Oh, let them be, Angela, it's a holiday. What does it matter how much noise they make?' and she had driven back to the pub from the bay where she went every morning before breakfast, leaving Ted still in bed.

She could not then resist the early morning light and the thought of the sea. In any case she was never sleepy and she had, this morning, gone down to a small enclosed sandy bay and paddled, getting her feet into seaweed, walking amongst the rocks and, idiotically, waving to a huge boat on the horizon. No one else was on the untrodden sand except a great shaggy dog which paid no attention to her, not even when she threw a piece of shell for him. He was on some business of his own which did not include her.

When she got back to the car and shut the door, the children began shouting. Their voices came from the back, two girls and a boy. She wasn't at all frightened. The only thing was that when she arrived back for breakfast she looked into the back of the car and saw the signs of sandy feet on the floor. That sand had not been there the day before, she knew, because she had spent an hour cleaning out the car. She shut the door and went in to find Ted, already eating cornflakes and drinking his coffee.

Now she was no longer frightened, though it was obvious to her that, at certain times, the car was haunted. She was completely certain of this the day the dog barked. It was at the same bay, at the same time of morning. She had driven down without Ted and it was all the same, though the sea was farther out. Even the same dog was running on the sand, only quite some way from her, over towards a building which she knew had once been a fish cellar and was now converted into a house. It was empty and she explored it, looking in at the windows, half expecting to see faces. But, it being a holiday house, there was no one, only furniture and beds in cellophane covers piled one on top of the other. It looked and felt sad and very end-of-season.

The dog was still running at the water's edge, chasing gulls, when she walked back, quite alone, picking up shells, pink scallops, tellins and cowries. When she shut the door of the car, however, she heard a dog bark from the back. It couldn't have been the dog on the beach, of course, for she looked at him out there immediately, still running after gulls, eternally hoping, eternally disappointed. She wasn't to be taken in again and did not turn round until she felt the rough tongue against her cheek. That did take her by surprise and she jumped round only to see that the car was completely empty.

Later that day she made what she thought of as a discovery; not that it had much effect on her. Ted had gone into the sea from what she called her pre-breakfast beach. The whole wide bay was before her and she could see him swimming in an otherwise empty sea. She pulled down the glove compartment and took the long, buff-coloured envelope out. Inside was the car's log-book which Ted had collected with other documents when he picked up the car. She remembered now that he had pulled the M.O.T. certificate from it, on the first day of their holiday, to allay her fears about the accident to the car before they bought it. And there were the names. It was quite incredible the peace of mind they gave her. All her fears disappeared now that she was able to put a name to the man who had a family and two girls and a boy and a dog with a rough tongue. She knew that she was right, since Ted hadn't said any children were involved in the car crash, only a man and a woman, and they must have been the last owners, if the car had recently been rebuilt.

There it was, 1st OWNER: JAMES SUTCLIFFE, 4 The Close, Salisbury. He had had the car for five years, it seemed, when the 2nd OWNER, took possession: HENRY OLIVER, 2 Maybrick Villas, Surbiton. She let the book fall to her lap, imagining the Sutcliffe family, their children and their dog. They were, then, very close to her. Well, they sounded nice. And it was only when she saw that the 3rd OWNER was TED BAXTER that she realised.

'So that's who you were,' she said, 'Henry Oliver, Mr Incubus with a beard. You'll never frighten me again.' How odd, she thought, that both former owners, in their own ways, haunted the car. And that Mr Sutcliffe, who lived in Salisbury, had not been the one to have an accident there, but Henry Oliver. Could it be that the first owner, by haunting the car (she had heard his voice admonishing his wife, Angela, hadn't she?) had caused the accident to the second owner? Even then she did not see the full implications. It didn't even seem to matter very much to her. She closed the book and put the documents back in the glove compartment. She ran across the sand with her picnic basket in the direction of the old fish cellars. When Ted joined her she was leaning against the warm rocks, half asleep.

'I'm famished,' he said, drying himself. A couple were now walking across the sand at the water's edge. 'Come on, I want some coffee and cake or something. It's time for elevenses, anyway.'

'Henry Oliver,' she murmured softly, looking up at his naked body, admiring the strength of it, loving it because it was hers.

'What the hell has he to do with anything? He's dead.'

She sat up with a jolt. 'He was the last owner of our car.'

'I know. He and his girl-friend, or maybe his wife, were killed in that accident I told you about. In Rampart Street, Salisbury. Garage man told me. Thought it might put me off, I suppose. I told him it didn't worry me. I mean you'd never buy anything, say a house for instance, if you were scared by people dying in it, would you?'

'But, but...' she stammered.

'Well?'

'I bet he had a beard and his girl had golden hair. Like that couple making love you thought you saw on our first night.'

Ted lay down in the sun, his body already the colour of sand. 'God, Meg, you do think 'em up! How the hell can you possibly know that?'

'I don't really, but I'm pretty sure that it was the first owner of the car who had a family and a dog, the Sutcliffes, and a wife called Angela. They sound as if they did. You can laugh but I bet I'm right.' A further idea was milling round her head. It had to be so; that grassy place they parked the car the first night of their arrival, her fright in the car and Ted finding the only pub in the little village so close. 'And what's more,' she declared defiantly, 'I'll prove it when we get back to supper.'

'Prove what?'

'That it was Henry and his girl you saw in the car that first night.'

And there, in the pub's visitors' book, it was, only a year earlier: Henry Oliver. Mr and Mrs, 4 Maybrick Villas, Surbiton.

'You're a bloody miracle,' Ted said. 'You ought to have been a female detective, not a librarian. I'll stand you a gin and tonic. You deserve it.'

Of course she should have realised and made Ted take a different route. But the holiday had been so happy that she wanted it all over and them back in London as quickly as possible once they had begun. She wanted to shut the album, as it were, on all the happiness, the sea, her early morning walks, the places they had driven to in their last week, the glory of the sunsets over the immense headlands. She didn't want it fragmented; she wanted to hold it all in her hands, like a brilliant apple and say to herself: 'My Holiday.'

Now that it was over and they were driving away, only the good things mattered, were to be remembered. And Henry Oliver, who had stayed in 'their' pub a year ago and was now dead, poor fellow, had not been a good thing. Not if he and that 'bitch' could come back ... She shut the picture from her mind. To hell with him. After all it was their car now and, and ... she suddenly remembered, also, that it was not only Henry and his girl who had come back, it was the Sutcliffe family as well.

They left it as late as possible on Saturday, bathing and picnicking on their favourite beach until after three o'clock. The roads would be freer then, Ted said, and it didn't matter what time they arrived home. They'd have all Sunday to recover before going back to work.

They reached Salisbury after dark. The street lighting was on. They drove up Exeter Street and right into St Anne Street, and then left to join the London Road. The road looked quite clear ahead and Ted accelerated. He suddenly swerved violently as the lorry bore down on them. Meg shouted and put her hands up to her face and tried to open the door. She heard quite clearly the barking of a dog and the voices of children as she wrenched at the handle. She knew then that this haunting by the Sutcliffes must have caused the crash to the Olivers. And now almost to themselves.

'Get down,' Ted yelled, as the car hit the kerb, too late and with too little space to manoeuvre out of the way of the lorry's cab. There was a fearful sound of breaking glass as it hit the side of the car, a tearing of brakes, and he was back in the deserted road, with only the street lights and shops ahead of him. The engine was still running. They were completely unharmed.

'It's all right, Meg, it's all right,' he kept on repeating in his shock, even though the car was shuddering under them, heaving and seeming ready to break apart. People were running past the car to something behind them.

They were shocked, and Meg very white. She could hardly stand when she got out on to the pavement.

'Look,' Ted said, 'the car isn't even scratched. God knows what happened. I thought it hit us.'

But Meg had gone back. She was standing a little way from the huge lorry now embedded in a shop front. 'Oh, no, no,' she was crying when Ted reached her. 'It can't be, it can't.' A lane opened in the crowd which had mysteriously gathered and he saw, lying on the ground, a man with a thin beard. Blood was trickling from his forehead, his body was squirming, half on, half off the pavement. Beside him, her head smashed like an egg, lay a young woman. All he seemed to recognise, as if in a dream, was her golden hair.

Ted understood the moment he took Meg into his arms and held her shaking body. Something was impelling him to look over her head at the sign above the last shop. RAMPART STREET, he read. He understood because the street was so silent, as silent as had been these two lovers in their car on that Cornish headland a fortnight ago. Even the crowd which had run to the scene of the accident was making no noise at all. All you could see—and he saw it very clearly—were their mouths opening and shutting, as if they were shouting. It was like looking at a TV set with the sound switched off.

A little later a police patrol car went slowly past them. The driver looked at him and Meg in each other's arms, and then thought better of it. Two lovers just met in a

deserted city street, nothing unusual in that, surely? Ted
half raised his hand as if to summon them but he knew
now, a year after the accident happened, that it would
be futile to call the police. They could not have seen
what he and Meg were seeing. They would have thought
him mad or drunk.

When he turned to look again at the dying and dead
bodies of Henry Oliver and his 'wife', the street was quite
empty but for their car standing by the kerb, waiting for
them.

JEAN STUBBS

Jarvey's Kingdoms

I knew when I made an offer for JARVEY'S that I should have to gut it from roof to cellar. Well, how can you build a new business on the ruins of an old one? JARVEY'S was a Victorian hardware store which had finally bankrupted its last owner, who tried to incorporate the character of the former shop. I could have told him he was wasting his time. The only way to get ahead is to have a clean sweep of the lot, even with a loan that makes you avoid your bank manager. Change the name, change the style, change the stock.

My wife Nell is a romantic, a sentimentalist. Those are the wrong words, but I can't think of words precise enough to describe something that is both lovable and impractical. She is the kind of woman who will save a few pence in the supermarket, and spend a few pounds on a shirt I don't need—which I said I liked. I do like it, of course. As for me, Nell can have whatever she wants within reason, and I never question her. But when it comes to business I'll hammer the table, because business is my living.

Business was Jarvey's living, too, at the end of the nineteenth century. No one can run a family store now as they were able to run it then. They had long hours,

cheap labour, even a personal dedication among the
staff. Or perhaps it was not dedication so much as neces-
sity, since Jarvey demanded blood and sweat. Nothing was
too much trouble to provide by way of service to the
customers. In fact, JARVEY'S provided everything from
nails to crockery, and performed any number of interior
and exterior jobs, whether they were qualified to do so or
not.

'You, lad!' Jarvey would say, pointing to his Mr Barker's latest recruit. 'You can lay linoleum in this lady's
kitchen, can't you?'

'Me, sir? Can I, sir?'

'Of course you can,' said Jarvey, hard and genial, with
an expression on his face that dared the boy to deny
it. 'You've seen linoleum laid many a time, I dare
say.'

'Yes, sir. I suppose so, sir.'

'Then go along to this lady's house, and make a good
job of it. Do you hear?'

And he turned away, satisfied.

'Sir, straightaway sir. Mr Barker,' in a lower tone, 'how
do you lay linoleum, if you please?'

'Measure it accurate, and cut it careful,' said Mr Barker.
'And may the Almighty help you if you make a mess of
it!'

'I never knew we laid linoleum, Mr Barker.'

'Mr Jarvey says we do. So hop it!'

Jarvey could track down anything. In that warren of a
building, where rooms led into rooms like a Chinese box,
and proposed eternal conundrums; where back stairs and
front stairs mounted and descended into labyrinths; he
knew his stock.

'This will require a very particular type of screw, sir,'
Jarvey would say, pondering on the scrap of rusty metal.
'It's quite a time since this article was made. Ah! The

old things last best, don't they, sir? Now, let me see.
Jeremy! Top shelf, lefthand corner, in the far back
room by the yard, there's a biscuit tin full of screws.
Take this with you for a match, lad. And, sharpish!'

'Mr Jarvey,' said one satisfied customer, 'you are more
than a good business man. You are a genius!'

'All part of the service, sir,' Jarvey replied easily, but
believed him.

Genius, as he knew, was the infinite capacity for taking
pains. He possessed that capacity. He took those pains.
His patience and tenacity and sense of purpose were a
part of that age which painted one quarter of the earth's
surface red, and named it the British Empire.

Everyone was pressed into service. His wife was his
cashier early in their marriage, before she began to breed
sons, and she always kept the accounts. As each boy grew
old enough to be trusted with the simplest task he was
pushed into the shop. The training they received was
merciless and invaluable. But they never forgot the hard-
ship of breaking ice in the water jug, at six o'clock of a
winter's morning; nor the long Saturday afternoons of
high summer, when other lads fished and swam, and they
delivered parcels by foot or bicycle. One by one they left
home, taking with them the ability to work and to endure,
and made their fortunes overseas. Gradually the family
rooms over the store emptied, and were resolutely filled
with stock by Jarvey, who would truckle neither to man
nor circumstance. But Mrs Jarvey withered, bereft of her
feminine vocation, and did not trouble to fight the influenza epidemic of 1890.

Alone then in fact, as he had always been in spirit,
Jarvey carried on and refused to delegate. Useless to point
out that his robust good health was waning, that his
splendid muscles would no longer heft boxes of iron-
mongery, that much of the stock was known only to him-

self, that the goodwill of JARVEY'S existed mainly through him.

'I'm fit for many a year yet,' he would reply briefly. 'My father died at eighty, God rest him.'

Though they had fought for a lifetime, and the store was Jarvey's answer to a penurious childhood, a declaration of wealth and independence. Still, the two men had always respected each other, and when the patriarch breathed his last there was no one big enough to raise Jarvey's blood pressure. Jarvey missed the old man from time to time, and fearing sentiment would mutter, 'Damn him!' whenever nostalgia threatened.

In his sixties, Jarvey became as much of a local legend as his store. He had been a handsome man, now he was distinguished also. His temper did not mellow. They could hear him halfway down the street, publicly enraged by slipshod service or workmanship. And they nodded one to the other in an agreeable manner, as if to say, 'What a character!'

His power was absolute. An honourable tyrant, a lovable despot, he reigned over his kingdom unchallenged, and refused to retire. The First World War was years away. No one could have guessed that long skirts, savage corsets and tight morals would be replaced by Women's Rights, and a general disenchantment with that state of life to which it had pleased God to call the poor. So, fortunately, Jarvey did not stay long enough to be tormented by something over which he had no control. Still decked in his butterfly collars, flowing ties captured by a gold pin, the frockcoat which was forever showing the dust, and his gold watch-chain looped across a stomach heavy with muscle rather than flesh, he left the world and JARVEY'S to fend for themselves.

The world stumbled on as best it could, but the store slowly foundered under one owner and the next. By the time I made an offer for it they were glad to be rid of a bad bargain. Nell and I stood before the battered mahogany front, and surveyed it with different emotions.

I said, 'This is going to be one hell of a lot of hard work!'

She said, 'You can't just wipe it out, Charlie. There's a century of living here.'

I said, 'Come inside and take a look at it, and just you tell me what else I can do.'

She said, in the dust, among the boxes, 'He's still here, you know.'

His name arched in flecks and streaks of ravaged gold across the gothic windows. It signed the brown bills of sale in a clerkly hand, and entered up the big ledgers. His swivel chair was pushed away from the heavy desk as though he had risen to take a turn about the shop. An old, cold iron kettle in the cold iron grate proclaimed that Jarvey had enjoyed his private cup of tea. No one had made any impression upon that place, except Jarvey. We walked from room to room, and she dirtied her gloves picking up this and that bit of antiquity, and exclaiming over it. I made the cash cylinders scuttle along the wires, to please her; and stood back, hands in pockets, watching them carry nothing from one end of the shop to the other. My cash registers would ring to some purpose. I found stuff in the back premises that even the Victorians would have thrown away, and they were great hoarders.

'Do you see what I mean?' I asked, rather hard and sharp, because I could see that she did not. 'This isn't a shop. It's a museum!'

'A museum?' Nell said, veering off on a different tack. 'Well, why not?'

'Because I've got an overdraft that would blench twenty Jarvey's,' I said. 'Because I'm not a museum-keeper. Because we have to live in the present, and for the future. This is past.'

She had a peculiarly obstinate air about her, like a child trying to have its own mistaken way. She knew better than to argue. When we argue, I win. The time that I lose is when she doesn't say anything and retreats into a world of her own. She retreated. I know the temporary answer to that one, too.

'Think it over,' I said. 'And do think, don't just feel!'

We were thinking two different things, and neither of them matched, but it gave us both time.

Time. I needed time, and time was shorter than money. The evening that JARVEY'S finally became mine I went there by myself. What I had paid for it was a crumb, compared to the loaf that must be spent making it a working proposition. Before I bought in the stock, let alone opened the door, the whole lot had to be cleared, re-fashioned and re-decorated.

Nell said, 'It will be like Psyche sorting the grains into separate heaps. You'll have to hope for an army of helpful ants!'

'To hell with Psyche. She lived a long time ago, and the only person who can help me is me!'

'Oh, you're quite right,' said Nell. 'Up to a point, that is.'

By myself in that deserted relic I could have done with a couple of armies to start shifting the machinery alone. There was a knife-sharpener in one corner that looked as though it was welded to the floor, and the floor would come with it, if it didn't fall through first. I sat in the swivel chair and opened the drawers of the desk, which were stuck.

'Some of us won't let go!' I said aloud, thinking of Jarvey who still reigned sixty years later.

'Some of us,' a dry voice replied, 'bite off more than we can chew, sir.'

I knew him, of course. The black frockcoat, dusty down the front. He must have been rummaging in his forgotten junk. The butterfly collar, very starched, very white. Who did that kind of laundry nowadays? He seemed hale and solid, but I knew him for what he was and what he had been. Only a jaw like that, and a pair of hard black eyes like that, could transform a shed full of cheap crockery into the biggest hardware store in the district. I knew him, all right.

'I know you,' I said slowly. 'You're Jarvey.'

'*Mr* Jarvey, if you please, sir.'

He made as if to sit on a packing case, and I offered him his swivel chair.

'Thankee,' said Jarvey, and took it. 'Now, sir, might I ask what you're about in my shop?'

'I've bought it. I'm going to make a clean sweep of it.'

'Very wise,' he said. 'Speaking from your point of view, sir.'

He considered me, head on hand, face impassive.

'Different line of business, sir?'

'Totally different, Mr Jarvey.'

'Very shrewd.'

We were both silent, waiting for each other. But he had been in business longer than I had, and had lived longer, and presumably could stall longer. So I spoke first, though it was a sign of weakness, and what I said was weaker still.

'You don't mind, I hope?'

'Mind? *Mind*, sir? Where shall I go when this is gone, do you suppose? *Mind*? Would you mind, might I ask, if a thunderbolt struck all that was dearest to you?' His was a ghostly shout, and I was glad of it. Full power and we should have had a policeman knocking on the door.

'I built this shop up from nothing, sir, and made it
something to be proud of. They came from twenty miles
about to see JARVEY'S. Aye, and further. I was a local
figure, sir, and a highly respected one, and you ask me if
I *mind*? I *made* this, sir!'

And he thumped the desk.

Something within me was sorry that neither of us could
hear the impact of that heavy fist, nor see the dust rise
from the silent mahogany.

'Still,' said Jarvey, calming down, 'I might get the better
of you yet, sir. I've made mincemeat of two or three
others, I can tell you. What year might it be, sir?'

'1973, Mr Jarvey.'

'H'm. Over half a century since I passed on, and my
name is still above that door, and the trade is still hardware. What do you think of that, sir?'

I could afford to be gracious, and in any case I liked
the old chap.

'I'm glad you're not alive, Mr Jarvey, or I might be
worried.'

He measured me for a full minute.

'I can buy you out,' he said quietly.

The inexorable face, the big muscles a little loose
with age, the air of authority. The spirit was indomit-
ably alive, but the flesh had died long since.

'How?' I asked, interested, and lit a cigarette.

Though it was a useless gesture, I offered him one.

'No, thankee,' said Jarvey. 'I prefer a good cigar. I had
a box somewhere. Now let me think.'

Astonishingly, he stood up and sniffed like a pointer,
then went straight to a corner cupboard and delved
behind a stack of account books.

'I can't seem to get at them, dammit!' he muttered, and
was hurt by his helplessness.

I walked over and brought out a box of Havanas.

'There should be half a dozen left,' said Jarvey hopefully.

There had been exactly half a dozen. They crumbled in my fingers like charred paper.

'I'll write to them about that,' said Jarvey dreadfully, and flung himself back in his swivel chair, underlip thrust forward.

'How are you going to buy me out, Mr Jarvey?'

'With the Gates,' he said, and a little smile warmed his mouth.

'Which gates, Mr Jarvey?'

He frowned, considering.

'Well, that's the difficult thing, sir, you see. I know they're a valuable piece of property, though I couldn't exactly tell you what they're made of. But I've dealt in metal all my life, and never seen any to touch this. I just know that if they would accept my offer—a fair offer, sir, though they don't seem to know the value and they don't have a use for them, as far as I can see—if they would accept my offer I could buy you out.'

'Tell me about them,' I suggested.

Because I was interested. Because he needed an argument badly and was enjoying the contest so much.

The gates were like nothing he had ever seen before, either in material or design. For one thing they shifted and changed as he looked at them, much as a kaleidoscope transforms the same scraps of coloured glass into infinite patterns. They were composed of something which seemed to be pearl in one light, silver or gold in another, and yet none of these things.

He touched them, but they might have been air. Nothing lay before or behind or to the sides of them. He could walk past, walk round. Nothing held them up.

They barred him from nowhere. Simply, they existed, and were beautiful beyond imagining, and this he could not comprehend.

'Who owns them?' I asked. 'And where are they?'

'Well, sir, that's another difficulty,' Jarvey admitted. 'There doesn't seem to be anyone there to keep an eye on them. As for where they are—they're all over the place, sir. For instance, the moment I walk out of this shop of *mine,*' he stressed the ownership courteously but firmly, 'they'll be standing there in front of me. And then again—I was born and bred in this part of the country, sir, so I like to take the air from time to time—then again I'll be walking miles away, and they suddenly come up.'

'Then to whom have you made your offer, Mr Jarvey?'

'Now that I don't rightly know, sir. There being nobody there—I shouted.'

'Fifty gold sovereigns for these Gates!' Jarvey roared into the stillness. 'My word is my bond, but you shall have a paper signed and sealed to that effect, by nightfall!'

An extraordinary quietness pervaded the place. Nothing seemed familiar, though a moment ago he had been sitting in his swivel chair, drinking tea. He longed for a good stretch of counter, with a bell upon it that he might stoutly ring.

'What happened then, Mr Jarvey?'

'Nothing, sir. Nothing ever has happened. Whenever those Gates turn up I make a bid for them. I've kept my eye on things here. I haven't been idle, sir. I have kept up with the changing times. Bless my soul, but money isn't worth what it was. I have offered everything within reason, and put up the price as the value of the sovereign went down. I have offered them cash, valuables. I never get an answer, sir, and I haven't got the Gates. Yet. But, by God, sir, when I do I *know* I can buy you out!'

I said nothing to Nell about Jarvey. She was occupied with some private crusade that needed no extra fuel from me: ringing up Councils and Planning People and Preservation Societies, and anybody else prepared to spend public money without hope of a return. She could manage very well without a tenacious old ghost to back her up. And Jarvey seemed to have wrecked his competitors so far, without any championship on her part. So I said nothing.

We were racing neck and neck, Nell and I, in the same race—but with different objectives. We have done it before, and survived. We shall always survive. Oil and water don't mix, they all said when we married. Well, they don't have to. Oil can calm a rough sea, and the sea is still there when the oil has floated away. Nell was hellbent to preserve JARVEY'S, and I was hellbent to change it. We both succeeded.

'I pay taxes for this sort of nonsense!' I said, throwing down the official letter.

'They are prepared to move the entire shop, from front to back, down to the last rusty nail and the last piece of paper—for *nothing*,' Nell replied. 'So why are you shouting?'

'I don't know,' I said. 'What will they do with it?'

'A Mr Jenkins has offered a building to house

JARVEY'S as a museum. It's perfect—and they'll keep it
up by charging an admission fee.'

'When are they moving the bloody stuff?'

'As soon as they can, but it will take time because
they don't want to spoil anything, and it will have to be
marked and docketed for setting up again. So don't make
difficulties, Charlie, will you?'

'How long? That's all I ask. How long?'

'A week or two. There's a very nice young man coming
round to see it, so please may I have the key? I'm saving
you money, really, Charlie. You won't have to move it all
yourself.'

'You're *costing* me money. I have to wait until they
move it, and I shan't get anything for the scrap metal.'

She said, very regally, 'What scrap metal is *that*?'

I gave her the key. I even made the young man a cup
of coffee when she brought him back, full of enthusiasm
for JARVEY'S. One thing comforted me. Jarvey hadn't been
able to buy me out, and I had moved his Victorian business off the premises: lock, stock, and literally barrel.

I walked round the shell afterwards. I am not unimaginative and I knew he had gone. But I am not
unimaginative. I was a little afraid that Jarvey might have
ill-wished us. I mentioned this in passing. Just in passing.
Only to Nell.

'Oh,' she said, 'you needn't worry about Mr Jarvey.
That's all settled.' She added, 'I thought you'd seen him.
I think you might have told me. You're very secretive,
Charlie, and it *is* a fault! I suppose you just talked
business?'

'When did *you* talk to him, then?'

'We had one or two conversations. I knew he was still
there. I said so, if you remember. I don't expect that
we talked about the same things, or saw the same person
—spirit. He was a very loving man, Charlie. You could

tell that from his mouth. He had a sensitive mouth.'

I said, 'What about his jaw?'

'He had a very good strong jaw, too. I liked him the moment I saw him. We got on famously. He's very like you, of course.'

With no more worlds to conquer, with his wife and children gone, Jarvey suffered. And since he could no longer expand the business, he expanded emotionally for the first time in his life. Jarvey had to grow. A curiosity for living and knowing possessed him, perilous and yet admirable. He who had lived as hard as he could now plunged ferociously into loving, with a fire that matched his early ambitions. He, who had taken to his Victorian bosom a worthy wife, now looked for the romance he had denied himself.

Life must have loved Jarvey, knowing itself to be so furiously courted. A widow, younger than himself by two decades, and with a little money of her own, succumbed to his determined siege. No woman, unless she loathes a man, can resist honest ardour. Jarvey, charmed by modesty and gentility, strove to please her in ways that were strange to him.

Spruce of a Sunday, in good grey broadcloth, he strode to her house bearing an awkward nosegay. He held her skeins of wool as she wound them deftly into balls. He sat back, eyes closed, as she read or sang to him of an evening. She led him into worlds gentler than the stout walls of his store. She brought forth ideas whose practicality he doubted, though he would have suffered much rather than said so. And in her turn, she drew strength from his knowledge of life. Though she secretly deplored his cynicism, it rendered her shelter more precious: protected as she had always been, and would be.

Their marriage surprised them both. A magnificent
first and last gift of passion on Jarvey's part: an unexpected revelation to her. The knowledge, in a prudish age,
that physical love could be shared and desired by both,
made her feel guilty in church. Her demureness over the
embroidery of an altar cloth was now veneer. She was
relieved, as well as happy, to find herself pregnant. It
seemed to justify the pleasure.

His adult sons had left JARVEY'S out of their reckoning,
and Jarvey had no heir for his kingdom. Now, on a Christmas Eve at the turn of the century, he surveyed the
store and dreamed of a boy on whom he would not,
could not, be hard.

'For we must move with the times,' said Jarvey to himself. 'And he will want to do differently. Quite right, too.
So he shall. I'll not stand in his way. No, indeed. I'll not
argue with him.'

Forgetting he would be in his dotage before the child
became a man.

'Shall I shut up shop, sir?' asked the lowest of his
staff. 'It's past nine o'clock.'

'I'll shut it myself, lad,' said Jarvey. 'Go your ways
home, and a Merry Christmas to you. God bless you.'

He mounted the stairs in an odour of mince pies, and
warmed himself in his wife's domain. The first Mrs Jarvey had been too mindful of his tongue and his am-
bition. The second Mrs Jarvey knew that no one was more
easily bidden than a masculine man. So she had coaxed
his stocks out of the top rooms, and furnished them with
a multitude of pretty articles, round which Jarvey trod
with fearful delicacy.

He drank one cup of tea, and watched her move
from table to cupboard and back again. All was well
with this world, and well as it had never been before.
Downstairs, JARVEY'S still provided and thrived, waiting

for young Jarvey to possess and expand it in ways unknown. Upstairs, was his other kingdom, and his heir in a sound flushed sleep.

'I'll take a second cup, my love,' said Jarvey, 'and a last look round the shop.'

He walked it from room to room, staircase to staircase, his mind docketing the contents of cases and boxes and packets and cupboards and shelves. And at last he entered the inner sanctum and sank into his swivel chair, quite winded. All about him were papers accumulated from the first day he had opened the store. Had a man possessed time, energy, and wit enough to read and memorise their contents, he would have known the place as Jarvey knew it.

'I am the happiest man alive,' said Jarvey. Then, with pride, looking round at the immensity of his achievement. '*I* made this!'

The tea cup tilted and fell, as he sprawled across the desk.

'I checked up in the local library,' said Nell, 'mostly out of interest, but partly to convince the museum-people that JARVEY'S was a genuine legend. His widow sold the shop. Well, she had to, you see. Every penny he owned was in the place. He hadn't taken insurance out for her or the child, or anything. He must have thought he would live and provide for ever. His son was killed at the end of the First World War, and *she* died soon afterwards.'

We have no children of our own, and there will be none now. So Nell comforts herself with the idea of spiritual heirs. I am too practical-minded. I wish I were not, sometimes. To be honest, I believe that there are a good many things we can't explain—take Jarvey, for instance. But if we can't explain them then let's leave them alone.

'I think you were meant to buy JARVEY'S,' said Nell. 'I know it will be a success. And you're so *like* him.'

'Did he tell you about the gates?'

'Certainly. They were the Heavenly Gates.'

'There's no such thing, of course.'

'Jarvey thought so. He believed in them, though he didn't recognise them—except as a wonderful bargain!'

'I suppose you advised him to have them taken over by the National Trust?'

'Don't be facetious, Charlie!'

'I'm sure you made some suggestion. The opportunity could hardly be missed.'

'I had to explain, you see.'

'I thought perhaps you might have to do that.'

'I explained,' said Nell, looking obstinate and very sure of herself, 'that the Gates of Heaven were not for sale. Mr Jarvey had two kingdoms, like all of us. One was the kingdom on earth, and that was JARVEY'S for him. The other was the kingdom of heaven, which is *in* us. Oh, you should see your expression! Call it whatever you like, then, since you won't admit to the words. Something that matters most, something that can't be named or described. You can't buy things like that, they have to be given.'

'You suggested that he asked the air to give him the gates?'

'No, of course not. I asked him if he had tried to open them and go inside.'

'He could go anywhere he wanted to, dammit. There was nothing round them.'

'No. Nothing *round* them. But he hadn't thought of going *through* them, had he?'

'Rubbish.'

'All right then, we'll agree to differ. What's on the television?'

It was the idea she had put into my head. I knew that. But all evening I didn't watch a thing on the screen. All I could see was that Victorian hardware merchant, in his frock-coat and gold watch-chain, marching up to the Gates. Only this time he didn't make a single offer, didn't shout. Simply pushed them open and walked in. I don't believe it for a moment, mind you. Only he isn't in the shop, and he isn't in the museum. And we thrive.

WILLIAM TREVOR

George and Alice and Isabel

Mr Mockler was a tailor. He carried on his business in a house that after twenty-five years of mortgage arrangements had finally become his: 22 Juniper Street, S.W.17. He had never married and since he was now sixty-three it seemed likely that he never would. In an old public house, the *Charles the First*, he had a drink every evening with his friends Mr Uprichard and Mr Tile, who were tailors also. He lived in his house in Juniper Street with his cat Sam, and did his own cooking and washing and cleaning. He was not unhappy.

On the morning of 19th October, 1972, Mr Mockler received a letter that astonished him. It was neatly written in a pleasantly rounded script that wasn't difficult to decipher. It did not address him as 'Dear Mr Mockler', nor was it signed, nor conventionally concluded. But his name was used repeatedly, and from its contents it seemed to Mr Mockler that the author of the letter was a Mrs Acland. He read the letter in amazement and then read it again and then, more slowly, a third time.

Dr Scott-Rowe is dead, Mr Mockler. I know he is dead

because a new man is here, a smaller, younger man, called Dr Friendman. He looks at us, smiling, with his unblinking eyes. Miss Acheson says you can tell at a glance that he has practised hypnosis.

They're so sure of themselves, Mr Mockler: beyond the limits of their white-coated world they can accept nothing. I am a woman imprisoned because I once saw ghosts. I am paid for by the man who was my husband, who writes out monthly cheques for the peaches they bring to my room, and the beef olives and the *marrons glacés*. 'She must above all things be happy,' I can imagine the stout man who was my husband saying, walking with Dr Scott-Rowe over the sunny lawns and among the rosebeds. In this house there are twenty disturbed women in private rooms, cosseted by luxury because other people feel guilty. And when we walk ourselves on the lawns and among the rosebeds we murmur at the folly of those who have so expensively committed us and at the greater folly of the medical profession: you can be disturbed without being mad. Is this the letter of a lunatic, Mr Mockler?

I said this afternoon to Miss Acheson that Dr Scott-Rowe was dead. She said she knew. All of us would have Dr Friendman now, she said, with his smile and his tape-recorders. 'May Dr Scott-Rowe rest in peace,' said Miss Acheson: it was better to be dead than to be like Dr Friendman. Miss Acheson is a very old lady, twice my age exactly. I am thirty-nine and she is seventy-eight. She was committed when she was eighteen, in 1913, a year before the First World War. Miss Acheson was disturbed by visions of St Olaf of Norway and she still is. Such visions were an embarrassment to Miss Acheson's family in 1913 and so they quietly slipped her away. No one comes to see her now, no one has since 1927.

'You must write it all down,' Miss Acheson said to me when I told her, years ago, that I'd been committed because I'd seen ghosts and that I could prove the ghosts were real because the Rachels had seen them too. The Rachels are living some normal existence somewhere, yet they were terrified half out of their wits at the time and I wasn't frightened at all. The trouble nowadays, Miss Acheson says and I quite agree, is that if you like having ghosts near you people think you're round the bend.

I was talking to Miss Acheson about all this yesterday and she said why didn't I do what Sarah Crookham used to do? There's nothing the matter with Sarah Crookham either, any more than there is with Miss Acheson or myself: all that Sarah Crookham suffers from is a broken heart. 'You must write it all down,' Miss Acheson said to her when she first came here, weeping, poor thing, every minute of the day. So she wrote it down and posted it to A. J. Rawson, a person she found in the telephone directory. But Mr Rawson never came, nor another person Sarah Crookham wrote to. I have looked you up in the telephone directory, Mr Mockler. It is nice to have a visitor.

'You must begin at the beginning,' Miss Acheson says, and so I am doing that. The beginning is back a bit, in January 1949, when I was fifteen. We lived in Richmond then, my parents and my brother, George, and my sisters Alice and Isabel. On Sundays, after lunch, we used to walk all together in Richmond Park with our dog, a Dalmatian called Salmon. I was the oldest and Alice was next, two years younger, and George was eleven and Isabel eight. It was lovely walking all together in Richmond Park and then going home to Sunday tea. I remember the autumns and winters best, the cosiness of the coal fire, hot sponge cake and special Sunday sandwiches, and little buns that Alice and I helped to make on Sunday mornings. We played Monopoly by the fire, and George would always have the ship and Anna the hat and Isabel the racing-car and Mummy the dog. Daddy and I would share the old boot. I really loved it.

I loved the house: 17 Lorelei Avenue, an ordinary suburban house built some time in the early nineteen twenties, when Miss Acheson was still quite young. There were bits of stained glass on either side of the hall-door and a single stained-glass pane, Moses in the bul-rushes, in one of the landing windows. At Christmas especially it was lovely. We'd have the Christmas tree in the hall and always on Christmas Eve, as long as I can remember, there'd be a party. I can remember the parties quite vividly. There'd be people standing round drinking punch and all the children would play hide-and-seek upstairs, and nobody could ever find George. It's George, Mr Mockler, that all this is about. And Alice, of course, and Isabel.

When I first described them to Dr Scott-Rowe he said they sounded marvellous, and I said that I thought they probably were marvellous, but I suppose a person can be prejudiced in family matters of that kind. Because they were, after all, my brother and my two sisters and because, of course, they're dead now. I mean, they were probably ordinary children, just like any children. Well, you can see what you think, Mr Mockler.

George was small for his age, very wiry, dark-haired, a darting kind of boy who was always laughing and had often to be reprimanded by my father because his teachers said he was the most mischievous boy in his class. Alice, two years older, was just the opposite: demure and silent, but happy in her quiet way, and beau-tiful, far more beautiful than I was. Isabel wasn't beauti-ful at all. She was all freckles, had long pale plaits, and long legs that sometimes could run as fast as George's. She and George were as close as two persons can get, but in a way we were all close: there was a lot of love in 17 Lorelei Avenue.

I had a cold the day it happened, a Saturday it was. I was cross because they all kept worrying about leaving me in the house on my own. They'd bring me back Black Magic chocolates, they said, and my mother said she'd buy a bunch of daffodils if she saw any. I heard the car crunching over the gravel outside the garage, and then their voices telling Salmon not to put his paws on the upholstery. My father blew the horn, saying good-bye to me, and after that the silence began and I must have known, even then, long before it happened, that nothing would be the same again.

When I was twenty-two, Mr Mockler, I married a man called Acland, who helped me to get over the tragedy. George would have been eighteen, and Anna twenty and Isabel fifteen. They would have liked my husband because he was a good-humoured and generous man. He was very plump, many years older than I was, with pleasant red hair and a fondness for all food. 'You're like a child,' I used to say to him and we'd laugh together. Cheese in particular he liked, and ham and all kinds of root vegetables, parsnips, turnips, celeriac, carrots, leeks, potatoes. He used to come back to the house and take four or five pounds of gammon from the car, and chops, and blocks of ice-cream, and biscuits, and two or even three McVitie's fruitcakes. He was very partial to McVitie's fruitcakes. At night, at nine or ten o'clock, he'd make cocoa for both of us and we'd have it while we were watching the television, with a slice or two of fruitcake. He was such a kind man in those days. I got quite fat myself, which might surprise you, Mr Mockler, because I'm on the thin side now.

My husband was, and still is, both clever and rich. One led to the other: he made a fortune designing metal fasteners for the aeroplane industry. Once, in May 1960, he drove me to a house in Worcestershire. 'I wanted it to be a surprise,' he said, stopping his mustard-coloured Alfa-Romeo in front of this quite extensive Victorian façade. 'There!' he said, embracing me, reminding me that it was my birthday. Two months later we went to live there.

We had no children. In that large Victorian house I made my life with the man I'd married and once again, as in 17 Lorelei Avenue, I was happy. The house was near a village but was otherwise remote. My husband went away from it by day, to the places where his aeroplane fastenings were manufactured. I used to think of him sitting at a desk drawing new fastenings on large sheets of paper and ordering that they should be manufactured and tested. There were—and still are—aeroplanes in the air which would have fallen to pieces if they hadn't been securely fastened by the genius of my husband.

The house had many rooms. There was a large square drawing-room with a metal ceiling, beaten tin, I believe it was. It had patterns like wedding-cake icing on it. It was painted white and blue and gave, as well as the impression of a wedding-cake, a Wedgwood effect. People remarked on this ceiling and my husband used to explain that metal ceilings had once been very popular, especially in the large houses of Australia. Well-to-do Australians, apparently, would have them shipped from Birmingham in colonial imitation of an English fashion. My husband and I, arm in arm, would lead people about the house, pointing out the ceilings or the green wallpaper in our bedroom or the portraits that hung on the stairs.

The lighting was bad in the house. The long first-floor landing was a gloomy place by day and lit by a single wall-light at night. At the end of this landing another flight of stairs, less grand than the stairs that led from the hall, wound upwards to the small rooms that had once upon a time been servants' quarters, and another flight continued above them to attics and store-rooms. The bathroom was on the first floor, tiled in green Victorian tiles, and there was a lavatory next door to it, encased in mahogany.

In the small rooms that had once been the servants' quarters lived Mr and Mrs Rachels. My husband had had a kitchen and a bathroom put in for them so that their rooms were quite self-contained. Mr Rachels worked in the garden and his wife cleaned the house. It wasn't really necessary to have them at all: I could have cleaned the house myself and even done the gardening, but my husband insisted in his generous way. At night I could hear the Rachels moving about above me. I didn't like this, and my husband asked them to move more quietly.

In 1962 my husband was asked to go to Germany, to explain his aeroplane fasteners to the German aircraft industry. It was to be a prolonged trip, three months at least, and I was naturally unhappy when he told me. He was unhappy himself, but on March 4 he flew to Hamburg, leaving me with the Rachels.

They were a pleasant enough couple, somewhere in their fifties I would think, he rather silent, she inclined to talk. The only thing that worried me about them was the way they used to move about at night above my head. After my husband had gone to Germany I gave Mrs Rachels money to buy slippers, but I don't think she ever did because the sounds continued just as before. I naturally didn't make a fuss about it.

On the night of March 7 I was awakened by a band playing in the house. The tune was an old tune of the fifties called, I believe, 'Looking for Henry Lee'. The noise was very loud in my bedroom and I lay there frightened, not knowing why this noise should be coming to me like this, Victor Sylvester in strict-time. Then a voice spoke, a long babble of French, and I realised that I was listening to a radio programme. The wireless was across the room, on a table by the windows. I put on my bedside light and got up and switched it off. I drank some orange juice and went back to sleep. It didn't even occur to me to wonder who had turned the wireless on.

The next day I thought about it, and I definitely remembered turning the wireless off myself before going to bed. In any case I was not in the habit of listening to French stations so that even if the wireless had somehow come on of its own accord it should not have been tuned on to a French station.

Two days later I found the bath half-filled with water and the towels all crumpled and damp, thrown about on the floor. The water in the bath was tepid and dirty: someone, an hour or so ago, had had a bath.

I climbed the stairs to the Rachels' flat and knocked on their door. 'Is your bathroom out of order?' I said when Mr Rachels came to the door, not wearing the slippers I'd given them money for. I said I didn't at all mind their using mine, only I'd be grateful if they'd remember to let the water out and to bring down their own towels. Mr Rachels looked at me in the way people have sometimes, as though you're insane. He called his wife and all three of us went down to look at my bathroom. They denied emphatically that either of them had a bath.

When I came downstairs the next morning, having slept badly, I found the kitchen table had been laid for four. There was a table-cloth on the table, which was something I never bothered about, and a kettle was boiling on the Aga. Beside it, a large brown teapot, not the one I normally used, was heating. I made some tea and sat down, thinking about the Rachels. Why should they behave like this? Why should they creep into my bedroom in the middle of the night and turn the wireless on? Why should they have a bath in my bathroom and then deny it? Why should they lay the breakfast table as though we had overnight guests? I left the table just as it was. Butter had been rolled into pats. Marmalade, Golden Shred and the ordinary kind, had been placed in two china dishes. A silver toast-rack that an aunt of his had given us as a wedding present was waiting for toast.

'Thank you for laying the table,' I said to Mrs Rachels when she entered the kitchen an hour later.

She shook her head. She began to say that she hadn't laid the table but then she changed her mind. I could see from her face that she and her husband had been discussing the matter of the bath the night before. She could hardly wait to tell him about the breakfast table. I smiled at her.

'A funny thing happened the other night,' I said. 'I woke up to find Victor Sylvester playing a tune called "Looking for Henry Lee".'

'Henry Lee?' Mrs Rachels said, turning around from the sink. Her face, usually blotched with red, like the skin of an apple, was white.

'It's an old song of the fifties.'

It was while saying that that I realised what was happening in the house. I naturally didn't say anything to Mrs Rachels, and I at once began to regret that I'd said anything in the first place. It had frightened me, finding the bathroom like that, and clearly it must have frightened the Rachels. I didn't want them to be frightened because naturally there was nothing to be frightened about. George and Alice and Isabel wouldn't hurt anyone, not unless death had changed them enormously. But even so I knew that I couldn't ever explain that to the Rachels.

'Well, I suppose I'm just getting absentminded,' I said. 'People do, so they say, when they live alone.' I laughed to show that I wasn't worried or frightened, to make it all seem ordinary.

'You mean, you laid the table yourself?' Mrs Rachels said. 'And had a bath?'

'And didn't turn the wireless off properly. Funny,' I said, 'how these things go in threes. Funny, how there's always an explanation.' I laughed again and Mrs Rachels had to laugh too.

After that it was lovely, just like being back in 17 Lorelei Avenue. I bought Black Magic chocolates and bars of Fry's and Cadbury's Milk, all the things we'd liked. I often found the bathwater left in and the towels crumpled, and now and again I came down in the morning to find the breakfast table laid. On the first-floor landing, on the evening of March 11, I caught a glimpse of George in the garden. Three days later, I saw Isabel and Alice.

On March 15 the Rachels left. I hadn't said a word to them about finding the bathroom used again or the breakfast laid or actually seeing the children. I'd been cheerful and smiling whenever I met them. I'd talked about how Brasso wasn't as good as it used to be to Mrs Rachels and had asked her husband about the best kind of soil for bulbs.

'We can't stay a minute more,' Mrs Rachels said, her face all white and tight in the hall, and then to my astonishment they attempted to persuade me to go also.

'The house ain't fit to live in,' Mr Rachels said.

'Oh now, that's nonsense,' I began to say, but they both shook their heads.

'There's children here,' Mrs Rachels said. 'There's three children appearing all over the place.'

'Come right up to you,' Mr Rachels said. 'Laugh at you sometimes.'

They were trembling, both of them. They were so terrified that I thought they might die, that their hearts would give out there in the hall and they'd just drop down. But they didn't. They walked out of the hall door with their three suitcases, down the drive to catch a bus. I never saw them again.

I suppose, Mr Mockler, you have to be frightened of ghosts: I suppose that's their way of communicating. I mean, it's no good being like me, delighting in it all, being happy because I wasn't lonely in that house any more. You have to be like the Rachels, terrified half out of your wits. I think I knew that as I watched the Rachels go. I think I knew that George and Isabel and Alice would go with them, that I was only a kind of go-between, that the Rachels were what George and Isabel and Alice really could have fun with. I almost ran after the Rachels, but I knew it would be no good.

Without the Rachels and my brother and my two sisters, I was frightened myself in that big house. I moved everything into the kitchen: the television set and the plants I kept in the drawing-room, and a camp-bed to sleep on. I was there, asleep in the camp bed when my husband returned from Germany; he had changed completely. He raved at me, not listening to a word I said. There were cups of tea all over the house, he said, and bits of bread and biscuits and cake and chocolates. There were notes in envelopes, and messages scrawled in my handwriting on the wallpaper of various rooms. Everywhere was dusty. Where, he wanted to know, were the Rachels?

He stood there with a canvas bag in his left hand, an airline bag that had the word *Lufthansa* on it. He'd put on at least a stone, I remember thinking, and his red hair was shorter than before.

'Listen,' I said, 'I would like to tell you.' And I tried to tell him, as I've told you, Mr Mockler, about George and Isabel and Alice in 17 Lorelei Avenue and how we all went together for a walk with our dog, every Sunday afternoon in Richmond Park, and how on Christmas Eve my mother always gave a party. I told him about the stained-glass pane in the window, Moses in the bulrushes, and the hide-and-seek we played, and how my father and I always shared the old boot in Monopoly. I told him about the day of the accident, how the tyre on the lorry suddenly exploded and how the lorry went whizzing around on the road and then just tumbled over on top of them. I'd put out cups of tea, I said, and biscuits and cake and the little messages, just in case they came back again—not for them to eat or to read particularly, but just as a sign. They'd given me a sign first, I explained: George had turned on my wireless in the middle of the night and Isabel had had baths and Alice had laid the breakfast table. But then they'd gone because they'd been more interested in annoying the Rachels than in comforting me. I began to weep, telling him how lonely I'd been without them, how lonely I'd been ever since the day of the accident, how the silence had been everywhere. I couldn't control myself: tears came out of my eyes as though they'd never stop. I felt sickness all over my body, paining me in my head and my chest, sour in my stomach. I wanted to die because the loneliness was too much. Loneliness was the worst thing in the world, I said, gasping out words, with spit and tears going cold on my face. People were only shadows, I tried to explain, when you had loneliness and silence like that, like a shroud around you. You couldn't reach out of the shroud sometimes, you couldn't connect because shadows are hard to connect with and it's frightening when you try because everyone is looking at you. But it was lovely, I whispered, when the children came back to annoy the Rachels. My husband replied by telling me I was insane.

The letter finished there, and Mr Mockler was more astonished each time he read it. He had never in his life received such a document before, nor did he in fact very often receive letters of any kind, apart from bills and, if he was fortunate, cheques in settlement. He shook his head over the letter and placed it in the inside pocket of his jacket.

That day, as he stitched and measured, he imagined the place Mrs Acland wrote of, the secluded house with twenty female inmates, and the lawn and the rosebeds. He imagined the other house, 17 Lorelei Avenue in Richmond, and the third house, the Victorian residence in the Worcestershire countryside. He imagined Mrs Acland's obese husband with his short hair and his aeroplane fasteners, and the children who had been killed in a motor-car accident and Mr and Mrs Rachels whom they had haunted. All day long the faces of these people flitted through Mr Mockler's mind, with old Miss Acheson and Sarah Crookham and Dr Scott-Rowe and Dr Friendman. In the evening when he met his friends Mr Tile and Mr Uprichard in the *Charles the First* he showed them the letter before even ordering them drinks.

'Well, I'm beggared,' remarked Mr Uprichard, a man

known locally for his gentle nature. 'That poor creature.'

Mr Tile, who was not given to expressing himself, shook his head.

Mr Mockler asked Mr Uprichard if he should visit this Mrs Acland. 'Poor creature,' Mr Uprichard said again, and added that without a doubt Mrs Acland had written to a stranger because of the loneliness she mentioned, the loneliness like a shroud around her.

Some weeks later Mr Mockler, having given the matter further thought and continuing to be affected by the contents of the letter, took a Green Line bus out of London to the address that Mrs Acland had given him. He made enquiries, feeling quite adventurous, and was told that the house was three-quarters of a mile from where the bus had dropped him, down a side road. He found it without further difficulty. It was a house surrounded by a high brick wall in which large, black wrought-iron gates were backed with sheets of tin so that no one could look through the ornamental scroll work. The gates were locked. Mr Mockler rang a bell in the wall.

'Yes?' a man said, opening the gate that was on Mr Mockler's left.

'Well,' said Mr Mockler and found it difficult to proceed.

'Yes?' the man said.

'Well, I've had a letter. Asking me to come, I think. My name's Mockler.'

The man opened the gate a little more and Mr Mockler stepped through.

The man walked ahead of him and Mr Mockler saw the lawns that had been described, and the rosebeds. The house he considered most attractive: a high Georgian building with beautiful windows. An old woman was walking slowly by herself with the assistance of a stick: Miss Acheson, Mr Mockler guessed. In the distance he saw other women, walking slowly on leaf-strewn paths.

Autumn was Mr Mockler's favourite season and he was glad to be in the country on this pleasantly autumnal day. He thought of remarking on this to the man who led him towards the house, but since the man did not incline towards conversation he did not do so.

In the yellow waiting-room there were no magazines, and no pictures on the walls and no flowers. It was not a room in which Mr Mockler would have cared to wait for long, and in fact he did not have to. A woman dressed as a nurse except that she wore a green cardigan came in. She smiled briskly at him and said that Dr Friendman would see him. She asked Mr Mockler to follow her.

'How very good of you to come,' Dr Friendman said, smiling at Mr Mockler in the way that Mrs Acland had described in her letter. 'How very humane,' said Dr Friendman.

'I had a letter, from a Mrs Acland.'

'Quite so, Mr Mockler. Mr Mockler, could I press you towards a glass of sherry?'

Mr Mockler, surprised at this line of talk, accepted the sherry, saying it was good of Dr Friendman. He drank the sherry while Dr Friendman read the letter. When he'd finished, Dr Friendman crossed to the window of the room and pulled aside a curtain and asked Mr Mockler if he'd mind looking out.

There was a courtyard, small and cobbled, in which a gardener was sweeping leaves into a pile. At the far end of it, sitting on a tapestry-backed dining-chair in the autumn sunshine was a woman in a blue dress. 'Try these,' said Dr Friendman and handed Mr Mockler a pair of binoculars.

It was a beautiful face, thin and seeming fragile, with large blue eyes and lips that were now slightly parted, smiling in the sunshine. Hair the colour of corn was simply arranged, hanging on either side of the face and curling in around it. The hair shone in the sunlight, as though it was for ever being brushed.

'I find them useful,' Dr Friendman said, taking the binoculars from Mr Mockler's hands. 'You have to keep an eye, you know.'

'That's Mrs Acland?' Mr Mockler asked.

'That's the lady who wrote to you. The letter's a bit inaccurate, Mr Mockler. It wasn't quite like that in 17 Lorelei Avenue.'

'Not quite like it?'

'She cannot forget Lorelei Avenue. I'm afraid she never will. That beautiful woman, Mr Mockler, was a beautiful girl, yet she married the first man who asked her, a widower thirty years older than her, an obese designer of aircraft fasteners. He pays her bills just as she says in her letter and even when he's dead they'll go on being paid. He used to visit her at first, but he found it too painful. He stood in this very room one day, Mr Mockler, and said to Dr Scott-Rowe that no man had ever been appreciated by a woman as much as he had by her. And all because he'd been kind to her in the most ordinary kind of way.'

Mr Mockler said that he was afraid that he didn't know what Dr Friendman was talking about. As though he hadn't heard this quiet protest, Dr Friendman smiled and said:

'But it was, unfortunately, too late for kindness. 17 Lorelei Avenue had done its damage, like a cancer in her mind: she could not forget her childhood.'

'Yes, she says in her letter. George and Alice and Isabel—'

'All her childhood, Mr Mockler, her parents did not speak to one another. They didn't quarrel, they didn't address each other in any way whatsoever. When she was five they'd come to an agreement: that they should both remain in 17 Lorelei Avenue because neither would ever have agreed to give up an inch of the child they'd between them caused to be born. In the house there was nothing, Mr Mockler, for all her childhood years. Nothing except silence.'

'But there were George and Alice and Isabel—'

'No, Mr Mockler. There was no George and no Alice and no Isabel. No hide-and-seek or parties on Christmas Eve, no Monopoly on Sundays by the fire. Can you imagine 17 Lorelei Avenue, Mr Mockler, as she is now incapable of imagining it? Two people so cruel to one another that they knew that either of them could be parted from the child in some divorce court? A woman bitterly hating the man that once she'd loved, and he returning each evening, hurrying back from an office in case his wife and the child were having a conversation. She would sit, Mr Mockler, in a room with them, with the silence heavy in the air. And their hatred for one another. All three of them would sit down to a meal and no one would speak. No other children came to that house, no other people. She used to hide on the way back from school. She'd go down the area steps of other houses and crouch beside dustbins.'

'Dustbins?' repeated Mr Mockler, more astonished than ever. *'Dustbins?'*

'Other children didn't take to her. She couldn't talk to them. She'd never learned to talk to anyone. He was a patient man, Mr Acland, when he came along, a good and patient man.'

Mr Mockler said that the child's parents must have been monsters but Dr Friendman shook his head and said this wasn't so. No one was a monster, Dr Friendman said in a professional manner, and in the circumstances Mr Mockler didn't feel he could argue with him. But the people called Rachels were real, he said, as real as the fat designer of aircraft fasteners: had they left the house, he asked, as it said in the letter? And if they had, what had they been frightened of?

Dr Friendman smiled again. 'I don't believe in ghosts,' he said, and he explained at great length to Mr Mockler that it was Mrs Acland herself who had frightened the Rachels, turning on a wireless in the middle of the night and running baths and laying tables for people who weren't there. Mr Mockler listened and was interested to note that Dr Friendman used words that were not easy to understand and quoted from experts who were in Dr Friendman's line of business but whose names meant nothing to Mr Mockler.

Mr Mockler, listening to all that, nodded but was not convinced. The Rachels had left the house, just as the letter said: he knew that, he felt it in his bones and it felt like the truth. The Rachels had been frightened of Mrs Acland's ghosts even though they'd been artificial ghosts. They'd been real to her, and they'd been real to the Rachels because she'd made them so. Shadows had stepped out of her mind because in her loneliness she'd wished them to. They'd laughed and played and frightened the Rachels half out of their wits.

'There's always an explanation,' said Dr Friendman.

Mr Mockler nodded, profoundly disagreeing.

'She'll think you're Mr Rachels,' said Dr Friendman, 'come to say he saw the ghosts. If you wouldn't mind saying you did, it keeps her happy.'

'But it's the truth,' Mr Mockler cried with passion in his voice. 'Of course it's the truth: there can be ghosts like that, just as there can be in any other way.'

'Oh, come now,' murmured Dr Friendman with his sad, humane smile.

Mr Mockler followed Dr Friendman from the room. They crossed a landing and descended a back staircase, passing near a kitchen in which a chef with a tall chef's hat was beating pieces of meat. 'Ah, Wiener Schnitzel,' said Dr Friendman.

In the cobbled courtyard the gardener had finished sweeping up the leaves and was wheeling them away in a wheelbarrow. The woman with the well-brushed hair was still sitting on the tapestry-backed chair, still smiling in the autumn sunshine.

'Look,' said Dr Friendman, 'a visitor.'

The woman rose and went close to Mr Mockler. 'They didn't mean to frighten you,' she said, 'even though it's the only way ghosts can communicate. They were only having fun, Mr Rachels.'

'I think Mr Rachels realises that now,' Dr Friendman said.

'Yes, of course,' said Mr Mockler.

'No one ever believed me, and I kept on saying when the Rachels come back they'll tell the truth about poor George and Alice and Isabel. You saw them, didn't you, Mr Rachels?'

'Yes,' Mr Mockler said. 'We saw them.'

She turned and walked away, leaving the tapestry-backed chair behind her.

'You're a humane person,' Dr Friendman said, holding out his right hand, which Mr Mockler shook. The same man led him back through the lawns and the rosebeds, to the gates.

It was an experience that Mr Mockler found impossible to forget. He measured and stitched and talked to his friends Mr Uprichard and Mr Tile in the *Charles the First*; he went for a walk morning and evening, and no day passed during which he did not think of the woman whom people looked at through binoculars. Somewhere in England, or at least somewhere in the world, the Rachels were probably still alive, and had Mr Mockler been a younger man he might even have set about looking for them. He would like to have brought them to the secluded house where the woman now lived, to have been there himself when they told the truth to Dr Friendman. It seemed a sadness, as he once remarked to Mr Uprichard, that on top of everything else a woman's artificial ghosts should not be honoured, since she had brought them into being and given them life, as other women give other children life.

'They're honoured here,' Mr Uprichard gently reminded his friend in the old public house. 'George and Alice and Isabel, God save the memory of them.'

They are honoured still. In the *Charles the First* in S.W.17 the story is told to strangers, how a woman wrote to a name in the telephone directory, anxious about her ghosts.

JOHN BURKE

False Harmonic

By the end of the first month he was beginning to feel he had been cheated. Or, worse still, that he was regarded as unworthy.

There had been no sound: not a whisper, not a hint, not a thread of melody. Here he was—waiting, receptive, attuned to anything the dead man might want to say— and still there was not the faintest resonance.

What made it so humiliating was that others heard. Heard, or saw, or in some way knew something he didn't. Others ... caring nothing for the great man or his work, yet somehow *knowing*.

And not telling.

Sometimes when he walked into the village pub he would catch a brief intimation before they knew he was there.

'Him again, last night. Or so my Margery reckoned.'

'Getting at you, like before?'

'Not this time. No, he was just sort of ...'

Then there would be a nudge, and a silence, and a sudden burst of talk about sugar beet and celery and drainage and next month's price review, and the landlord would smile with false benevolence. 'All right, then, Mr Bickford? Getting on all right up there?'

On one occasion when there was no one else in the bar he tried to get the landlord to talk. But the man was too good at his job to be drawn if he didn't want to be. No politics, no religion in this pub, gentlemen, please—and apparently no music.

'The composer feller? Oh, but honest now, sir, that was long before my time.'

'I'd have thought you might have heard things from some of the older folk. There must be several who can still remember him, and still talk about him.'

'Nothing much to talk about, from all I did hear.' The landlord busied himself polishing a glass which was already sparkling. 'Kept himself to himself.'

'Until he died,' Mark Bickford prompted.

There was an echoing silence, like a single beat rest before the resolution of a cadence. Then the landlord said:

'Well, folk don't do a lot o' visiting when they're no longer with us, like.'

'No? That's what I've been wondering.'

Behind him the latch rattled. The landlord twitched a smile of relief as one of his regulars came in.

'I'd have thought'—he moved away, pulling a pint without waiting to be asked, turning towards the newcomer and politely but decisively finishing with Bickford—'you'd be the one most likely to know all about him, any road, with all that stuff you got up there in the house.'

The house was a late eighteenth-century rectory on one of the shallow islands on which churches and monasteries had long ago been built in the Fens. The church itself had crumbled and finally collapsed during a land subsidence when new drainage channels were being dug. Now gap-toothed ruins overlooked the line of a dyke laid straight to the northern horizon. There was no other landmark apart from a tall grey silo five miles away, and that would not have been there in the composer's day: Saul Gregory had chosen a home without distractions. Whichever way he looked, there was nothing to take his mind from his work. When he went for one of his long walks there was no hill or cathedral or scenic extravagance to divert him from his one obsessive task—which was to write music equally free from all excrescences and all falsifying touches of colour and emotion.

Saul Gregory had bought the rectory in 1884 and did not leave it for more than a few days at a time during the next fifty years. When he died he left instructions that his ashes should be scattered along the footpath leading to the dyke, under the shadow of the featureless green wall. He had been an only child, his parents were long dead, and he had never married. The house was left to a second cousin, a dry little woman who took it over just as it stood and moved nothing from the places which Gregory had appointed. It became what many of the island buildings had been centuries ago—a retreat, an austere cell, remote from everything save the implacable east wind. And then, in the late 1950s, it became a shrine: a shrine to which only the most devout pilgrims came.

As the record companies poured out long-playing records, someone rediscovered Saul Gregory. Two of his string quartets were enthusiastically reviewed by critics surfeited not merely with Vivaldi but with Schoenberg. 'The ultimate refinement of musical expression,' wrote one: 'or, perhaps one should say, of flawlessly musical non-expression.' A three-record box followed. The BBC Third Programme devoted three two-hour recitals to his orchestral music, which Saul Gregory himself had never heard: he had never bothered to attend the few public performances of his work in London and Manchester, answering one invitation to do so with the brief note, 'I hear it in my own head, and am content to hear it only there.'

When the shrivelled old woman died, she left the house to the nation just as she had found it. The fabric, however, was in danger of collapse on the north-east corner, and new damp courses were needed to check the quickening deterioration of several rooms. A trust was established; urgent renovations were carried out; a curator was advertised for, and it was announced that the house would be open to the public three afternoons a week, or by special appointment.

A few enthusiasts from Ely, and some driving across country from the Kings Lynn Festival, came to inspect the study and the meticulously preserved relics—Saul Gregory's steel pen, the neatly docketed drawers of manuscripts, the scrubbed kitchen table at which he worked in preference to a desk, and the large oval portrait of his father and mother, the only picture in the entire house. There was no musical instrument anywhere. Gregory had never worked at the piano: music evolved by composers sitting at the keyboard, he claimed, whether meant as orchestral or chamber music, always *sounded* as though it had been worked out at the keyboard—and this was the faultiest music of all.

In a glass case were spread out the sheets of the composition on which he had been working when he died. It was his ultimate foray into an ascetic unknown: the quintessence of Saul Gregory, the distillation and triple, quadruple distillation of ideas so refined that they had eliminated every predictable cadence or resolution, eerily making more of silence than of sound. The music was in four-part open score, but there was no indication whether it was designed for string quartet, organ, or for some combination existing only in Gregory's mind. Perhaps he had wished it to exist only in itself. 'It makes Webern sound like Franz Lehar,' said a catalogue note contributed by a fervent disciple.

Fervour was something which Gregory would surely have disapproved of.

The first curator of the house and its contents was a middle-aged scholar engaged in writing what was to be the definitive treatise on atonalism. He had plenty of time for concentration on this work. Visitors were few, but those who did come were in no way an irritant: anyone who troubled to come off the main road and along the bumpy track to the house was inevitably someone who spoke the same language and could discuss the same abstruse theories.

In his first annual report to the trustees, the curator recorded the number of visitors, recommended widening and surfacing the track to the house and providing a small car park if possible, and coyly admitted that he had spent a great deal of time trying to complete the unfinished quartet.

A few weeks later he wrote a much less formal, rather confused letter in which he said: 'I don't think I can stay here. He obviously thinks I'm not good enough. He gets very angry when he can't get through.'

Edwin Toller, secretary to the trustees, drove down to see what was wrong, but learned little. The curator was sheepish and apologetic. It was lonely here, he must have been imagining things: it wouldn't happen again.

What did happen was that he was brought up before the local magistrates on a charge of assaulting a seventeen-year-old girl on the path from the dyke to the village.

After a scathing denunciation from the local land-owner who dominated the bench, ending with the advice to get out in the fresh air and take some healthy exercise —which caused a few sniggers among those who considered that this was precisely what had got him into trouble in the first place—he was bound over for a year.

He resigned, and departed so hurriedly that Saul Gregory's house was left empty for six weeks.

The trustees considered installing a married couple, but felt it was somehow out of keeping with the Saul Gregory ambience. When they got round to interviewing Mark Bickford, he was able to assure them that loneliness was no problem whatsoever. It was all a matter of temperament. For himself, he would welcome the isolation. Toller felt it only fair to quote to him the disturbed phrases of his predecessor's letter; but the remarks about not being good enough, and of the anger when *he* couldn't get through, incited rather than discouraged the younger man.

He...

Mark Bickford was confident the great quartet could be finished. Then perhaps there would be more. That liberated genius, working on in its fleshless world, communicating with someone sensitive enough to pick up the vibrations: what masterpieces might not yet be created?

The older man, niggling away at his own treatise, had been too set in his ways. He had been neither humble enough nor responsive enough. Things would be different this time.

But mortifyingly, as the weeks went on, there was no word.

Bickford sat motionless for hours, in the evenings, hardly daring to breathe. Time after time he thought he detected a faint shrill of melody; only to find it was the rise and fall of the Fenland wind. Time after time he drowsed off by the fireside and then jerked awake afraid that the trailing thread of a dream might have been a message which he had just failed to grasp.

Not good enough ... had the judgment already been passed on him?

Reverently he took the sheets of music from their glass case and pored over them. Other devotees had tried to finish the quartet, or written articles about it in the musical press. Perhaps by handling the originals, the very staves on which Saul Gregory had worked, he would catch a lingering reverberation. His predecessor had tried and failed. But if he cleared his mind of every other thought, let it see and hear only that strange, ethereal counterpoint over and over again until the moment came when he would go on hearing it after the notes on the staves finished ... surely he could bring the work to the conclusion Saul Gregory had planned?

Silence.

He went out walking as Gregory had done, averting his eyes from the distant silo and trying not to hear the puttering of tractors riding the rims of the vast fields. Several times he dawdled over the stretch of path where the ashes had been scattered more than a quarter of a century ago. Once—just once—he thought he heard a dry, derisive laugh. But it must have been a sudden, wind-whipped plop of water against the dyke wall.

On a bright day in high summer he followed the dyke itself to Three Waterings. He was about to turn back, realising that the lock gate and the pool beside the tributary lode were new since Gregory's day, when he saw a small figure crossing the gate and slithering down towards the water. Idle curiosity held him for a moment, watching the boy drag off his clothes and throw them carelessly aside before splashing into the pool. He swam from one side to the other and then back again, unperturbed by the disintegrating verge of green scum.

There was the smell of dry, dusty earth, and heat from the woodwork and oily metal of the lock gate; a tang of brackish water, and grass turning papery brown under the sun.

Abruptly the boy floundered and went below the surface. He reappeared, gasping and shaking his head. Then he struck out more vigorously, churning up the pool, lashing himself madly from one bank to the other. It looked as though he was trying to shout something, to protest. At last he grabbed a tuft of grass and hauled himself out of the water. Clutching his towel and dabbing at himself, he glared accusingly at Bickford.

'What d'you want to let *him* loose for?'

Bickford slid a couple of steps down the slope. 'I'm afraid I don't know what you—'

'Him. The one you brought with you.'

'I've been on my own all morning.'

'He wouldn't have come this far on his own.' The boy towelled his head, then shivered in the sunlight. 'He was ... right inside me. Making me swim, making me ... Right inside, like part of me.'

'Who? Who was?'

Bickford exultantly knew the answer, but wanted to hear it said out loud.

The boy reached for his shirt. 'Who d'you think?'

'Tell me,' Bickford insisted. 'Tell me.' Say it, he silently implored. 'Does this happen often? To you—and other people?'

He was too eager. He had shown too much. The boy was more alarmed by him, now, than by what had possessed him a few minutes ago. He dragged his trousers on. 'It was just a feeling.'

'Is this the first time? Or—'

'Funny old sort of day.'

The boy hadn't done up all his buttons, he hadn't dried his feet and legs properly before dragging socks and shoes on. He was in a hurry to be away.

'*Who?*' Bickford cried.

The kid was scrambling off up the slope. 'Well, he's with you, isn't he? You're the one should know.'

When Bickford was alone, he stood quite still and waited for some intimation that in fact he was not alone. Once, very carefully, he looked over his shoulder. There was a shimmer in the air—but it was only the heat of the day.

He listened. And heard only the whispering of grass and water, and the fading glissando of a jet plane far away across the sky.

Slowly he walked home.

As he approached the house another figure came to life in the dazzling landscape. Their paths converged. She was following the edge of a field, walking towards the village from a farm cottage set below the level of the road half a mile away. He was on the dyke when she crossed it and went down the path, slowing and glancing back at him.

She had bold brown eyes, and there was a lazy arrogance in her walk. The top button of her check shirt was undone. Sweat glistened on her throat and forehead.

'Good morning,' he said.

Her eyes widened, as though she unexpectedly recognised him; or recognised his voice. She stopped and smiled warily, almost ready to break into a laugh—as if she had reason to taunt him with something, but was afraid to risk it.

Then she looked away and hurried on towards the village.

In the late afternoon he had a phone call from Edwin Toller, who suggested coming down to see how things were going. They had some estimates for the car park and for tidying up the fencing. And there was a question of advertising in some tourist brochures.

And, thought Mark Bickford wryly, the question of whether I'm feeling the strain, and whether I'm likely to do anything silly, here all on my own.

He thought of the girl he had passed this morning. And there was that crackling laugh again, instantly suppressed. Nothing but old woodwork in the house, creaking and settling.

Toller arrived at noon and took him to lunch in Ely. The clatter of traffic and the bustle of people going in and out of the shops were disconcerting. He felt frightened, not so much of the unaccustomed noise as of the possibility that he would lose touch with Saul Gregory—for he was sure, now, that Gregory had been very close, had perhaps been just on the verge of speaking.

Back in the house, Toller took a parcel from his case and unwrapped a small bronze statuette. It was the figure of a slender, blandly faceless creature playing the lyre. He set it on the mantelpiece in Gregory's study, not far from the portrait of his parents, and stood back to survey it.

'From the Swabian Society for the Advancement of Experimental Sonority,' he said. 'Awarded posthumously to Saul Gregory.'

'They're catching up,' said Bickford approvingly.

Toller folded his arms and contemplated the room. A faint line of puzzlement deepened across his brow. He unfolded his arms, put out his right hand; and stopped it.

'No.' It was dragged out of him, a plea to someone unseen.

Bickford tensed. He demanded to hear. It was unfair, monstrously unfair that he should be shut out.

He said: 'What is it? What's happening?'

As though of its own accord Toller's right hand reached out again. It took the statuette from the mantelpiece and calculatingly, deliberately hurled it across the room.

Toller said: 'He doesn't like it there. Doesn't want it.'

Bickford found himself shaking uncontrollably. 'You're in contact! He's ... getting through.'

Toller paced across the room in a trance. He picked up the statuette and came back towards the fireplace. He looked at the framed oval portrait of Gregory's mother and father; and, raising the bronze figure above his head, pounded it into the glass. A flying sliver cut his cheek, but he ignored it. The statuette went on smashing and raking the picture until the yellowing photograph and its mount were slashed and buckled into an unrecognisable pulp.

'Always wanted to do that.' The laugh was loud and unmistakable this time. 'Always wanted to.'

Toller stood rigid for one more moment, then his arm fell to his side and the statuette thudded to the floor.

Bickford said: 'Tell me—'

'Why did I do that?' It was Toller himself again, Toller shaken, Toller appalled, backing away from the mess.

'He made you!' cried Bickford jealously. 'It was him, wasn't it?'

Toller stared. 'You've had it too, then?'

'No. Not me. Why not me?'

Toller began clumsily to tidy up the pieces, babbling as he did so. He must have had a brainstorm, it had been a hot day, he wasn't himself, couldn't make it out. There was something about the house. Not safe. Must be off. 'And you'd do better to come with me. Get out while you can.' He hardly heard Bickford's refusal, but went on to plead that the other trustees mustn't hear about this, that he would find some explanation for the shattered picture.

'Must be off. Look, do come with me. I'll see your salary's continued until we—well, decide what to do. Square it with the others. For your own sake, come with me now.'

All Bickford wanted was for Toller to go and leave him in the silence that was quiveringly ready to cease being silence. He was impatient for this blundering intruder to be off the premises.

'He's never come through to me'—he couldn't help blurting it out again as Toller got into his car.

'Maybe,' said Toller shakily, 'he's saving you for ... something special.'

Bickford went back indoors and sat down to wait.

As twilight crept in from the vast horizon he took the sheets of music out again and stared at the last few bars, where they petered out into tantalising nothingness.

He waited. And at last it came. Came as a derisive sigh, not in his ear but within his head.

'Oh, all right. But it's a waste of time.'

Behind the sneer he heard something else. Heard four distinct strands of sound, weaving and blending, running together and coming apart in a pattern that no one but Saul Gregory could ever have devised.

'Wait,' he said aloud, trying to retain his sense of the oneness of it while scribbling one line, desperately jotting a note here, a bass phrase there to keep him on the track.

But the music ran ahead of him. It was greater than he could ever have imagined; and it would not wait for him.

'Please—please give me time.'

It was becoming a grotesque cacophony. He lost his grip even on the treble line, and began to sob. And the music was overwhelmed by a roar of contempt, and a voice was shouting, 'Why bother, why bother? All the time I wasted—the years I wasted. Wasted.'

His own hands were picking up the sheets and tearing them across, then tearing them again, halving and quartering and finally ripping corners off and tossing them madly to all corners of the room. He sobbed with horror at what he was doing, but at the same time there was something within him rocking with uncontrollable joy.

When the manuscript sheets had been reduced to confetti, he waited. There was more to come. That much he knew.

He found himself on his feet. It was a cool evening, after the heat of the day, but he did not take a coat with him when he went out.

Conversation in the pub sagged and then built up again as he entered the bar. He had no idea what he ordered, but it was soon gone. And there was another; and another. The landlord looked at him dubiously. 'All right, sir? Getting on all right?' Another one, and wasn't he trying to sing a song into the face of an old mole-catcher? 'Time, gentlemen, please'—and he was arguing with someone, and they were making a dour joke of it and he was laughing himself silly.

It was much colder on the homeward way, but he went on laughing.

'So that's what it feels like!'

He wanted to be sick, but still it was so funny. Better than spending your life cooped up struggling to express what no one wished to hear. Better to be warm, and cold, and strong and weak; better to know what it was like to be drunk and to vomit in a ditch than never to have breathed.

Against the skyline there was a shadow. It drifted to one side as he lurched along the last stretch of path before his own rickety gate.

Even in the darkness he knew who it was.

He sensed her breathing.

'Go on,' said the chuckling voice alongside his reeling mind.

No. He tried to say it decisively, but it was only a thought. And again the stronger voice urged him on.

It was the same girl. He knew it, ought to have known it from the way she glanced at him yesterday morning. The girl who had been assaulted by that older man, wrenched from his pathetic treatise on atonality and driven out to seek her.

'Go *on*.'

He felt the mounting appetite, the dead man's greed for what he had denied himself in life. He fought against it. And Saul Gregory raged. *He gets very angry when he can't get through.* Desperately Bickford clung to a thread of music, as though holding out a charm to drive off an evil spirit. Gregory's furious derision resonated through him, as Gregory's music had obstinately refused to do.

His eyes were growing used to the shadows below the dyke. He saw the girl's eyes faintly, gleaming and watchful. She was breathing hard, and he knew with a knowledge not his own that she was scared and greedy at the same time—a greed that answered Gregory's.

'No,' he shouted.

'You fool,' raged Gregory. 'You're no use. No use at all, damn you.'

The beam of a torch stabbed out from somewhere behind him. Footsteps quickened along the path. His throat went dry and he thought of another accusation, another magisterial denunciation. He broke into a run, and went past the girl, but a man came on even faster, and there was a hand on his shoulder spinning him round.

It was a young man he had seen in the pub. From one

of the neighbouring farms, he thought. 'Charlie, it's all right,' the girl was saying huskily. The man shook Bickford and said: 'Just keep your hands off her, y'hear me?'

'Let go of me. I—'

'We had enough of that last time. The other one. If *you* start, by God, I'm warning you—'

'I was simply walking home from the inn.'

'Charlie, it's all right. Honest.'

'And what were you waiting here for, anyway?' He turned on her.

'For you, like you said.'

'Yes, well.'

Bickford pulled himself free. Still there was this insatiable clamour for the girl in his head and, shamingly, throughout his body.

'Just stay away from her, all right?' growled Charlie.

Bickford stumbled on, through the gate and up to the front door. He fought against the screaming demand to turn round and knock the young man aside and get his hands on the girl.

The door closed behind him.

And he felt the invading spirit, the otherness he had so long sought, draining away out of him.

'No use'—a last derisive cry racing off into the night—'no use to me at all.'

He slumped into a chair. Now the sickness really gripped him. He waited for the room to stop going round before pushing himself dizzily upright and staggering towards the bathroom.

When it was over, he was utterly empty. Empty of everything. The throbbing in his head was pain, not music.

He would write to Edwin Toller in the morning.

Or telephone him now; right now.

The girl screamed.

It was a sound so piercing, so animal in its agony, that his stomach contracted and he would have been sick again if there had been any sickness left in him. He groped for the door and opened it, letting the light flood out.

She let out another cry, as if calling a blurred name, and then dropped into a steady whimpering. Of pain or of unendurable pleasure, he couldn't tell.

Bickford tried to steel himself to go out down the dwindling river of light.

After a moment Charlie appeared at the end of the path. His face was slashed by a set grin.

Bickford said: 'What have you done to her?'

'Why don't you go to bed?' said Charlie in a voice that was no longer Charlie's.

'That girl—'

'She's fine. She's happy. Which is more than you'd ever be able to make her.'

'Clear off,' said Bickford. 'Go away, before I—'

'Before you do what?'

'Go away.'

'From my own house?'

'Charlie,' the girl called faintly, 'who are you talking to?'

Charlie advanced slowly towards the door, his face sharpening as it came fully into the light. He looked puzzled, putting one foot hypnotically in front of the other until he had reached Bickford. His eyes begged an answer; but the grin was set and remorseless.

Bickford, too late, tried to close the door. Charlie's right hand smacked out and held it open.

He said: 'I don't think you're right for this place. You won't do at all, my boy. Wasted too much time. No use to me. Can't bear any more waste. Not any more.'

'Charlie,' said Bickford desperately, 'don't listen to him.'

'I don't like being let down. Surely somebody mentioned that to you?'

Bickford lashed out with his fist but was pushed with contemptuous ease into the room. The voice went on:

'You'll never learn, not where you are. Perhaps if you came over to this side ...'

One hand ran like a spider up Bickford's arm and settled on his throat.

'You can't...'

'Another experience I've never had. Dying, yes. But not killing. So many things I never dared to try when I was alive.'

The other hand came up and clamped into place.

'No,' choked Bickford. And 'No,' clamoured Charlie's wide, terrified eyes; but Charlie's hands continued to tighten on Bickford's throat, and the derisive roaring in Bickford's head throbbed up to an intolerable pitch beyond which there must, soon, be merciful silence.

Or—it was his last anguished thought—would there be not silence but Saul Gregory's laughter, taunting him with all that he, too, had missed in life?

GILES GORDON

Crampton Manor

The front door bell rang.

Mrs Florence Humphreys was immediately aware of the fact, and began to move across the living-room. After she had taken three or four steps, she stopped. The bell was still ringing. There was thus something insistent about it, a sense of foreboding. Did whoever was ringing assume there was no one in the house? But why then were they ringing at all? Or did they think that whoever was at home was deaf? If they had known Mrs Humphreys, they would have known that her hearing was excellent, if anything better than it had been when she was considerably younger. Certainly no visitors were expected, which didn't necessarily mean that there wouldn't be callers.

The bell continued to ring.

'All right, all right, I'm coming,' Mrs Humphreys muttered to herself, though she didn't move from where she was standing. The cheek of it, ringing the bell like that. She'd a good mind not to answer. Maybe they'd go away —but maybe they wouldn't; then she'd be the worse off. At once she was struck with remorse for having such a thought. Perhaps some unfortunate had casually placed his finger on the bell, and the instrument had jammed.

How embarrassed he would be as desperately, despairingly he attempted to put an end to what he had accidentally begun. But she knew this was unlikely. The bell had not gone wrong since she had been living in Crampton Manor, and that was before she married Herbert, her second husband. If it hadn't gone wrong in thirty-two years, why should it go wrong now?

The noise was not actually getting any louder. She just had the impression that it was. It was surging about her head with the compulsion and inevitability of a whirlpool, it was spinning around behind her eyes, boring into the sockets like a catherine wheel setting fire to the universe and refusing to burn out. She raised her hands to her ears, to blot out the ringing, to expel it from her presence, as if that act of silencing it in her own frame would destroy it in the exterior world. The noise throbbed through the palms of her hands, pierced her ears even more urgently than had previously been the case.

She dropped her hands down. It was still ringing. *It was still ringing.* Whoever was standing outside the front door must have placed his finger on the bell, pressed the instrument and held his hand there, causing the sound to continue and continue, to grow, to grow, to grow. Florence Humphreys wondered whether if, at this moment, she hurled open the front door, the person ringing wouldn't go on ringing, having become so used to the activity.

She couldn't stand there any longer, in the centre of her living-room. She had to do something, to act, as otherwise the ringing could and might go on for ever. With the back of her right hand she touched her forehead, then walked quickly across the room, which was on the first floor of the large, Victorian-restored Elizabethan house. She had only to take eight or nine steps to the window, but by the time she was there she was panting, unaware that her breath was not coming to her easily. She hardly dared to look out to see who it was—assuming it was someone she would recognise. What if it was Edward, back again? If he could appear behind her in the mirror, through her, he could surely appear at the front door? But the thought was foolish: he would use his own key. The lock hadn't been altered, not during all those years.

As she lowered her head to look down, she closed her eyes. She wasn't praying, she was afraid. Her eyes were shut for only a few seconds, but during those seconds the noise seemed to be inflating her head, blowing it up like a balloon being filled with air. As her head seemed to be on the point of exploding, she looked.

There was no one there.

Whoever had been so anxious to attract attention was not visible. Whoever had pressed the bell was not there, was not in sight. And yet the bell was still ringing. Soon the very stones of the house would cry out, 'Stop, stop!' Mrs Humphreys couldn't take her eyes away from the doorstep. She was certain there was someone there, that if she looked for long enough, if she concentrated sufficiently on the invisible presence, whoever it was would be revealed to her. He must still be there, the bell was still ringing.

She wiggled the fingers of both hands. They were clammy, sweaty. Then she thought the ring of the bell, its cacophony, was ascending the staircase; that somehow it had poured through the keyhole and was taking over the house. It was now in the landing, outside the living-room. What would she do when it came through the door, began to go for her? She couldn't look round, she didn't dare look round. She couldn't envisage its three dimensional presence.

This sensation gave way to another. While still looking at the doorstep, she wondered if there was a solitary finger pressing the bell, the possessor of the finger having been divorced from it. If it had been neatly, cleanly severed she wouldn't mind too much, though it might be distasteful; but if it was dripping with blood, staining the doorstep, then more than a bucket of soap and water might be required to wash away the memory. But the doorstep was not stained with blood, wet or dry; not that she could see, or imagine. Besides, would a single finger have sufficient strength when not part of a hand, part of an arm, part of a body to remain for so long pressing a bell?

She lifted her head up slightly, slowly. Her eyes stared at the bell itself. They seemed to have lost the ability to blink. She could see the button of the bell clearly as it was a bright, crisp October afternoon. No one was touching the bell. Nothing was touching the bell. Not anything nor anyone visible. Please, bell, stop, she thought to herself. Please.

She wasn't becoming used to the noise, but she was— she acknowledged with extreme irritation—becoming able to cope with it, to absorb it into her system if not to accept it. In a flicker of time, a flash of her mind, she imagined the remainder of her life—however few years were left to her—being spent against the noise of the bell: it would accompany her permanently, awake or asleep. The thought appalled her but she accepted that it was possible, that it could happen. She moved her head away from the bell, from the doorstep. She was breathing more regularly now, her hands were no clammier than they had been a few minutes ago.

Fifteen feet to the right of the front door was a pantechnicon. It was motionless and could have been there for days. There was no driver to be seen, nor anyone else. Mrs Humphreys couldn't hear if its engine was running.

As she thought this, she frowned. She *was* growing senile: she couldn't have heard the Concorde had it flown above the house at this moment. She wouldn't have heard Vesuvius erupt had she been standing on its crater. She wouldn't have noticed the explosion of the bomb destroying Hiroshima. The front door bell of her house was the only noise there was, the only noise there could be. All else was silence.

She looked carefully at the pantechnicon. Orange in colour, it had no markings. There was no indication as to who owned it, which she knew to be illegal. Herbert hadn't been manager of an insurance company all these years without her picking up a few of the tricks of the trade, as he chose to put it. Normally it wouldn't have worried her, though it probably would have occurred to her, but the lorry was in her garden, on her drive, in front of her house—and the front door bell was ringing, *still* ringing.

If the pantechnicon was there, and it *was* (and recollection made certain that it hadn't been two hours ago), someone must have driven it there. Was the driver in the back, searching for something, moving gigantic packages, clambering over grand pianos or clocks? The back of the vehicle seemed to be locked. Certainly it was shut, so that seemed unlikely. She looked back from the pantechnicon, above it and beyond it. She searched with her sharp eyes the expanse of the garden— there was probably an acre and a half in front of her, though it trailed away out of sight near to the gate. But as far as she could see, there was no one there, no one skulking or walking around.

The clang, the yowl, the screech, the din of the bell. Her head was throbbing. She felt as if she were bouncing up and down, as if suffering from what she imagined to be the sensations of electric shock treatment. Then she remembered what happened to Edward. The same must not happen to her. The comparison would not have occurred to her a few years ago but now, well, other people did seem to be getting younger. She had survived more summers, more Christmasses than most people. She had no immortal longings—far from it: this was why she took such pride in her appearance, why Herbert bought her a new wig twice a year, why most people who knew no better thought she was ten or even twelve years younger than she was. It was those ten or twelve years that worried her, that made her wish sometimes that she had spent them differently.

Her eyes glazed over, her recollections of the reluctant past mingling with fear of the present. She turned round, away from the window, facing into the living-room. She darted her eyes around it. Anybody could have come in without her hearing. Anybody could have been crouching behind one of the high-backed chairs, or at the side of the huge oak bookcase. Herbert was hopeless in this kind of situation. Practical and down to earth in his work, he didn't see why he should be at home. Anyway, he wasn't here, which bore out her contention. Of all things, he'd gone into town to see old Parsons about his will. He'd drawn it up only a couple of years ago, and now he wanted to change it. She'd told him from the beginning that she would outlive him—nothing unusual in that situation—but only now, or so she surmised, would his vanity allow him to accept the likelihood. Had Edward been here, had it been in his time, the servant would have gone to the door long since, and somehow have stopped the bell ringing. In those days they knew how to do things like that, practical, useful things. But Edward was not here, and no servant would stay in a house like this, miles away from anywhere.

The noise. The noise. The noise. The noise.

The loud, shrill, unmusical, relentless bell.

Did it have a new battery, or would it wear out soon? She'd no idea. Edward would have known ... She hadn't thought of him for a year or two in this kind of way, of how he'd have handled a particular situation.

She looked into the mirror on the wall opposite the fireplace, near to the door. Strange, she'd no recollection of having moved from the window, across the room. Trying to concentrate on the steps she must have taken seconds ago, she couldn't recall them, they were not stored in her memory. And yet she had moved from the window to the mirror. In the mirror, her eyes. She looked at them, at herself. Light was beginning, just beginning, to seep from the sky. Not everything seen in the mirror was defined as it would have been when the sun was at its zenith. Her eyes, she looked at her eyes. The sound of the bell, the ringing, bored through them, into the mirror, out of the mirror.

All she had to do, all you have to do, is to leave this room, walk across the landing, down the staircase, take twelve or thirteen steps through the hall, open the door. There is nobody else in the house, in all its rooms. There will be nobody outside the door. The pantechnicon is a figment of your imagination—or if it is there there's a perfectly straightforward reason for its presence. The bell is not ringing.

All the while looking in the mirror, she thought of something. Anything to keep her mind from the present, from what was happening. Something occurred. A memory, a vision, a moment of intuition, of making connections that usually mightn't be made. Of having something pushed into her mind. My God, she thought. A hand went up to her neck, she looked in the mirror, saw it. My God, she thought. Fingers fluttered in front of her lips, and her lips were moving. *That* was why Edward died: the bell hadn't rung, and he'd been the only one asleep. Had it rung it would have woken him and he'd have escaped. But it didn't ring, it couldn't have rung— that must have been the explanation. Why had nobody thought of that?

Her eyes grew bigger, larger. There was more and more of them. They would pop out, fall out, like immense boulders crashing over a clifftop. My God, she thought, and the palm of a hand flattened in front of her face, stifling her mouth. The man behind her, to her left, was not Edward. He was someone she hadn't seen before. Young. Thirty. Fair hair. Reminiscent of that miniature by Hilliard, the one there was a reproduction of in the hall. He was smiling, slightly, ever so slightly, and his head was bent forward, at his shoulders, as if greeting her, acknowledging her presence. As if it was his house, as if he was the host and she was the visitor.

She opened her mouth wide, having clasped her hands in front of her. Her tongue wobbled about from side to side, her head rolled. Her tongue felt for something outside her mouth, again and again, but seemed not to find it. No sound came out of her mouth, or if it did it was enveloped by the sound of the bell. Because her scream was noiseless, it was no less a scream.

She faced the man, but the man was not there. She had turned round. The mirror was behind her. The man was not there. Neither, of course, was Edward who sometimes, in moments of extreme contentment or stress, was revealed by the mirror, through the mirror. In front of her was the portrait of one of somebody's ancestors, maybe hers, which had, longer than she had lived in the house, hung on the wall, next to the fireplace. He was dressed in Elizabethan clothes, was aged about thirty, smiled slightly, with his head bent forward as if about to say something to whoever was admiring his portrait.

Mrs Humphreys frowned, looked away from the painting. She was shaking and felt hot. No, cold. No, hot. She must take a grip of herself. The bell was still ringing —of course it was.

Was the pantechnicon there? She walked to the window, looked out. It was.

But something was wrong. Something new was wrong. There was a hollow, ringing sound in her ears, like waves crashing on rocks, or booted feet echoing down cloisters. In an instant she realised what it was. Her ears were going to burst—they had burst.

The bell had stopped ringing.

She breathed in deeply, held her breath, expelled it. She could hear it. The bell had stopped.

She looked at it, the bell press, out of the window, through the glass. It was as it always was.

She smiled to herself, and began to walk away from the window. She listened, for a sound, for a sign—of anything.

The phone began to ring.

She moved hurriedly to the instrument which was situated on an occasional table by one of the two armchairs by the fireplace. She stretched out her hand to pick up the receiver, placed it against her ear. She was far from certain that she'd be able to hear any sound other than the door bell ringing, the memory of the bell, the echo, the ripples.

'Hallo?' she said.

'Is that Ryesmuir 69?'

'Yes. Yes, it is.' Normally she gave the number when answering the phone. 'Who is it?'

'Oh, I'm phoning about the advertisement.'

Mrs Humphreys wondered what Herbert had been up to now, then was sure there must have been a mistake.

'Hallo? Are you there?' the caller asked.

'Yes, I'm here. I think . . .' Her voice trailed away.

'I'm phoning about the advertisement. You know, in the *Journal*. Your advertisement.'

'I'm sorry. There seems to have been a mistake. We haven't placed an advertisement.'

'But you are selling your house?'

'No! Why should we be?'

'But you've advertised it?'

'No, of course we haven't. My husband and I live here . . .' There was a loud knock. Mrs Humphreys knew it was the back door. 'Look, I'm very sorry. There's someone at the door. There's no one else here, I'll have to let them in.'

'I really don't understand this. Is your house Crampton Manor?'

'Yes, it is.'

'Then it's for sale. It's advertised.'

'Look, I'm sorry, it's not for sale.'

'I've often passed your house, by car. Admired it from the road.'

'It isn't for sale,' she shouted; then more quietly, 'I should know, I live here. My husband and I own the house.'

'But Mrs Humphreys . . . ?'

'How do you know my name?'

There was a further knock on the door.

'It was given in the advertisement.'

'Well, I'm sorry, there's been some mistake. I must answer the door.'

She replaced the receiver in its cradle, not giving the man an opportunity to say or find out more. She hoped Herbert would bring home a copy of the *Journal*. He sometimes did. The door was banged on again, more insistently this time. She walked out of the living-room, through the house to the kitchen, where she unlocked the back door.

'Good afternoon, madam. We thought there'd be someone at home,' said one of the two men standing there.

Mrs Humphreys looked at them, completely bewildered. 'Have you come to read the gas meters? They usually send only one man.'

'No, no,' said the other man, laughing a little. 'We're not gas men. We've come for the furniture.'

'What furniture?' Mrs Humphreys almost screamed.

'Excuse me, dear, but are you the caretaker?'

'My husband and I live here. We own the house,' she said, sensing the words were familiar.

One of the men looked at her as if she were intentionally trying to provoke them:

'The new owner, or the old owner?'

'I will not be asked questions like that.'

'Lady, have you just moved into this house, or are you about to move out?'

'Do you mind telling me what's happening?' she asked, barely in control of her senses.

There was a pause. Both men obviously thought she was insane.

'Certainly, madam,' said one. 'We tried the front door, but the bell wouldn't ring. As the house is so big, we thought there must be another door, so here we are. There's no bell here that we can see, so we knocked. Three times. Then you came.' A slight pause. 'Would you rather we took it out by the back door, or the front door? It's all the same to us. We can bring the van round. We've parked it in front.'

Mrs Humphreys breathed deeply, looked closely at the faces of both men before answering. She was sure they were not playing a practical joke on her. Somehow they were here in error. There would be no point in being rude to them.

'I'm sorry,' said Mrs Humphreys, 'there's been a mistake. The furniture you're looking for is somewhere else.'

One of the men put a hand inside his jacket, and produced a heap of papers. He began to rifle through them, but soon stopped. He began to read, then said:

'This is Crampton Manor?'

'Yes, it is.'

'Well, then. We knew it was. Don't make mistakes of that kind. Anyway, it said so on the gate. And is your name Mrs Humphreys?'

'Yes, it is.'

'Look.' The man thrust the piece of paper in front of her eyes. Beneath her name, and Herbert's name, and the name of the house, was an inventory of their furniture, of their belongings. There were the armchairs in the living-room, and the elephant tusks, and the escritoire that his godfather had left Edward. There was even the portrait of the ancestor in the living-room. Mrs Humphreys looked up and down the list in amazement, bemused.

'And look, more on this sheet, and this,' said the man, holding them out to her. In response she handed the first sheet back to the man.

'It *is* our furniture,' she said. 'Most extraordinary. I can't understand it.'

The other man said: 'We don't make that kind of mistake. We don't get the wrong house.'

Mrs Humphreys ignored the remark and said to the other man:

'Where did you get that inventory?'

'Given it, we were. Back in the office.'

She looked from one man to the other, and back to the first again. The time had come for her to take control of the situation, to show who was in command.

'Gentlemen,' she said. 'I regret that your journey has been in vain. What it says there is correct, it is our furniture listed. But we haven't asked you or anyone else to remove it. We haven't sold this house. We aren't going to live anywhere else. I'm sorry you've been troubled. Good afternoon.'

'So you won't let us take it away?'

'No, of course not. I've told you so.'

'Come on, Bob. We'll have to leave it now.' And to Mrs Humphreys: 'We'll be back, madam. I'm sure we will. We don't make mistakes of this kind. Not with a full inventory.'

They turned away from the back door and began to walk round the house to where their van was parked. Mrs Humphreys closed the door, lent against it for half a minute. She was exhausted, worn out. She would make herself a cup of tea. Herbert should be home any minute now. He would be able to explain about the furniture, and that phone call. Then she thought that she didn't really want tea. She'd have a glass of brandy instead. Otherwise, she'd still be a shaking wreck when Herbert walked in.

Parsons, the solicitor, drew up in his Morris Oxford just after six o'clock. Presumably he'd been wearing black all day, hadn't returned home and donned it specially, before coming out to Crampton Manor. Mrs Humphreys had the front door open before Parsons had reached the doorstep, before he could ring the bell. She knew straightaway what had happened, though not the circumstances.

'In my office, sitting in front of my desk, just before he was going to sign the new will. We'd been going through it for an hour or so,' said the solicitor. 'Suddenly slumped across the desk. Not a movement, Mrs Humphreys. Not a twitch.'

'I'm sure you did all you could, Mr Parsons,' she said.

She hadn't known that he hadn't paid his taxes for so long, though she didn't mind having to sell the house and its furniture. It would have been much too big for her to have lived in on her own. It had really been much too large for the pair of them.

What was curious though was that the man she had seen in the mirror (at the exact time Herbert had died, it was later established), the man standing behind her, was the man who bought Crampton Manor. His name was Grierson, and he was new to the district. He viewed the house three weeks after Herbert's death, and said that he felt he'd always lived in it, it seemed so familiar.

JOHN MOAT

Chope's Retreat

Chope turned his back on the sun, and started into the valley. There was eagerness about him, the excitement of a native returning. His compact figure seemed to relish the weight of his rucksack as he strode, almost skipped there was such spring in him, in time to his whistling of 'Hallaballoo'. Or else he whistled in time to the stride and ring of the iron heel-bits of his boots on the steep broken lane. As he whistled his breath fizzed on the still, frozen air.

He was entering the valley from the South. Only a few yards the liquid winter sun shone on his back before he left it behind him, ditched over the hill. Sunk between high hedges of hazel and blackthorn, the lane, as if to cope better with the steep descent, fetched west across the hill-face towards the sea, now glimpsed slate-grey through the cleft of the valley. In the banks there was yet some frosted green, moss and fern and on the briar a few failing leaves, but mostly now it was the brown of old leaf and the ochre of the fallen sedge. The air had been crisp in the sun; here it was weighted with the tang of earth, and smelt damp. Chope stopped. On tip-toe he looked down the valley at the sea, and changed to whistling between his teeth.

Just then a goldcrest with an indignant cheep, flicked

into the hedge beside him. Immediately there was a flurry and a mob of tits, blue and longtail, invaded the lane, scolding one another and jumping from twig to twig with great show of haste and purpose. Chope watched them keenly, his brown eyes bright with attention, his lower lip stretched taut against his bottom teeth, and his head alive to match the movements of the birds. One flew almost at his head and he ducked and then swung round to follow its flight up the hill and over the hedge. He was about to turn back, but hesitated.

Twenty yards above, in the gateway he had just passed, the man was leaning on the five-bar, gazing inland over the fields away to the moor. Maybe he had just climbed out of the field, but this was unlikely since about his figure there was the heaviness and inertia of someone who has been still a long time. As Chope watched, the man pushed back with his forearms on the top bar of the gate, and stood up stiffly. He seemed to chew on the air for a moment. Then he looked down the lane. Chope, over his shoulder, nodded to him. But the man didn't notice, or affected not to. He turned about, put his hands in the pockets of his old blue macintosh and spat viciously into the hedge. He then walked heavily away up the hill, his wellingtons, the top six inches turned down, dragging the gravel.

Near the bottom of the hill, where at last it was sheltered from the prevailing South-westerly gales, Chope reached the first stunted trees of the oak-wood, and at the same moment came on the sound of the stream. Even from here the stream's clatter was loud, and it was so clear that it set the stillness of the wood in strange relief. The trees seemed curiously still, every twisted branch and twig somehow alert in the clear winter light. One magpie, stark white and black, falling away through the top branches, appeared by its movement to reduce the definition of the entire wood—until it had flown out of sight, and then the intense stillness was reasserted. Where the ivy grew on the pitted grey trunks its life was green and startling. A blackbird made great racket as it hopped here and there through the frozen leaves. But this was apart from the noise of the stream.

The hill was steepest at its very foot, and here Chope allowed himself to run the last yards down, and then up and on to the hump of the small bridge. He stood for a time, one foot on the low parapet, looking down through the coils of his breath at the rush of grey water. Then he stood up and was about to leave the bridge when suddenly he glanced back up the lane, the movement, to judge by his expression, being not a response but merely some small involuntary reflex.

The cottage was immediately on the right and opposite to the entrance to the farm. Chope, as he bent to try to solve the secret of the old wooden gate, was whistling again, softly between his teeth. Finally he had to lift back the gate, the lower hinge having rusted through. He left it propped open, and had started up the path when he stopped and looked down in apparent surprise at the pitting of heavy bootmarks in the mud. He then looked through the small orchard of bent and grey-bearded apple trees, and across the unkept lawn to the stone and slated cottage. The surrounds to the windows had recently been painted white. Clearly the place was shut up, and yet there was to it the same staring quality of the ivy in the wood. Its stillness and vacancy had extraordinary presence, as if in some way occupied.

From across the lane in the farm came the sound of a churn dragged over cobbles, and the ring of lively whistling. Chope smiled. He turned and made his way back out into and across the lane and into the yard of the farm. The door to the kitchen was standing open. He put his head round. The woodfire in the Rayburn whined and hissed, but the warm kitchen was empty. Chope looked round the yard and then walked its length to the door of the shippon. The heat of cows drifted out from the dark, and yet when Chope entered he found it empty. In a corner, new piled, was a heap of steaming straw and dung. Two large brown chickens were raking it with their toes and pecking distastefully whatever life they uncovered. They stopped to take stock of Chope. They eyed him broodily, and one gave a subdued croak of alarm.

Chope went out again into the yard. He looked down the valley at the meadows that skirted the right bank of the stream. There was no sign of the farmer, or of the cows. As he turned back he faltered a moment. A man and a woman were leaning against the wall of the house. They were not looking at Chope but staring with exaggerated fixedness across the yard at the base of the shippon. Yet it seemed certain it was he that held their attention. Both were wearing grimed trench-coats and trousers, old, well-darned, the woman's too big, and old leather boots. Their hair, dark and long to their shoulders, looked filthy too. The man had an old blue woollen skull-cap on the back of his head. Their features were strangely flaccid and heavy; their eyes were dark, and both had the same complexion, very pale with what seemed a bluish luminosity to it, particularly the man's around the rough stubble on his chin.

Chope looked at them, as if hoping to catch the eye of one before asking some question. But they didn't look up, and in the end, walking back up the yard, he passed through the line of their gaze. They never moved. At least not until they were virtually out of Chope's vision, then they raised their heads, looked at each other, and smiled.

Chope again set out up the path to the cottage, and again at the same point he stopped and looked about him. The noise of the stream was suddenly extraordinary, like a rope of sound down the valley, very loud, very distinct. It was somehow apparent that the pronounced definition and the stillness were a response.

There was another sound too, quite apart. Chope searched for it. A hundred starlings were busy on the lawn, stabbing and bickering. As they moved, their oily plumage caught colour and flickered. When Chope continued up the path, suddenly, like one thought, they lit off and, in a black shifting cloud, whirred away over the winter trees.

Chope, as he crossed the narrow parapeted stone terrace between the cottage and the lawn, took a key from his pocket. He entered the small beamed and slated porch and then bent, apparently to examine the lock before he tried the key.

It required the strength of both his wrists to turn the key in the lock.

There were two rooms downstairs, a kitchen and a sitting-room. A staircase led up from the sitting-room to a small landing between two bedrooms, one end of which had been recently converted into a lavatory with washbasin. In each room the main window, wood-framed with lead-latticing, looked out down the valley, over the terrace and the lawn. One of the bedrooms was empty, and in the rest of the house there was little furniture and that old and mostly in need of repair: a chair and bed in the other bedroom, in the sitting-room a sofa in front of the large open fire and two armchairs, and in the kitchen a table, a stove and two cylinders of gas, and a small dresser which contained the few pans and bits of crockery. There were no curtains in any of the windows, and the entire cottage smelt damp, damp soot and masonry downstairs, and upstairs damp wood and plaster. At the back of the cottage there had once been a vegetable patch. This was now overgrown with gorse and young thorn and beyond that was the oak-wood.

Soon after his arrival Chope made two trips out into the silent oaks for firewood. In the valley the evening settled early. With the dusk a blackbird several times sounded its repetitive, strident alarm. Otherwise there was no movement apart from the cold emphatic sound of the stream.

Chope had trouble with the fire. The wood was sodden and the slow heavy smoke veered away from the damp chimney and into the room. At last he coaxed a small flicker of flame. But by the time he had lit the oil lamp and settled on the sofa to read, the flame was gone, its energy dwindled to a hiss and a dull failing issue of smoke. He read for a time and then went into the kitchen and heated some soup.

Some time in the night he woke suddenly. The window had rattled. He lifted his head fractionally from the old coat he was using as a pillow. The cottage was completely quiet, and outside there was no wind. However now, beyond the valley and quite apart from the steady wash of the stream, the sea was sounding. A swell must have risen because the waves broke in slow time; there was the crash and then after a few moments the drag of the pebbles back down the beach, and then before the next crash a considerable silence. Sometimes a large wave, tumbling its full length on to flat water, can create an explosion of air—it was possible that such a blast might have rattled the window.

He lay back, and pulled his sleeping-bag up to his ears.

Chope woke early, and dozed until it was light. He then struggled out of his sleeping-bag and went to the window. The day seemed warmer, but it was grey and still entirely without wind. The sea was calm again, or at least it could no longer be heard beyond the clatter of the stream. Chope, after looking around, leaned forward and opened the window. The way the stream's noise seemed to break into the room was quite startling. Chope's attention fixed on the lawn. There, coming from the orchard, was a line of heavy boot-prints. They appeared to end in the middle of the lawn. Whoever it was had probably come that far, stopped, and then retraced his steps.

From over at the farm came the untroubled sound of the farmer's wife calling the chickens for their corn.

After his breakfast he stopped indoors and read until mid-morning. He then took a jug from the kitchen and went over to the farm to fetch milk. He knocked on the kitchen door which was standing ajar. When there was no answer he looked in. As he did so a cat jumped down from the draining board beside the sink. It was black, with torn ears, presumably a tom. It arched and backed away from him, spitting. The room was cold. The oven door as usual was open, but the ashes were dead. Again he walked down to the shippon. It too was empty; the pile of straw and dung and the chickens were gone. As he walked back up the yard he whistled softly between his teeth. Once, as if he heard something behind him, he looked over his shoulder, and then more casually

about him. There was a watchfulness about the silent
house, and something in the shape of the yard seemed to
hold the sound of the stream and to give it an added
resonance.

On his way back up the path to the cottage he stopped
for a moment, as if to listen. He then left the path and
made his way through the stunted apple-trees on to the
lawn. For a time he stood looking down at the last of
the deep boot-prints. Somewhere nearby a blackbird had
started its insistent call of alarm, half cheep, half croak.
He looked up. A stocky figure in a long black PVC mac
and a brown cap, carrying an old rope in one hand,
was walking up the path. His head was down and he
appeared to be staring intently at the ground in front of
him. He disappeared round the back of the cottage. A
moment later came the snap of twigs, presumably as the
man forced his way over the bank into the oakwood.

Chope looked around the valley, somewhat hastily, and
then went indoors.

Early that afternoon he left the cottage. He walked
quickly down the path and then over the bridge and up
the lane. Some way up the hill he paused and looked
back. In the gloom at the bottom of the hill by the
bridge there stood three figures, dark in the distance.
They were apparently watching Chope climb the hill.
When he looked round they separated and went to the
parapets of the bridge, two to one side and one to the
other, and stood looking down into the water. Chope
continued up the hill, out of the valley.

Helped by a couple of lifts he made his way the fifteen
miles to the town. There he went into a number of
shops to restock his provisions. The day was still mild
and windless, but overcast with heavy brown clouds and

a drift of fine fret in from the sea. In the town, an old
port on an estuary whose channel was no longer dredged
for the shipping, there was little traffic, and few people
were about. Chope found his way into a narrow street
that had been set aside for pedestrians. He walked slowly,
looking into the shops on either side, and finally went into
a small green-grocers. He bought a cabbage and a few
apples.

Coming out from the shop he stopped on the step.
He appeared to experience some surprise, and looked
up and down the street almost as if he failed to recognise
where he was standing. The silence of the afternoon was
imposing, the whole town seemed strangely dormant. But
more strange was the imminent sound of the sea or,
since that was unlikely, a flooded stream; a thrashing
sound, not very loud, but seemingly very much to hand.
Something immediately across the road seemed to take
Chope's attention. When, after a few moments, he
walked away down the road he appeared pale and confused.

Opposite the greengrocer's was a tea-shop. At a table
in the window two men were sitting. There was through
the heat-misted window nothing clearly remarkable about
them, except both appeared dark and unshaven and
seemed to share a certain thickness of jowl. They both
wore heavy outdoor clothes. They evidently had finished
eating, and although they were not talking they were
looking at each other and appeared to be smiling.

It was dark when Chope returned to the cottage. With
kindling bought in the town he succeeded in lighting a
fire. He cooked himself supper, and then sat by the fire
and read.

As he was going to bed he heard a car come down the

hill and draw up at the farm. He stopped undressing and listened carefully. One of the car doors opened, and after a moment he heard above the noise of the engine the farmer's voice shouting a cheerful goodnight. A door slammed and a second later the car drove away.

Some time in the night Chope again woke with a start. On this occasion there had been no noise. And yet there was that shock to the silence which at night follows for instance the fall of a picture in a downstairs room. He raised himself on to one elbow and listened. From outside there came a sound which at first seemed that of a number of people whispering. But after a time it became clear that this was merely a trick of the night, and that the sound was the distant rasp of the sea. The drier weather of the last two days must have affected the level of the stream: tonight it was barely audible.

When Chope woke next morning there was already light in the valley. He lay on his back for a time with his hands behind his head. He stared up through the thin light at the ceiling and, from the way he moved his eyes, appeared to contrive some interest in the pattern of cracks in the plaster. At the same time he whistled absently between his teeth.

Suddenly he stopped whistling and looked towards the window. The day was still as before, except that a skein of gulls was going overhead, crying with a strange bitter fury. In some way the sound suggested there was menace in the day's stillness. When they had gone, pursued by their keening, away to the sea, they left the silence disturbed. It was now clear that the night's impression had been unreliable; the stream's sound might have receded a little, but it was still as sharp, as finely etched, and it was still as insistent.

He got up from the bed and went over to the window. He stood there for a time, his hands on his hips, staring down the valley. Then he yawned.

It was as he yawned he appeared to catch at his breath. The lawn, from end to end, was pitted with footprints. It looked as if people in boots had been dancing reels on the soft turf, or else had been playing some game like basket-ball.

He stayed in during the morning. He sat in the sofa beside a sluggish fire, reading and occasionally gazing vacantly out of the window. At around midday he went into the kitchen and had something to eat, and then he went out.

For a time he stood on the terrace, looking at the sky, apparently in two minds. The tops of the hills on either side of the valley were in steady cloud. There was the finest drizzle, felt on the face and in the lungs, but not visible. He turned, walked to the back of the cottage, followed a path between the gorse and thorn, and made his way over the bank into the woods.

Somewhere high above to the left a man shouted, and a moment later came the abrupt mutter of a chain-saw. But it was as if inside a cathedral a motor-bike was heard being started without: the sound entered, but was apart from the contained silence, or the sharp measure of the private ritual. In the sanctuary of the wood the stream sounded with two clear tones, the surface rush of the water, and an understrain, hollow and more musical. Chope picked his way carefully, as if to disturb as little as possible leaf and stick underfoot. He kept close to the stream, but as he went on the sides of the valley began to close in and to become steeper. At one point, as he was climbing to go round a dark and brilliant berried holly tree, the ground seemed to shift beneath him, and then took to the air. The woodcock never made a sound as it ghosted away between the trees. He shook his head, and smiled self-derisively. And as if on a whim, he looked about him, maybe to be sure no one had witnessed his nervousness.

Only one of the four was actually watching, looking down over his shoulder from the shelf or small dingle in which, some thirty yards above, they were standing. They stood more or less side by side facing the hill, and appeared occupied with some activity in the dingle. There was a certain uniformity about them, a heaviness in their stance, or else in their mud-spattered black oil-skins or heavy overcoats. But it was also in their complexions. These were pale and, though flaccid and greyish, seemed to glow with a blue luminosity. All four were listening, but only the one, his face set with malicious humour, was watching Chope. As Chope's eyes met his he looked away. It was just noticeable that he nudged with his elbow the man on his left, and at the same time he hunched his shoulders and raised his right hand to his face as if forcibly to restrain rude laughter. Momentarily the palm of his hand before his face was visible to Chope, and in the wood's grey stillness it appeared wet and to scream the colour of blood. The stream's splatter burst in the valley, almost as if it sounded in the brain. At the same time the air was filled with a sweet, rancid stench, like a tannery on a hot day; and from the dingle came a scrambling, and a moan or croak of an animal's terror.

Chope didn't quicken his pace, and although he did not look back, more than once he started and his eyes raced left or right to some shadow or movement on the ground. After a few hundred yards the sides of the stream became sheer to form a narrow gorge and he was forced to climb away on to a small plateau. Here the wood ended and opened into a field. Some ten feet into the field there was a large fallen branch. He went to this and with his back to the wood sat on one of the limbs, staring inland east to the upland of moors. He sat quite still, his shoulders bent forward a little, as if from the cold. When the twig snapped in the wood behind him, he didn't start, but after a moment he turned his head slowly. The figure, dark in the wood's gathering twilight, moved from the cover of a tree and with impressive stealth retraced the path that Chope had taken.

Chope stood up. He strode quickly inland, across two fields, until he came to a track. He followed this south, and then by means of a long detour made his way back and at dusk entered the valley as usual by the steep lane. He allowed himself to run the last yards down, and then up on to the hump of the small bridge. He stood for a time, one foot on the low parapet, looking down through the coils of his breath at the rush of grey water. Then, as if on a sudden determination, he strode from the bridge and into the farmyard. He paused outside the open door to the kitchen. The house was dark. More than anywhere else it was here there was something maddening about the constant thrash of the stream. He looked in at the door. After a moment he backed away, his face drawn, almost devoid of expression. Not only was the kitchen empty and the Rayburn cold, but just visible in the last light were the few remaining pieces of furniture, upturned and broken. Near the ceiling the damp paper was hanging away from the walls. There was something alive, scuttling in the cabinet under the sink. The place was not merely deserted, it felt it had not been lived in for a long time.

Chope glanced down the dark yard to the lifeless shippon, and then turned and walked quickly across the road and up the path to the cottage.

That night he lay awake for a long time; till well after midnight. The valley was filled with the deafening sound, not of the stream, but of the boom and drumming of the sea.

He slept late the next morning. As soon as he opened his eyes he sat up. He looked at his watch. It was after nine. Then he looked over to the window. He narrowed his eyes, and appeared to be listening. Apart from the roar of the stream there was nothing—an occasional tick in the rafters, nothing else. He drew himself slowly from his sleeping-bag, stood up somewhat stiffly, massaged his hands one with the other, and then walked fast to the window.

There were certainly seven of them; maybe more. They were standing singly or in twos, or sat on the wall of the terrace—unmoving, and having, perhaps for their heavy mud-spattered and soiled clothes, a dark aspect to their stillness. Or perhaps it was something to do with the heaviness and pallor of their features, or perhaps simply with their measured patience. One at least was a woman, high cheek-bones and a wide thin mouth, built broadly as a man. She was sitting, her hands in her trouser pockets, on the wall facing the cottage. As soon as Chope came to the window she glanced up. She lowered her head immediately, and turning slowly and smiling she looked out of the corners of her eyes at the man beside her. None of the others moved, and yet it appeared that they tensed, as if there'd been conveyed to them some tremor of expectancy. Immediately be-

neath the bedroom window Chope could see the back of
a man in a marine blue trenchcoat. His head was not
visible because he was stooped forward against the cottage.
His arms were raised, and it was clear from his attitude
that his hands were shielding the light so that he could
see more clearly in through the downstairs window.

Chope drew back. He went and sat down on the bed,
leaned forward, his clenched hands held between his
thighs. Once he looked up at the ceiling, almost curiously, as if assessing its shape or area, but otherwise he
simply sat and stared vacantly out of the window.

And then he was listening. There was an unfamiliar
sound. For the first time in days the wind was stirring. It
was still some distance down the valley, but clearly it was
on its way. It hit the cottage with a rattle of hail. The
wind sounded in the one chimney; a door slammed downstairs. In less than a minute it had gone—the squall and
hail, but not the wind. As it continued the air felt transformed. With no longer the silence framing the sharp
measure of the stream, it seemed an oppression had
lifted from the entire valley. Chope stood up and went
cautiously to the window. They were gone.

At mid-morning Chope left the cottage. Without hesitating he started down the valley, making his way
through the meadows to the sea. His stride was brisk and
had recaptured its spring. When he reached the cliff he
stood for a while at the head of the long series of falls
by which the stream tumbled to the wide stony beach,
watching as the strong wind from the sea tugged and
snatched at the cascading water, and drew from it coils
of spray which it splayed and towed inland. After the
last few days it seemed unreal to be so near to the stream
and yet to be unable to hear its sound: here it was

smothered by the roar of wind and sea. He turned his back on the stream and, climbing to the higher cliffs, set out North along the wild coast.

For the next two hours he followed the cliff path, stopping now and then to watch a squall blow in from the sea. It would trail the sharp rain, and this, seen from the height of the cliff, appeared to dull or even erase the edge of the waves. The sea had risen, and now as the tide brought it against the cliffs it leapt white, as if reaching for a hold on the face. The exuberance seemed to infect Chope. As he lengthened his stride he whistled, and the gale pilfered the sound from his lips.

He climbed down at length to the cove and among the few cottages set around the sheltered quay. Here in the small, slated pub he stopped for bread, cheese and beer. He leaned on the bar and as the beer took him he laughed with two fishermen and the landlord, and argued at length when they told him like as not to be ready for snow.

When he started back and had climbed again to the high cliffs, he found that the wind had changed to the North West, had dropped a little but was now blowing steady. The sky had turned leaden, though out to sea to the West it appeared lightened by a magenta glow. The air was cold and not so cold; it was likely the fishermen were right.

When he arrived back at the cottage it had been dark some time. He built a fire, and tonight, with the wind to draw the flame, it was soon brilliant and lively. On the fire he cooked himself a large pot of soup. He ate it eagerly. Then he picked up his book. But after the day's walking and wind he was full of sleep.

Upstairs, as he was undressing, he heard a car in low gear descending the hill. It stopped outside the farm. A moment later, above the sound of engine, he heard the farmer and his wife calling goodnight. Two doors were slammed, and the car drove away.

Chope was smiling as he blew out the oil-lamp.

It was already light when he woke. He lay back for a moment, looking about the room. The wind was still blowing, buffeting the sides of the cottage, but the place felt warm. Certainly no other sound in the valley was audible. The light was strange, muffled and yet in some way glowing. He jumped from his bed and went to the window. The valley was deep in snow. It lay thick on the lawn, obliterating every trace of the footprints. Chope chuckled, and leaning forward he opened the window. As the cold air started in he put his head back and breathed deep through his nose.

Hurriedly he put on his clothes, and then went into the little wash-room at the head of the stairs. While he shaved in the icy water, he hummed or, when he could open his mouth, he whistled 'Hallaballoo'.

As he jumped down the stairs he all but fell over the two figures sitting side by side in the half dark three steps from the bottom. He stopped himself and drew back. But from where he was he could see the others seated motionless on the chairs, the sofa and the windowsill. A number were crouched on the floor. Their backs were leaned against the walls and their heavy forearms rested on their thighs.

GEORGE MACKAY BROWN

Brig-o-Dread

When thou from hence away art past
Every nighte and alle
To Whinny-muir thou com'st at last
And Christe receive thy saule

From Whinny-muir when thou may'st pass
Every nighte and all
To Brig-o-Dread thou com'st at last
And Christe receive thy saule

From Brig-o-Dread when thou may'st pass
Every nighte and all
To Purgatory fire thou com'st at last
And Christe receive thy saule

'I should say at once who I am, in case it is necessary for me to make a statement soon. My name is Arkol Andersvik. I have been married for twelve years to my dear good wife Freya. We have a son, aged 11, called Thord, a clever fair-haired boy whose craze, at the moment, is science fiction. His school reports are promising—I will say no more. We live in a fine old house in Hamnavoe, and I have a garden that slopes down from the hill to the street. My shop is in the town centre.

Out of whalebone we—my brother and I—carve souvenirs and mementos, and I deal in a variety of sealskin articles. We do a fair business in summer, when the islands are filled with tourists. I am a councillor. I am fifty years old.

'I try not to neglect the cultural side. For the past ten years I have imposed a discipline on myself. I have striven to acquaint myself with the best that has been sung and thought and written. You might call it a quest for truth and beauty. At the moment I am engaged on reading *Hamlet* for the third time. A poem that I chanced on last week really delighted me—the *Ode on a Grecian Urn* by Keats. It gave me a feeling of great purity and peace.

'My brother says this pursuit of culture is a substitute for the kirk pew. He may be right. I am not a religious man.

'Something strange has happened to me. That is why I am preparing this statement. I am not at home, nor in the shop. I don't know where I am, that's the truth. I am sitting on a bench in a bare room, like a prison cell. (But that is impossible.) Or it could be like a room where witnesses wait until they are called to give their evidence. It is worrying. I have never been involved in any kind of legal process. I intend to get to the bottom of it. It is a waste of my time, to put it mildly. I have a business to attend to. I have council work to see to this very evening. Freya will be very worried indeed.

'I have just discovered, with a certain relief, that I am not in prison; they have not removed my tie and bootlaces. I will go on writing in my notebook. That might help to clarify the situation in my mind.

'Wistan and I went seal-shooting yesterday afternoon, it being early closing day in the town. (Wistan is my younger brother.) We took our guns and motored four miles along the coast to a certain skerry where the seals come and go all summer. Some people wax sentimental over these animals. They invoke all the old legends about the selkie folk, half man and half seal, and their fondness for music. They denounce those who slaughter them, forgetting that they are voracious beasts that eat half the fish in the sea. The legends are charming, but most of that kind of talk is slush. Every man has his living to make. (What about the beasts that are slaughtered for our Sunday joints?)

'Wistan and I got out of the van at the cliff top and, carrying our guns, made our way carefully down salt broken ledges to the sea, only to find that the skerry was bare. The seals were away at their fishing. That was disappointing. We decided to wait for an hour or so, seeing that it was a fine afternoon and still early. I laid my gun along a ledge of rock. Wistan said he would take a walk round the coast, to see if he could find some shells or stones that—properly decorated—might tempt the tourists in search of souvenirs. He offered me his whisky flask. I declined, of course.

'A word or two about Wistan. He helps me in the business. I might have made him a partner but the truth is that there is a certain waywardness about him, an unreliability. He went to sea as a lad—came home after two years. My father used his influence to get Wistan work in a lawyer's office in Kirkwall, but he left, saying he couldn't bear the thought of scribbling and copying all day and every day, maybe for the rest of his life. For the next year or two he was a ne'er-do-well, spending his mornings in the pub, his afternoons in the billiard hall. Most evenings he would take his flute to dances in this parish and that. Wistan's conduct clouded our father's last years—I am certain of that.

'In the end I employed him in the shop. What else

could I do? He is my brother. I did not want to see him wasting his life entirely. Wistan has talents. No one can make more handsome sealskin bags and slippers than him, and the way he paints birds and flowers on stone is masterly. He, not I, is the whale-bone carver. I pay him twelve pounds a week. He has a small house on a pier and lives there alone. (In case somebody should say, "That is a poor wage to give a man", I reply, "That is all the business will stand. Give him more, he would simply squander it..." Besides, who but myself would employ him?)

'Poor Wistan! He is not highly regarded in the community. He was a delightful child, but some kind of raffishness entered into him at adolescence. It has never left him—the dreams, the deviousness. He drinks too much. Freya does not like him. I inflict him on her all the same—I insist that he comes to dinner every Sunday. In that way I can be sure that he gets at least one good meal in the week. He lounges about in the house all Sunday afternoon while I retire upstairs to my books and gramophone records.

'I thought to myself, between the crag and the skerry, "How on earth can Wistan afford whisky, on his wage?" I am not a skinflint, I hope, and I have nothing against a dram in the evening—but to booze in the middle of a summer afternoon! So I shook my head at the offered whisky flask. Still holding his gun in the crook of his arm, Wistan took a sip or two.

'A sleek head broke the surface fifty yards out. Large liquid eyes looked at the hunters. I whistled. Wistan whistled, farther off. The creature stirred and eddied towards us. "Come on, my beauty", I remember saying. The water was suddenly alive with seals. And that is all I remember, until I found myself an hour ago in this cell-like room.

'It is very strange. Where am I? Where is Wistan? Where is the seal, the shore, the gun?'

Mr Andersvik had no sooner closed his notebook than he saw that the door of the mysterious room now stood open. It was a summer day: there was blue sky and white clouds. He was free to go, it seemed.

Outside a signpost pointed: TO THE MOOR.

The landscape was strange to Mr Andersvik. The moor stretched, a wine-red emptiness, from horizon to horizon. It was eerie, to say the least. 'Well,' he thought, 'I'm bound to meet somebody who can tell me the way to Hamnavoe.' Indeed, when he took the track that wound into the moor, he saw a few people, and they too, like the landscape, had a remote dream-like quality. They moved like somnambulists. Every heathfarer was solitary and did not appear to be going anywhere. The moor was a slow soundless dance of intersections and turnings. The faces were down-tilted and preoccupied. It was soon obvious that the moor-dwellers wanted nothing to do with Mr Andersvik. As soon as he tried to approach one or other of these lonely ones, to ask the direction, they held out preventive hands—they had nothing to say to him, they did not want to hear anything that he had to say to them. Mr Andersvik was a bit hurt to begin with at these rebuffs. But after he had walked a mile or two a kind of contentment crept through him. It was quite pleasant out here on the moor. What contented Mr Andersvik particularly was the account he had written in his notebook in the court-room—he had set it down defensively (as if he was actually going to be charged with some offence) in order to put a good face on things, to cover up certain shames and deficiencies in his life that were, after all, his own concern. But here, on this moor, the images and rhythms of his prose pleased him very much indeed; he could savour them with extraordinary vividness in the solitude and silence. The remembrance was all pleasant, a flattering unction. He began the cycle of his life again—Freya and love and the garden, Thord and promise, Wistan and responsibility, the shop and sealskins and money, the council and honour, the temple of culture where he was a regular devoted worshipper... The second round of meditation was if anything sweeter than the first ... This delight, he thought, might go on for a long time. He very much hoped that it would.

Mr Andersvik discovered, by certain rocks and a certain gorse bush in the moor, that he had drifted round in two wide circles. He was learning to behave in the manner of the moor-dwellers. He halted.

'This will never do,' said Mr Andersvik to himself, breaking the lovely idyll. 'I must get back. These memories are not entirely true, I'm afraid. I must open the shop. There is this council meeting tonight.'

He turned. He strode on across the moor, frowning and purposeful. He was aware that his ankles had been rather badly scratched with gorse-thorns—he had not noticed the pain till now.

One of the moor people loomed close, with a tranced preoccupied face, drifting on, smiling, in a wide arc across the path of Mr Andersvik.

'Please,' said Mr Andersvik. 'One moment. I'm wanting to get to Hamnavoe. Could you tell me if I'm going in the right direction?'

'What's wrong with this place?' said the dancer on the moor. 'What greater happiness could there be than this solitude? If you leave the moor you'll never get back. Beware, man. Your journey will end in ashes and smoke' ... The man drifted on, smiling, feeding deep on the honey of his past.

A finger of fear touched Mr Andersvik. To go on like that for ever, nourished on delusions! He was sure of one thing now, he wanted to break out of these endless self-flattering circles. He hurried on. Gorse tore at his ankles. Once he fell in a blazing bush—his hands bled and burned. He picked himself up and went on. Clumps of gorse blossomed here and there on the moor—it was impossible to avoid them entirely. Freya would have to put some disinfectant on a multitude of scratches.

He came over a ridge and saw with relief that the track gave on to a road.

It was strange. Mr Andersvik thought he knew every road in the island, but he had never been on this particular one. He came after a mile or so to a crossroads. The signpost said: TO THE BRIDGE. He walked on. Soon familiar hills and waters came about him. He recognised Kringklafiold and the twin lochs with the prehistoric stone circle. And over there was the farm where his sister Anne had gone to live and toil when she married Jock Onness thirty years before. Alas, Anne had been dead for four years. That death had been a blow to Mr Andersvik; Anne was one of the few folk he had ever had affection for. He felt a pang as he looked at the widowed farm. Should he call in and have a word with old Jock? He thought, not today. The shop—souvenirs, sealskin— he was losing pounds. Besides, he did not feel in a mood to explain to the old man all the strange things that had happened to him. Jock was very deaf, and not too bright.

He walked on. Ahead was the little stone bridge that divides sea from loch, parish from parish. Under the triple arch salt water mingles with sweet water twice a day. A woman was standing at the hither end of the bridge. She beckoned to Mr Andersvik. Her face was tranquil, as if a quiet flame had passed through it.

It was his sister Anne.

He tried to speak, but his mouth locked on the words.

'Arkol,' she said, 'I've been expecting you. You've been on the moor a long time.'

'An hour or two,' he whispered.

'Longer than that,' said the dead woman. 'Oh, much longer. Well done, Arkol, all the same. Only a few folk have the strength to tear themselves away from that moor.'

Mr Andersvik took his first dark taste of death.

'I had to come and meet you,' said Anne, 'before you cross the bridge. Otherwise the pain would be too sudden and terrible.'

The half-ghost understood nothing of this. Death, in his understanding, was a three-day feast of grief, a slow graining and seepage among roots, the last lonely splendour of the skeleton—but all enacted within a realm of oblivion (except for a few fading fragrances in the memories of friends). An eternity of harps, or flames, had always seemed to Mr Andersvik an insult to the human intelligence.

He could not by any means accept his present situation. Yet here he was, in dialogue with a kindly riddling ghost.

'Arkol, you've chosen the truth,' said Anne. 'That's splendid. But the truth is cruel, Arkol. A poor naked truth-bound ghost has a terrible journey to go.'

'What happened to me?' said Mr Andersvik after a time.

'A gun-shot wound. In the head. The court said "Self-inflicted. Death by misadventure." Poor Arkol.'

'My gun was six yards away on a ledge of rock!' cried Mr Andersvik. 'That's impossible!'

'Poor Arkol,' she said again. 'But that's only the start. Are you willing to be dead?'

'No,' he cried. 'I don't believe it. Don't touch me. I can't be dead. I have years of work in front of me. Thord must be given a good start. Freya must be provided for. There's the housing committee and the graveyard committee. I am going to extend the business. I haven't made a will.'

His sister soothed him. She spoke to him with all the tenderness and kindness that in the old days had persuaded Mr Andersvik that, for example, he must really not be so pompous, he must learn to laugh at himself a little; that he must give Freya a more generous housekeeping allowance, she was having to pinch here and patch there—it was a shame, him with all that money and all these pretensions ... Now Mr Andersvik sensed a new depth in his sister's concern. He bowed his head. He yielded to her wisdom, there on the bridge between the dead and the living. Anne kissed him on the mouth, and so sealed his death for him.

Arkol crossed over the bridge then.

In darkness the dead man returned to the dimension he had left. Time is a slow banked smoulder to the living. To the dead it is an august merciless ordering of flames, in which the tormented one must learn at last to be a dancer.

His fellow-councillors were sitting in the council chamber. There was a new member seated in the chair he normally occupied—his brother Wistan. The provost was making some kind of formal speech ... 'welcome our new councillor, Mr Wistan Andersvik, to this chamber. We welcome him doubly in that he is the brother of the late councillor Arkol Andersvik, who died in such tragic circumstances a month ago. The late councillor was a highly valued member of this assembly. His wisdom and his humanity will be greatly missed. Some said that maybe he was over-cautious in this matter and that, but my reply to that was always, "Arkol Andersvik is a true custodian of the public purse" ... A more prudent man never walked the streets of this burgh. We trust, indeed we know, that his brother will be in all respects a worthy successor. He will bring imagination to our debates where the lamented elder brother gave us abundant practical sense. I will ask you, fellow-councillors, to be upstanding for one minute as a token of our respect for that good man who was taken so suddenly from our midst...'

They stood there, a lugubrious circle, and Wistan stood among them. Arkol felt for the first time the pain of the wound in his head. He cried out that they had taken a murderer into their fold, a brother-killer; but no one heard him. They passed on to the next business on the agenda...

Arkol shook himself clear of that flame. Darkness beset him again for a while (he did not know how long); then, far on, a new flame summoned, a white splash of time. He eddied like a moth towards it ... What shuttered place was he standing in? Light sifted through slatted window blinds, and of course he soon recognised it: it was his shop. The clock ticked on the shelf, spilling busy seconds into his timelessness. It was a quarter past ten in the morning, and still the door hadn't been opened to the public. So, it had come to this. How had Freya ever allowed it! She ought to have sold the business as a going concern. It had been a small gold-mine. Plenty of folk would have given a handsome price for 'A. Andersvik— Novelties, Presents, and Souvenirs'.

The key shrieked in the lock. The street-door opened. A familiar shadow stood there, carrying a heavy bucket.

Arkol saw in the new light from the street that there were no longer any painted pebbles or sealskin on the shelves. In their place were pieces of baked hollowed-out clay, garishly decorated. So Wistan had set himself up as a potter? The shop was a shambles—it reeked of burnt earth.

'You killed me,' he said sternly. 'But you're too loutish and lazy to enjoy the fruits of murder. How dare you ruin a good business! Filthying my shop with your mud and fire!'

Wistan set his bucket of clay beside the warm kiln. He moved over to the bench. He began to knead a lump of clay with knuckles and fingers. He was humming happily to himself...

Arkol came out of the flame singed and trembling.

He stood on Celia's pier in the first light of morning. (Time here was, as always, surely, a limpid invisible burning.) The old women arrived with their cats and basins while the fishermen (just back from the west) handed up the steps baskets of haddock. It was a famous place for gossip and opinion and elegy. Gulls, savage naked hungers, wheeled between the boat and the pier.

They were speaking about a death.

'Accident,' Maisie Ness was saying. 'That makes me laugh. You can't shoot yourself by accident. He was in trouble, if you ask me. He was on the verge of bankruptcy. So I heard. There was nothing else for him to do but shoot himself.'

'Well,' said Andrina Moar, 'he isn't that much of a miss. The swank of him! The strut of the creature along the street!'

Not one face on Celia's pier stilled with sorrow for the dead man. Instead the women, old and young, began to tear at Arkol's death like gulls among fish guts.

The haddocks gulped and shrugged in their baskets: dying gleams. Cats mewed. Sea and sky and stone was an asylum of gulls. The voices went on and on in the sunlight...

The darkness wrapped him away, trembling, from the slanders of the living.

He emerged into fragrance and sweetness. A peaceful green rectangle sloped down from the hill to the clustered roofs of Hamnavoe: his garden. What man was that sitting on the bench under the sycamore tree? It was, again, Wistan. Years had passed. Wistan's face was thin and sick and grey. Was he perhaps on the point of accomplishing his suicide by alcohol (an end that Arkol had more than once prophesied)? Then Arkol saw that Wistan was somehow injured—his right hand (the one that had pulled the trigger) was white and thick with bandaging. Wistan looked very seedy indeed in that net of green wavering shadows. (So Freya, out of the foolish kindness of her heart, had taken the creature into her house, for cure or for death.)

Freya came out of the kitchen into the sunlight. There was an extra decade of flesh and capability on her now. She was carrying a tray with salves and bandages on it. Wistan looked up. Blackbirds sang here and there in the bushes. It was a marvellous summer morning. The man and the woman smiled at each other. But immediately the shadow fell on Wistan's face again.

Freya set down the tray on the bench. She bent forward and kissed him on the forehead.

The ghost stirred in its flame.

'So, dearest,' said Freya, 'this is one of your black days, is it?' ... She knelt on the grass and began to undo the bandage on Wistan's hand.

There was a passionate outpouring of song from the rosebush at the bottom of the lawn.

'It *was* an accident,' said Wistan in the shivering silence that followed. 'The gun went off in my hands. But, dear, he'd done such terrible things, anything he could think

of—you know—to make me eat dirt, that sometimes I
think...'

'We've been through all that before,' said Freya the
comforter. 'I know. You've told me hundreds of times...'
She kissed the scarred hand. 'There, if it helps you. Of
course it was an accident. Just as you didn't mean to put
your hand in the kiln last Friday. You were aiming for
the seal. You might as well argue that *I* killed Arkol. If
I didn't particularly want him to die, that was just because I'd got used to him. I realise that now ... You
wedged the gun into his arms—that's all you have to re-
proach yourself with, love. It was nothing. It was clever
of you, in fact. It saved a lot of trouble, a lot of fuss and
anger and suspicion.'

Wistan closed his eyes. Freya began to spread the un-
guent over his charred palm.

Freya said, after another blackbird interlude, 'I don't
think now, looking back, that I ever really liked Arkol.
The meanness of him, the arrogance! That horrible flesh
lying beside me all night and every night! But you, dear,
the first time I ever saw you...'

The ghost smouldered in the garden, among the siev-
ings of birdsong. It glowed. It reeked. It longed to be
anywhere, in any darkness, away from this incestuous
place. Then it remembered, and acquiesced in the stake.
The flames thickened. The ghost burned terribly. Yet it
forced itself to look while Freya wrapped Wistan's wound
in new bandages, swiftly, delicately, tenderly; and even
afterwards, when the man and the woman enfolded each
other on the long bench.

If only a ghost could die ... It bore into the darkness
terrible new scorchings.

Arkol came to a room that had a stale smell in it. It
was the study where he had sought to improve his mind
with good music and books. A reproduction of Van Gogh's

'Sunflowers' hung over the mantelpiece. Freya, it seemed, had sealed the place off like a mausoleum. The dust whispered to him from shelf and record-player, 'What good was it to you, after all? You went through life blind and dense and hoodwinked. Here we are, Chopin and Jane Austen and Shelley, and we tried to tell you many a wise and many a true thing, but it only served to bolster your self-importance. Go and look for some peace now, poor ghost, if you can...' No one entered the study. *Hamlet* was lying on the table, just as he had left it the day before his murder, and *The Oxford Book of English Verse*, open at 'The Grecian Urn'. The ghost bent over the grey page. The poem was, as never before, a cold pure round of silence; a fold; a chalice for the transmutation of all sublunary vanities and grief.

But that solace was not for him. New flames—white splashings of time—summoned him. He was as hungry as a moth now for the anguish and the healing.

Arkol passed deeper into the charred ruins of his life. In another room a youth was sitting at a table, making notes of some kind. Thord had grown into a pleasant-looking young man. Bits of *Hamlet* drifted through the ghost: 'Thy father's spirit...' 'He took me grossly full of bread...' 'Avenge his foul and most unnatural murder...' The ghost smiled, in spite of its pain. As if this ordinary youth could ever be roused to such eagle-heights of rage, assoilment, passion! What had Thord done with his life? Arkol had had high hopes of the shy eager boy with his pile of science fiction books on his bedside table. Thord, he had thought, might well become a physicist, or a writer, or even a seeker among the stars. The ghost bent over the warm shoulder. Thord was filling up a football pools coupon. On the door-hook hung a postman's cap. To this favour the clever little boy had come: knocking at doors with white squares of gossip, propaganda, trivia. It did not matter. The ghost drank the beauty of his son's face—and saw, without rage, how like his mother he was now. He longed to linger out his time in this flame. But, shadow by slow shadow, he was folded in oblivion once more ...

This was the rock, right enough. Coldness and heaviness and poise lay across the ghost, a gun-shape. It oppressed him. He wished he were free of it. Another man was walking on the loose stones of the beach fifty yards away. The man stooped and picked up a stone or a shell every now and again. The man uncorked a flask and tilted it towards his mouth. A sleek head broke the grey surface—a seal, with large dark brimming eyes. The ghost whistled, but no smallest sound was added to the wash of the waves, the sliding of stones, the click of a bolt. There was another louder whistle farther along the shore. Suddenly the bay was musical with seals; they clustered about the off-shore rock; their sea-dance was over, they clambered awkwardly on to the stone. 'Come on, my beauties ...' Whitman's song came on the wind:

> I think I could turn and live with animals,
> They are so placid and self-contained.

A line of Coleridge flowered: 'he blessed them in his heart ...' The ghost raised an invisible hand seaward. He greeted the clean swift beautiful creatures of the ocean. He acknowledged the long wars of man against that innocent kingdom. He whispered for forgiveness. Then he turned calmly to face the blaze and the roar.

The day began with streams of blood. All the village followed the white-robed priest and the heifer whose horns were hidden under wreaths and clusters of blossom. Children danced and shouted. The throng of people disappeared beyond the last house of the village.

The only man who did not go to the ceremony sat in his cell and waited. The door had been open since first light.

He heard, after a long loaded silence, a whisper on the hillside, a fierce flailing of hooves, a surge and a spattering; then a wild ecstatic cry.

Presently the folk returned to the village. The lonely celebrant went with his red arms into a small house at the shore. The village street was soon empty. Family by family, purified, was eating its morning meal.

Not long afterwards the prisoner was summoned out to the village square.

A court of some kind was assembled and waiting. The square brimmed like a well with light. People of all ages sat here and there. Arkol was invited to station himself beside a sun-warmed stone.

The interrogator faced Arkol. Four people sat apart from the others, against the wall of the pottery-maker. Arkol took them to be a panel of judges. They consulted together. Occasionally one looked across at him and smiled.

The interrogator began with a reading out of the statement that Arkol had originally made: 'trust of the townsfolk...' 'quest for truth and beauty...' 'intend to get to the bottom of this...' The interrogator was interrupted every now and again by wondering laughter.

The older men and women sat in their doorsteps. Children—hidden voices—shouted in the gardens behind the street. The sound of the sea was everywhere. A young man went round the people in the square carrying a tray with a pitcher and tankards. An old man nodded approval over the white blown fleece of foam. An old woman shook her head reprovingly at all the raised tankards.

The voice of the interrogator—austere, measured, and melodious—reached into the bright morning. The villagers were rather bored with the proceedings, on the whole. Arkol could tell by their faces that they would much rather have been down at the fishing boats, or on the hill with their sheep, than wasting the day with such a trivial case. But at the end, he supposed, the villagers would have to give some kind of a verdict in the square.

Some young folk had got out of it by bathing. Arkol could hear shouts along the beach and the splash of bodies in the surf. There were mocking harp-like cries, then a sudden silence. A young man, naked and gleaming with sun and water, passed hurriedly through the square and entered a small steep alley. Children shrieked at the sea drops that shivered and showered over them. Voices from the rocks called for the insulted one to come back. A girl with wet hair appeared at the mouth of a sea-ward close. 'We're sorry, Adon,' she called. 'Please come back. Please.'

'Silence,' said the interrogator sternly. 'Go back to the sea. We are considering an important application.'

The girl withdrew bright hair, bright shoulders.

The case suffered no more interruptions. The interrogator paused upon this phrase and that: ... 'a word or two about Wistan...' 'I am not a skinflint, I hope'. An old man laughed above his ale. Arkol smiled ruefully.

A boy called from a hidden garden that he had caught a butterfly—he had—but it had wriggled out of his fingers and was free in the wind once more.

What intrigued Arkol more than anything that morning were the faces of the four judges who, he supposed, would finally decide whether his application should be granted or no. They sat on a long bench in front of the

interrogator. It was as if old woodcuts and frontispieces
and dead music had trembled and quickened. These were
the jurors: a man with wild hair and a wild mouth—a
young woman who in spite of merry mischievous eyes
looked rather prim—a man with a russet beard and a scar
at one ear—long lank hair over a lank dark cheek, a
velvet jacket, lank fingers: the hollows and shadows
scattered whenever the man smiled, which was often.

There was silence in the square. The reading of the
statement was over.

The cup-bearer had spread a white cloth on a long
trestle table. He reappeared in the square now, carrying
a tray with steaming fish on it, and bread. He began to
arrange seats.

'The statement, it is a tissue of lies,' said the hollow-
cheeked juror in a foreign accent. All the jurors nodded.
They looked at Arkol and smiled.

'The wonder is how he ever managed to escape,' said
Van Gogh. 'I took him for a typical moor-dweller as
soon as he arrived here last night.'

'He is a hero,' said a girl in a doorway who was feeding
a baby at her breast.

The bathers came up from the sea. The girl whose
face had been glimpsed for a moment between the
houses looked anxious now. Her companions tried to
reassure her. They went in an agitated troop up one of
the alleys.

The cup-bearer carried from the inn a huge pitcher—
both his arms were round it—some wine slurped over
on to the cobble-stones. An old man cried out in alarm.
But the pitcher was safely deposited at last among the
fish and the bread.

'As one of the villagers,' said a man who was leaning
against a wall smoking a pipe, 'I think he must at least do
this before we give him the stones to build a house—he

must alter the account of his life so that it comes a bit nearer the truth.'

The villagers shouted their approval.

'You can't eat or drink with us, you understand,' said the interrogator to Arkol, 'or stay here in this village, until you have paid your debt to the truth. You must revise your statement in certain respects. You will be given pen and paper. Now that you've been through the fire, I think you may enjoy doing it.'

The villagers turned away from Arkol. They began to gather round the table. The bathers, all but two, came down the alley and joined the others. Mugs and pieces of bread were passed round—there was a mingling of courtesy and banter. Three seats were empty.

Arkol sat on a sunlit step. He poised his pen over the paper. He wondered how to begin.

The children's voices drifted down from the hillside. They were filling baskets with blackberries. Pure echoes fell into the square. The children shouted that they would not be home till sunset.

The lovers who had quarrelled on the sea verge stood in the mouth of the close. They were tranquil and smiling now. They moved into sunlight. Folk rose up at the table to let them pass on to their places.

Arkol wrote. Phrases with some beauty and truth in them began to come, with difficulty. He longed to sit among the villagers, and share their meal. But the feast was eternal. He hoped that he might be able, before it was over, to present to the elders the poem of his life.